Black Light

by

A H Jamieson

This is a work of fiction. Names and characters are the product of the author's imagination and any resemblance to actual persons, living or dead, is entirely coincidental.

ISBN: 978-0995639508

Peerie Breeks Publishing
www.peeriebreeks.com

Thank you

Abigail Wetton - Sorry I killed you off!

Becky Stannett - For words that kept me going.

Joan Brunnick-Ryan - For saying the truth.

Gerry Donovan - For not saying the truth!

Karen Pinkerton - For all the good editing advice.

Stephen McDonald - For agreeing with your wife-to-be.

Marie O'Keefe - For telling me where I could stick my commas!

Rhona Pinkerton - For being my Verity.

xxx

Prologue

One large figure and two small stood in the darkness and rain atop a lonely hill. Dark Oak Orphanage waited at the bottom.

"Wait here," the hooded figure said.

The hooded figure had a womanly shape.

The rain beat down soaking their skins.

Two made their way towards Dark Oak.

"What about Perfidy?" the little girl asked. Her tears mixed with the rain on her cheeks.

"You will be safe here."

"What about Perfidy?" she asked again.

"You will see her soon," the hooded figure lied.

"You must stay here for a little while. It's no longer safe for you to be with me. I will come back for you soon." The woman thumped the door with her fist. The rain fell.

"But, I will miss Perfidy. I don't want to leave her," the little girl said. She was no more than five. Her blue eyes shone through the darkness and her wet black hair clung to her cheeks.

"You won't remember her or me after this my child." She handed the little girl a small gourd of liquid to drink. She thumped the door again. This time a large woman answered.

"No children tonight," she said gruffly.

"Please reconsider," said the hooded woman handing her a pouch of gold coins.

"You had better come in," the large woman said.

"No." said the hooded woman.

"Take down your hood so I can see your face," the large woman said.

"No." came the reply.

"What's her story?" the large woman asked.

"She has none," the hooded woman replied.

"What about the wretch you left on the hill?" the large woman sneered.

"Her place is elsewhere," came the reply.

The hooded woman bent down and whispered in the little girl's ear. "I will send a friend to find you when the time is right." She kissed her gently on the cheek. The little girl looked groggy.

"Does it have a name?" the large woman asked.

"Her name is Verity."

Chapter 1
Dark Oak

'Three things cannot be hidden, the sun, the moon and the truth.'
Buddha

Dark Oak Orphanage for Girls was quiet.

Twenty to midnight.

Verity lay in her bed wide awake. She had a slim curvy face and had been told she was beautiful although had never once felt it. Her raven black hair lay on her shoulders like silk. Her face was pretty, her skin was pale and unmarked other than a small dark mole on her cheek near her nose and her blue eyes would have pierced the bluest sky. Her frame was slender but strong.

The room was still. A small shimmer of moonlight crept through a crack in the thick brown curtains casting a velvety pale shadow across the wooden floor. Verity scanned the gloom to see what she could make out. The only two shapes in the room looked like strange versions of what they really were. The wardrobe and the small wooden chest of drawers made soft shapes and were splashed with tiny dabs of moonlight. She enjoyed this time of night. She thought of her friend Frances who hated the darkness, "It creeps me out!" was her favourite phrase at the moment and the "things that wait in the dark" definitely gave her the creeps. Verity did not share this feeling. When the darkness came she felt a strange sense of peace. The noise and worry of the day melted away and she could think clearly, without stupid girls or annoying adults bothering her. The only one who didn't bother her was Frances. Verity had every reason to dislike the inhabitants of Dark Oak Orphanage for Girls as they were a beastly crowd. She remembered reading somewhere that girls were supposed to be like sugar and spice and all things nice. Well whoever wrote that had clearly never been to Dark Oak. Life was tough and was made worse by the fact that the Carers were nasty and spiteful, led by the Matron, Ms Krankle.

Verity closed her eyes gently and listened.

Nothing.

Beautiful nothing.

Happy nothing.

She could only hear the rise and fall of her own breathing which was peaceful and calm.

Fifteen minutes to midnight.

Verity started to relive the events of the day. This is where her and Frances differed. "When I go to bed, I go to sleep," Frances would say, "not to fret and worry about stuff you can't change anyway." Verity was often jealous of this ability to fall asleep as she often found her head whirling in the darkness. It was as if the thoughts would not let go until she had thought them away a thousand times. Today had been dominated by Briony Grime. She was one of the older girls, two years older than Verity, and had been in the orphanage for years. She was a large girl, both tall and broad, and she used her size to bully the other girls. Her hair was dirty blonde, shoulder length and always tangled. She never wore tights and usually had dirty knees in the middle of her lumpy legs. Her mouth was small and puckered as if she had just sucked a lemon, and her eyes were sharp and wicked. The only person who had ever stood up to her was Verity and she despised her for it. There had been a problem at lunchtime. Briony had taken young Martha Tweet's tray and tipped her lunch on the floor in order to establish fear in the little one which had worked brilliantly until Verity had stood between them. Her large blue eyes had stared hard at Briony. Briony, livid, had picked up a glass and raised it with the purpose of smashing Verity over the head when Ms Krankle had finally decided she should intervene.

In the dark Verity was troubled. Not because an unpleasant thing had happened. She didn't care about Briony and she wasn't scared of her. That was the problem. She wasn't scared. She had stood in front of Briony and looked in her eyes and watched her raise the glass. She had not moved a muscle and her heart had beat as calmly as it did in the peaceful darkness now. She thought she should have been scared.

Ten minutes to midnight.

Verity sat bolt upright. The silence was broken. Quiet at first. A scuffling, a snuffling, scratching, scraping outside the bedroom door. Verity listened hard. The doorknob started to turn. Whatever was turning it was doing it achingly slowly. Verity breathed deeply and fixed her gaze on the door. Her muscles tensed. The door creaked open a fraction. Whatever was opening it didn't want the sleeper to wake it seemed. The corner of Verity's mouth curled into a smile. They picked the wrong room tonight she thought. She slid out of her pale green duvet and moved like a cat effortlessly across the floor and positioned herself behind the door that was still gently creaking open. A shadow started to form on the floor from the light on the landing. A figure crept in. A hand first, followed by an arm, then the shape put a leg through the door. Verity waited patiently, quietly. The figure made its way into the room and the door slowly creaked shut behind it. Verity's voice cut through the darkness, "Don't you know it's rude not to knock!" she pounced towards the figure and tumbled it onto the bed.

"OWWWW!" it cried. Verity recognised the voice and let go. "You really do give me the creeps!" croaked Frances.

"What on earth are you doing?" whispered Verity.

"The dark was giving me the creeps so I came here, although goodness knows why!" grumbled Frances.

Verity looked at her friend. She wore glasses which she was now trying to push back on to her nose. Her red hair was always untidy but never made her look scruffy. Her nose was dotted with freckles and her green eyes were warm with kindness. Her mouth was the thing that fascinated Verity most of all and was what had drawn her to Frances. It was always smiling, always happy. Verity was in awe of that mouth. How could she smile so much when life had been so cruel to her? Her parents had been lost in a car accident. The family were driving down the motorway; Frances and her big sister Abigail were in the back. A lorry driver didn't look and the car ended up smashed at the side of the road. The doctors said it was a miracle Frances lived. Frances was told her parents were gone and she ended up at Dark Oak; nobody would speak to her about her sister.

"If crusty old Krankle catches us we are for the chop. I already have litter duty for a week after the Briony thing," said Verity.

"I know, I'm sorry. That was so unfair, you didn't even do anything. Lots of the girls are on your side you know. They hate Slimy Grimey," Frances replied.

Suddenly, the clumping of Doc Martin boots could be heard. That could mean only one thing, KRANKLE.

"Which dirty little urchin is up at this time of night, I will make them pay for interrupting my beauty sleep!" she muttered. Krankle would need to sleep for a thousand years to start making a difference to her beauty. She was horrible inside and out. A big round woman with piggy little eyes. Her hair was jet black although everyone knew she was as grey as a mule and she dyed it with boot polish. It was scraped back and tied in the tightest bun it seemed possible to tie. She only dressed in grey. Her trousers were way too tight and she had a blouse that defied the laws of physics to hold her massive upper half in. She carried a cane which she was fond of using to scare the children. There were rumours that she once lost her temper with a girl called

Sara Butler and lashed her so hard she had to go to hospital and she never came back.

The footsteps stopped outside Verity's room. "This little wretch is always causing trouble," she spat the words out in a whisper.

Verity acted quickly. She put her hand on the back of Frances' head and shoved it down into the mattress, then in a wink she swirled the duvet over them both and lay down as if asleep. Krankle strode in flicking the light switch as she did. "What exactly is going on in here child!" she bellowed.

Verity rolled over and squinted as if just wakened. "Mrs Krankle?"

"It's Ms Krankle to you, child!" she shrieked.

"Oh sorry, I keep forgetting, over and over again," Verity delivered with a sickly smile.

"I heard noise, I know it was you." her attitude changed, "If you admit it, I won't think badly of you," her words were hollow.

"No noise from here MS Krankle, not from here," said Verity.

"NOT FROM HERE! NOT FROM HERE! Then what is this little worm doing in your bed!" with that she tore the covers off to reveal a sniffling Frances. "You are going to meet the cane girl!" Krankle sneered at Frances. She raised her right hand and the cane was ready to strike. Frances cowered and managed to let out a whimpering "Please!" the cane was raised in the air and was about to beat down when a cry filled the room.

"STOP!"

Krankle, who had been holding the cane above her head, slowly brought it down.

Her gaze was fixed on Verity. "The reason you are about to give better be phenomenally good child," a small amount of spit dribbled down her chin as she spoke.

"It's my fault miss. I mean, I tricked Frances. I went to her room and told her you wanted to speak with her and that you were here and she came. I thought it would be amusing."

"Amusing! AMUSING! You have landed yourself in a world of trouble girl!" she pointed a crooked finger. "You, Frankie!"

"It's Frances Ms."

"Don't correct me child, back to bed, NOW!"

Frances looked at Verity with those big green eyes and Verity gave her a knowing nod. She sloped off the bed and scurried out the room. The door closed.

Three minutes to midnight.

"I've been watching you." Krankle's friendly tone was almost scary, "You came to us in quite a mysterious fashion. Your guardian brought you and told us not to ask questions. No family, no past, no story. She did have another little girl with her but she only wanted to leave you. We could not accept a child under those circumstances you understand but she was very persuasive."

"I don't want to be here," Verity was cool and calm.

"Perhaps not, but here you are, and I want to make sure you have the most miserable time that I can! You sit there with your pretty face and your sneering looks. You have always been different from the others. You think you're better than us don't you, I can see it and I'm going to take great pleasure in using the next five years to beat it out of you!" Her mouth twitched at the edges as the words splurged out.

Verity's blue eyes looked at her carefully. Her blood was boiling and every fibre of her body was telling her to stand up to this bully. She knew however that it would do no good. When did kids ever win against adults?

"Hold out your hand!"

Verity did as she was told. The cane made the air crack. It split her hand. "Could I have another please?" Verity blurted through the pain, she was determined to show it didn't hurt. The blood ran off her palm.

"Ha, why don't you clean that, and don't you dare get any on your sheets!" Krankle was smiling as she left and shut the door. Verity was glad to have the darkness back.

One minute to midnight.

Verity pressed down hard on her palm with her washcloth. She was annoyed. She hated herself for not standing up to Krankle. Her hand stung and made her eyes water. She was able to wrap and tie the cloth tight round it. It hurt but it also felt good to have the pressure on it. She flopped back in her bed. What a day! What else could go wrong?

The dusty old grandfather clock that stood in the hallway began to chime.

Midnight.

There was a scuffling, snuffling, scratching scraping outside Verity's door. Frances! Verity leaped out of bed. She was in no mood for 'the creeps' now. She was ready to make her red headed friend understand it was time for bed and she didn't mind using bad language to tell her. She pulled the door open and was ready to rant but all she was met with was an empty hallway. She was wondering what was happening when she heard a scuffling, snuffling, scratching scraping noise coming from behind her somewhere in the room. Spinning around she caught sight of a shape that dived into her bed. Her hand trembled a little as she closed the door and tried to make her eyes adjust to the dark. There was a lump in her bed. A small child sized lump under the duvet. Verity slowly moved towards it. Something was on the floor, she tripped and the shape from the bed jumped on top of her. She was on her back and the shape was sitting on her tummy. She squirmed and wriggled. She managed to sit up and push the shape across the room. She clumsily clambered on to her bed and clenched her fists. "You picked the wrong room!" she croaked.

"Messenger," came a voice. "Messenger," came again. It was a frightened voice, "Messssssssenger." It was holding something above its head. Verity moved closer and grabbed what was a piece of paper. The paper was crunchy. She scrambled to her bed light and switched it on. The messenger covered its face and dived beneath the bed. Verity held up the piece of paper; it was yellow and torn. It simply read,

I know where she is…

That was it. Verity was shaking. She reached under the bed and grabbed a handful of furry flesh and dragged the small creature out. The creature was light and Verity lifted its face to hers and growled, "Who is SHE?"

The creature splurged and gurgled its words,

"She is your sister!"

Chapter 2
Cellar

'It's not what you have on the outside that glitters in light, it's what you have on the inside that shines in the dark.'
Anthony Lecconi

Dark Oak was a very large, very grey building. It had been an old country estate once but when the owners disappeared it had fallen into disrepair. Nobody knew who had bought it to create the orphanage. The day-to-day running was left to the Matron, Ms Krankle. The roof needed repaired and the windows and doors rattled when the wind blew. It was surrounded by a rotten old fence and the garden, if you could call it that, was overgrown with weeds and jaggy nettles. It sat in the middle of a bleak countryside. There were no other buildings in sight. A forgotten house in a forgotten place. A great place to hide something or someone. Verity's messenger last week had caused several problems. The week had gone much as usual except for a few key things.

One - The messenger had vanished from Verity's room and seemingly left through the front door, which it then left open. Ms Krankle went crazy as the door was always locked at night and she kept the only key on a chain round her fat neck.

Two - Krankle suspected Verity was up to something and was now watching every move she made and if she wasn't, one of her minions would be there, sneering and watching.

Three - The messenger hadn't just left a note. It had rekindled a feeling that Verity had hidden deep down within her. Far away inside her, behind a high wall, in a house with no doors, in a black room, hidden in a box locked with riddles. It was a feeling she tried to ignore but couldn't. It burned in Verity's heart and would not let her go. She did not feel complete. She had to escape from Dark Oak.

Lunch time. It was the usual scene, girls trudging in a slow but perfectly formed line while they waited for the cook, Mrs Pussle, to dole out whatever slop she had decided to mix that day. All this was overseen by Krankle and her minions. Krankle was very proud of her straight slow lines, the order of it all pleased her.

"STAND TALL! DON'T SLOUCH! LIFT YOUR SHOULDERS GIRL!"

She barked at the girls but didn't need to. She had broken them all a long time ago. They were little obedient creatures and nobody wanted to incur the wrath of Krankle. Nobody except Verity. She looked at Krankle and saw everything she hated in people. Selfishness, spite, greed and cruelty. She thought Krankle was very ugly but not because of what she looked like but because of the things inside her.

Verity trudged in the line with everyone else. Frances was behind her.

"I heard that Sarah Peters said that Briony was out to get you." she chittered excitedly. "Then, I heard that Gemma Winters was ready to stand up for you!"

"Oh, that's interesting," Verity lied.

"Yes! and Emma Jackson said that she heard Krankle say she would find out who had been able to open the door and, and, and lock them away! Guess who is number one on her list!" said Frances wildly.

"Father Christmas?" smiled Verity.

"Father what…? No you dope it's you!"

"I got that idea, thanks. I'm sure everything will be fine, now be quiet before we get caught whispering." snapped Verity.

"TOO LATE!" screeched a voice from behind them, "Ms Krankle, oh Ms Krankle." Everything stopped. "I have a snotty little girl here who seems to think she is sooooooo much better than the rest of us and that it's acceptable for her to break the rules!" Krankle's minion sneered as she spoke.

Krankle was at the other side of the canteen. Her nasty gaze fixed in on Verity's location. "WELL, WELL, WELL! Which, dirty, little oily tick is it?" she bellowed. She knew full well who it was but wanted to deliver a little performance in front of everyone. She was delighted with the chance to punish Verity publicly.

"This one here Ms Krankle!" the minion said excitedly. She poked out a crooked finger at Verity. The minions all looked the same, sharply pointed faces which looked old although not all of them were. Grey hair, tied back with grey hairpins, grey blouses, grey below the knee skirts, thick grey tights, grey shoes, grey socks and grey personalities. They were all terrified of Krankle.

"OH MY, OH MY, oh my, what a shame," Krankle's voice was sickly as she spoke, "one of our little family has decided she is better than the rest of us, has she?" Verity stood calmly not taking her steely blue eyes away from the large beastly woman. "SHE, thinks she is better than all of us, does she?" Krankle's face was becoming nastier with every word she spoke. "SHE, thinks she is so wonderful that we are all not worthy, does she! SHE, is so ungrateful for everything we have done for her that, SHE, wants to throw it back in our faces, DOES SHE!" Krankle's words fired like bullets from her mouth.

"THEN SHE CAN BE LOCKED IN THE CELLAR!"

Gasps erupted round the canteen. Nobody dared to move. Verity had not reacted yet and stood still and calm. Verity was a humble girl and despite being in a place where there were few, her manners were important to her. She hated conflict, it always made her feel awkward so she avoided it but she also believed fiercely in the truth. She couldn't help it; it was a feeling that came from deep inside. She sometimes wished she didn't feel that way, it would make life easier, but she had to stand up for what was right. Krankle was not finished. "That is of course unless SHE wants to apologise." By this time Krankle had made her way across the canteen and stood uncomfortably close to Verity. Krankle lent in and whispered, "If you beg in front of the hall, I will spare you." Verity could feel her vile breath on her face, it smelt of fish. Krankle spoke to the room again, "If you can show how sorry you are, we MIGHT forgive you!" There was a pause. "Well?"

Verity looked at her. She knew what she should do. Keep her head down, apologise, steer clear of trouble, but something was bubbling within her. "WELL?" Krankle's eyes flashed as she smiled manically.

"I was wondering," began Verity.

"YES," replied Krankle. turning to her audience, smiling, waiting for her victory.

"I was wondering…" Verity paused for what seemed like an age. Everyone held their breath.

"I was wondering why you think I would ever want to apologise to a dry old trout like you?"

Krankle was stunned into silence her eyes wide and her mouth gaped open. Wild chattering spread like wildfire around the canteen. The minions looked at each other unsure quite what to do.

Finally Krankle screamed, "SILENCE!" The room obeyed. "LOCK HER IN THE CELLAR!"

The way out of the cellar was through a hatch in the ceiling underneath which was a pull down ladder which Verity could not reach. Even if she could have reached, she was still stuck because Krankle had locked the hatch. Verity sat cross legged in the darkness. The floors and walls of the cellar were made of stone and it was largely empty other than an old rusty bike and some empty paint pots in the corner. Verity had seen these things just before Krankle had taken out the light bulb. Krankle thought she was being cruel but she didn't know how at peace Verity was with the blackness. Verity was also not bothered by the rats that hurried and scurried, going about their business in the dark.

She didn't mind the damp musty smell that lingered in the air, but the cold was something Verity wasn't so keen on, and the cellar was cold. She was annoyed. The messenger had lit a fire inside her. A fire that burned for the truth about her past. She didn't remember anything before Dark Oak. She knew there must be something. She had planned to escape Dark Oak to find it. Now, she was stuck. She couldn't even escape the cellar never mind anywhere else.

She got up and started to stretch her legs. She tripped over something and tumbled to the ground.

"Devon help us! Why don't you watch where you is goin'!" came a grumpy voice, "here I is minding me own beeswax and I gets tramply boots all over myself." The voice seemed to be grumbling to itself. "A bit of quiet and peace is all I asks, can't even tiddle on me toilet withouts somebodies botherin' me bones. That's the trouble with folky peeps now, no respect for old wrinkles like me."

"Er, sorry." Verity said sheepishly.

"Mmmmm, we is all sorry. Sorry, sorry, sorry." it grumbled.

A match flared and illuminated the small wrinkled face of what looked like a mole.

"Are you all right?" she asked.

"Now, where are you, where did I leaves you?" it muttered.

"You won't find much in here I'm afraid." Verity said.

"Here you is little waxy one!" the mole creature exclaimed. He lit a candle, which to Verity's surprise was sitting on top of a dusty old bookcase crammed full of books. "Come little waxy ones," the mole muttered as he went round and lit more candles. The room was now entirely illuminated except for the far corner. Verity could not believe her own eyes. The rusty bike and paint tins were no more and the bare room she had been in was full of bookcases that lined the walls top to bottom. They were all full to bursting with old dusty, cobwebby books that were all kinds of different colours. Reds, blues, browns, greens, purples and greys, they just went on and on.

"What is this place?" Verity said as much to herself as to the creature.

"You, me little girly peep, is in me Toiletery!" the moleman announced proudly.

Krankle moved down the corridor swiftly for such a large lady. She stopped at a brown wooden door with large iron hinges. She looked over both shoulders before pulling a small silver key from her pocket. The lock gave a satisfying clunk as she turned it. She looked over her shoulder again, pushed the door open and slipped in. Once inside she locked the door behind her then moved towards a small cauldron which sat at the other end of the room. The room had no windows and no furniture. It was only big enough for one, perhaps two people to sit comfortably in. She got down on her knees and pulled a match from her pocket. She struck it on the floor and threw it into the cauldron. Thick plumes of coloured smoke started rising from it. The smoke changed from red to green to orange then to black. Once black, it thinned and became wispy. A face started to appear in the centre. The room suddenly felt icy cold. Krankle started to speak, "Hail oh lord of all, Hail oh wonderful one," her head was touching the ground.

The voice that came back was cold, it spoke slowly as if picking every word with care.

"What of the girl?"

"She is under control. I have seen to it personally, just as you asked oh great one." Krankle's voice was shaking.

"Where is she?"

"I have locked her away oh special one. Away safe so no-one will reach her." Krankle sounded pleased with herself.

"Do you know she has already been visited?" the voice said.

"Impossible." Krankle replied shakily.

"Are you a failure Krankle?" said the voice.

"No master." Krankle whimpered.

"Failure is not an option with me," it said slowly.

"I won't let you down oh majestic one."

"I believe you won't. It is time."

"Time for what my lord?" she asked.

The face in the smoke spoke four last chilling words.

"For her to die!"

Verity was sitting uncomfortably on an incredibly small chair holding a beautiful blue and white patterned china cup and saucer. "More coffee?" the moleman asked.

"No I'm fine thanks." said Verity with a smile. Had she been given coffee, she might well have said yes, but after being given a cup of what seemed to be mud with dandruff sprinkled on top, she decided she wasn't as thirsty anymore.

"I is still thinking why you has come to me. I means, most times I is alone in the dark, alone as an alone thing what has just won best prize in an alone test."

"I don't know why." said Verity.

"You needs to squinkle up your coffee and tootle away back and fronts to where you came. I hasn't got the times to be twittering to alls the little whatsypops what might winkle their ways to my hideyhole. Go on missy, off you tiddle." The moleman turned his back and muttered something to himself about tiddlers not toddling old wrinkles or something like it.

"Wait!" blurted out Verity. "I need to know the truth!" Her voice was desperate. She knew she must have a past, a family. She knew she must have parents. She couldn't remember them, couldn't feel them, couldn't feel anything. Yet the fire burned inside. Right now this little moleman was all she had. "Please!"

"Wonderings, happenings, we is all thinking we is special," said the moleman as he shuffled towards the dark corner.

"Please!" Verity felt so lost inside.

"Goings and comings, isn't we all learning we has our place," it muttered.

"Please," her voice seemed as small as it had ever been.

21

The moleman had nearly disappeared into the dark corner. "We has all got our troubles which is creakin' our backs and bending our bones. We must busy on, yes yes, busy busy busy. We can't all be sitting round waitin' for Verity." The moleman slipped into the blackness.

Verity flopped to the ground, cross legged and had her head in her hands. "How do you know my name?" she said through her fingers.

A small twitchy, whiskery nose poked out of the gloom. "What is you sayin' girly peeps?"

"How do you know my name?" Verity repeated lifting her head.

The moleman reappeared, "You is Verity?"

"Yes," she said quietly.

"Oh my daisy aunt! By jingo and by lingo! Oh happy days and a lovely good pinch of salt!" the moleman cried excitedly. "Verity! My little girly peep!

"The truth is savin' us all!"

Frances had felt terrible ever since sneaking to Verity's room a week ago. She felt as though it was all her fault. She never looked for trouble but it always seemed to find her. Today in the canteen had only made it worse. She thought the world of Verity. She looked at Verity and saw a girl who was prettier than most but never said it, in a world where being beautiful seemed to be the only goal. She saw a girl who tried hard to do the best thing, the right thing. She had never known anyone so strong, with nerves of steel yet never had a bad word to say about anyone. She also saw what most didn't, the sadness that Verity carried. It was like a large weight sat squarely across her shoulders. What made Frances saddest of all was that Verity never laughed. Frances couldn't see her best friend locked up. Especially not because of her. She knew where the cellar was but she didn't have the key!

Krankle snored loudly. Her bedroom was grey and dull. One bed, one wardrobe, one grey rug, and one bedside table. "Anything else would just be an extravagance!" she would say.

Tonight, something else was in the room. One Frances! She crouched in the corner trying her hardest not to breathe too loudly. Her heart felt as though it might beat right out of her chest! She crept slowly towards Krankle's bed on her hands and knees. The old boot snorted and spluttered as she slept. Frances inched her way to the bed. Krankle kept no secret of the fact she kept her keys on a chain round her neck. The key chain was lying on the bedside table. Next to the table lay a large, empty syringe. Frances crept closer. Krankle grunted loudly and rolled onto her side. Frances was right next to the bed now. Very slowly, she reached a small shaky hand out towards the keys. Her trembling fingers inched closer and closer. Krankle snorted and rolled over. Her flabby arm fell on top of the bedside table and the keys. A word appeared in Frances head that didn't make her feel proud! She saw the little key she wanted, the skeleton key. Matilda Tench had told her about it. Matilda had said that a skeleton key was a special key that opened many doors. This one had a small silver skull on the end. Her hands were trembling as she slid it off the key chain. Krankle snored loudly. It eventually slipped off; she had done it! Suddenly, there was a loud knock at the door! Frances' blood froze. "Ms Krankle." there was another knock. Krankle stirred. Frances did the only thing she could. She quickly scampered under the bed.

"Enter," mumbled a sleepy Krankle. She sat up in her bed. Underneath the bed Frances held her breath. The door opened and she watched a pair of grey shoes and socks walk in.

"You said to tell you immediately when it was ready," the voice said.

"Yes. Did you prepare it exactly as I asked?" Krankle enquired.

"Exactly," came the reply.

"Thank you, you may leave."

The grey shoes turned and started to walk away but stopped at the door. "Ms Krankle?"

"Yes," she answered.

"You are aware that the mixture would be very dangerous for anyone who took it, I mean, you do realise it could kill them in quite a horrible way?" she asked nervously.

"You have been one of my most loyal servants," Krankle answered. "I have come to think of you as someone I can trust," she continued. The minion smiled. "But if you question my wishes again, I will make you howl for your mother! Do you understand!"

"Yes Ms Krankle." and with that the grey shoes and socks left the room. Frances stayed as still as a stone under the bed. She heard Krankle shuffling about then getting up and leaving the room. Frances waited for a minute before crawling out of her hiding place. She looked around. The rest of the keys and the syringe were gone. In their place was a small glass bottle half full of an inky black liquid. Frances moved quickly for the door. She had to get to the cellar before Krankle!

Chapter 3
Escape

'Walking with a friend in the dark is better than walking alone in the light.'
Helen Keller

Verity and the moleman had left the cellar. He had fetched a wobbly old wooden ladder and when he climbed it the hatch was no longer locked. "Ah it's been dusty long times since I has been up here," he said. Verity had been asking him to explain what was going on but all he seemed to do was hurry around and mutter till he found the ladder, now here they were. The belly of Dark Oak. The room they were in was familiar to Verity as she had already been there yet nothing about it was the same. When she had been dumped in the cellar earlier, this room had been full of junk. Mostly cardboard boxes piled on top of each other as well some old bits of furniture and a few rolls of carpet. Those things were gone. Instead, it was empty and there was a large brown door which Verity had not noticed before. Moleman saw her staring at it. "So the gores can gets fro and to," he said.

"What?" replied Verity.

"The gores, they is big ol' blighters so needs a big door," he said, as if Verity must be stupid.

"I don't get it?" Verity was puzzled. "Where are all the boxes? The furniture? Where did all the books in the cellar come from?"

"Girly peeps, girly peeps, let I stop you tracks an' all. You has come through. I is not knowin' how you has gotten through but through you has gotten! You has never seen things as they really are before," he said.

"Through where? I'm still right here!" Verity moaned.

"Right here is you! Here is right where you is! That is what's right!" The moleman's tone suddenly became quite serious. "Does you like the dark Verity? Does it make you feel different, like your little bubbles and troubles are gone and you feels peace at last?"

"Yes." Verity's eyes were wide.

"Most peepsy folks don't like it, no no no, they is not so pleased."

"What is wrong with me?" Verity pleaded.

"Wrong? Wrong? Ho de ho ho. Nothing wrong, all is right! You has a secret, oh ho ho, a big woopsy secret and I is going to help you."

"This isn't making any sense. I don't have a secret. I'm just Verity."

"Yes you is lovely one, yes yes yes, and never forget it. You has come through your darkness and now we needs to tiddle over here and close our little mouthy holes." He pulled Verity by the arm and dragged her into the far corner of the room. He then produced a black cloak and swirled it over them. The door opened and Krankle walked in. She closed it behind her and made her way to the cellar entrance. Verity could see a syringe full of black liquid in her hand. She opened the cellar door and started to climb down.

"Hello my little petal, where are you?" she called as she climbed down.

"She is wickeder than the wicked witch of the vest!" whispered the moleman. "I would rather push hot bananas up my nose than speak to her!" he continued.

"How do you know Krankle?" Verity asked.

"Shhhhhh." hissed the moleman. "Watch what I does! I is on the move!" With that he waddled quickly over to the hatch. Verity could still hear Krankle down in the cellar.

"Let me just get this pesky little light bulb back in my sweet. Then, I can see your lovely little face. I have a present with me you lucky little girl."

The moleman reached the cellar hatch. Krankle switched the light on. "Where are you, you little maggot?

Come out from behind those boxes and take your medicine little worm!"

The moleman shouted down the hatch, "You is a soggy old sock Krinkle!"

"Morton? Is that you Morton? What are you doing out? I will make you sorry when I get up there. Where is the girl?"

"You isn't getting up warty one! I is closing the door and ooops and loops I is lockin' it tight!"

"MORTON!" she bellowed.

"Tatty bye byes." Morton slammed the door and produced a little silver key from his pocket and locked it. "This is the best day ever!" he said happily. "Now girly peeps, I is knee-deep as a dodo in do do, let's go!"

"I can't," said Verity, "I have to get out of the orphanage, I have to find someone."

"Ho de ho girl. I has no plans of staying here. Out we must be. Someone you needs to meet."

Krankle was banging the hatch.

"Let us wiggle away lickety quick, she won't stay there long." They were about to move when the door handle began to turn. Verity flashed a look at Morton. She grabbed his arm and pulled him behind the door then quickly pushed the light switch. The room clicked into darkness. The door creaked open and Verity got ready. She waited till the figure was in the room and jumped out and kicked it hard in the leg. It crumpled and fell to the ground. Verity clicked the light back on.

"Ow!" came a familiar voice, "I really wish you wouldn't do that!" groaned Frances.

Verity looked at her lying on the floor rubbing her leg. "What on earth are you doing here?" she asked.

"Well obviously, I am saving you!" Frances replied.

"You are an idiot. You will get yourself in so much trouble." Verity said a little crossly. Frances looked a bit hurt. "But you are a brave idiot," Verity added with a smile. She pulled her friend up and hugged her. "Thank you," she said.

"Ehh hem," coughed Morton.

"Verity I think I must have bumped my head, I am seeing things," said Frances.

"No, I'm afraid not. Frances meet Morton, Morton meet Frances."

"Morty, if you pleases Mrs Frances," he gave a little bow as he spoke.

"This is all lovely but shouldn't we get going?" Verity added. The cellar hatch burst open and a hand appeared.

"Who is that!" Frances called out.

"Trouble!" Verity replied, "Lets go!"

The trio rushed out the door. They raced down the corridor that was lined with doors left and right. They burst into the last room on the left. Verity clunked the door shut. The three of them were breathing hard.

"What do we do now?" asked Frances, "she is bound to find us and then she's going to, going to, going to..."

Frances was terrified.

Verity put her hands on Frances' shoulders and looked calmly into her big green eyes. "She won't do anything because she won't catch us. We are getting out of here, me and you. I'm going to look after you. Right now, you need to trust me." She tried her best to make her voice reassuring. Frances nodded.

Morty was grumbling. "All right for girly peeps, they is not old as dragons' wrinkles. I has wonky knees and squeaky hips. All this fussin' and buzzin' about is no good to me!"

Verity wasn't listening. She was thinking hard about how to get out. They had hidden in the laundry room. There were big baskets filled with bedclothes and linen. "We could hide in these!" Frances said excitedly, "and then wait till… Well, till…" her voice tailed off as her idea disappeared.

"Till we come out and are still stuck in the middle of Dark Oak?" Verity said sarcastically.

"Well I don't hear you coming up with anything better," replied a grumpy Frances.

A door slammed further down the corridor. "Come out, come out little ones!" came Krankle's voice. "Time for your medicine! Don't worry, the needle won't hurt too much although you might get a little sleepy. In fact, you might feel like sleeping FOREVER!" She sounded slightly manic as she sang out. Another door slammed.

"It won't be long before she is here, I mean, my plans are clearly far too stupid, so what do we do smarty pants?" said Frances with her arms folded.

"Bones creakin' an crackin', I is goin' to need me cod liver oils tonight," grumbled Morty.

"Ok," said an exasperated Verity, "your plan was a very good one, everything about it was extremely clever except for the tiny niggle that it wouldn't work. Apart from that, it was a winner. Morty, I'm sorry your hips are sore and I will personally see to it that you get the very best of medical attention just as soon as we get out." Another door slammed. "That is of course, as long as Krankle doesn't mince us first, so please, pretty please, with a cherry on top, could we all think of a way out of here!" Verity huffed.

Frances looked at Morty. "A little touchy wouldn't you say?"

"Yes yes yes Mrs Frances, needs more fibre in the diet me thinks," he replied.

"Morty, you must have been here forever. You must know a clever way out. Can't you think of anything?" pleaded Verity.

"Ways out, ways in, yes yes yes. We is right at the bottom of Dark Oak. There is no ways out down here, only ways in," he said. Verity knew this made no sense but didn't think trying to reason with him would help. "Up and up we needs. Up to the attic. We can gets out and be safe as a bug in a jug from there."

Another door slammed. Krankle was close. "If you turn her in Morton, I will make sure you are well rewarded!" she called. She was one door away now. Verity looked around the room desperately, no windows, one door and the large bins of laundry. The three friends flashed worried looks at each other. Krankle's footsteps were nearly outside.

Morty spoke quietly to Verity, "Find the cauldron in the attic. Throw these in and walk into the smoke." He pushed some dried leaves into Verity's hand and before she could say anything he disappeared out the door closing it behind him. Verity and Frances rushed to the door and pressed their ears hard against it. Both voices outside were slightly muffled. "Hi De Ho Mrs Krinkle. How is you diddlin'? Did I hear you talky peepin' about a reward?" Morty said.

There was a thump against the door as Krankle hammered him against it. "Get me the girl and your reward will be that I don't end your miserable little existence," Krankle snarled.

"Yes yes yes Mrs Krinkles my honour. Come with me, I am showing you where girly peeps hides."

Verity held her breath. "Winkle this way," she heard him say.

Their footsteps slowly disappeared. Frances looked at Verity. "What if he's not ok? What if..."

"You heard him, he wants us to get to the attic and that's where we are going," Verity interrupted.

"We won't leave him though will we?" Frances' green eyes grew large. Verity thought for a second. She had only known Morty for about an hour but he had already been more of a friend to her than anyone except Frances.

"We won't leave him," she said boldly. "Now let's go!"

They opened the door and Verity checked that the corridor was clear. They ran to the stone staircase and headed up.

"Where is everyone?" asked Frances. "The place seems deserted."

"I bet Krankle has locked them all in while she does her wickedness," Verity said.

Up they climbed till they reached the first floor.

"We need to go through the main hall to get to the stairs." Verity grabbed Frances' arm and they hurried across the hall. The wooden floorboards creaked and groaned as they went.

Just as they got to the bottom of the stairs, they heard Krankle shouting in the kitchen. "They are not here you pipsqueek! I should have done this a long time ago!"

"Now now now Mrs Krinkle. You be careful with that sharpy knife. You could be putting it down now!" came a frightened sounding Morty. Verity looked up the stairs. They had nearly made it, they just needed to hurry upstairs and find the hatch to the attic. She looked at the kitchen door. Could she risk something happening to Frances? Frances looked at her with her big green eyes.

"Take these," Verity said pushing the dried leaves into Frances' hand. "Get to the attic and do as Morty said."

"What about you?" pleaded Frances.

"I will be right behind you but I don't want you to wait for me. If I don't appear, you don't hang around. Now go!" she pushed Frances towards the stairs. Frances glanced back at her before running up. Verity ran to the kitchen door, took a deep breath, and made her way through.

Morty was trapped in the corner of the kitchen and Krankle was heading towards him with a large kitchen knife. "I will start with your nose," she crowed, "then, I will start nipping off your little fingers till you tell me where she is!" She towered over little, cowering Morty.

"Right here you crusty old boot!" Verity shouted as she burst into the kitchen.

Krankle spun round on the spot. "Well, well, look who has come to join us. You are just in time sweetness. I was just preparing dinner. A delicious mole soup with chunky mole pieces on the side." Krankle's voice turned nasty. "I don't mind putting that off for you though, Verity," she said the name as if she had some dog dirt in her mouth.

"I don't know what you want but we are leaving and won't be back so you don't have to worry about us bothering you again," Verity said calmly.

"HAAAA HHAAAAA," Krankle screeched, "How right you are, I won't need to worry about you because you will be dead!"

"But why?" Verity pleaded, "I'm just Verity, why me?"

"For my master, child," with those words, she turned and thrust the knife in and out of Morty who yelped helplessly and fell to the ground. Then, she fixed her gaze on Verity and charged towards her. Verity moved before she even thought about what she was doing. She dived under the large metal table in the middle of the room and crawled till she came out the other side. The table was now between Krankle and Verity.

"You are a monster!" Verity hissed.

"You are the monster!" Krankle replied. "It is you not me, that must be stopped before you poison the world!"

Krankle swiped the knife across the table but her reach was not long enough. Verity looked around frantically for something to defend herself with. There was nothing to hand. Trust me to be in the tidiest kitchen in the land, she thought. Krankle placed both hands on the table and used her huge weight to shove it as hard as she could. The table caught Verity in the stomach and she was forced backwards till she hit the metal shelves behind her. She ended in a heap on the ground. Her head was fuzzy and there was a sharp pain in her back. She groggily pulled herself up into a sitting position. She could see little Morty lying in the other corner. Krankle loomed over her, knife in hand. "This is for the Master!" she said as she pulled the knife back ready to strike. Verity was too dazed to react properly. She saw the glinting knife and closed her eyes softly and waited for the pain.

THUNK! An almighty clang filled the air. Verity quickly opened her eyes to see Krankle falling like a tree to the floor. The knife skittled across the tiles. In her place stood Frances clutching a large iron saucepan.

"What are you doing here?" Verity was still a little groggy.

"Obviously, I am saving you!" said Frances who had appeared to surprise herself. "Where is Morty?" she asked.

Verity pulled herself to her feet and stumbled over to the corner.

"Oh Morty!" wailed Frances.

"Come on Morty!" Verity whispered desperately as she shook him a little. She buried her head in his chest and sobbed.

"What is you doin'!" Morty croaked. "Rattlin' me bones then soakin' me fur! Get orf," he groaned.

"Morty!" cheered Frances as she leaped over for a hug.

"OW wow ow! Keep your little wiggly feelers to yourself!" Morty groaned. He had a nasty wound just below his shoulder where it met the body.

"It's bleeding too much, get me something to cover it," Verity said quickly. Frances scurried round and came back with a white dishcloth. Verity wound it round the wound and tied it as tightly as she dared. Morty groaned several naughty words.

"Should moles use words like that in front of girls?" Frances asked innocently.

"Never mind that now, it's time to go before she wakes up," Verity said, pointing at Krankle who was now groaning.

Frances picked up the pot and swung it again. *THUNK!* Another clunk to the head. "Oops," said Frances, smiling. The two girls helped Morty to his feet and made their way out of the kitchen. Morty wasn't very heavy and it didn't take too long to get him up the stairs and into the attic.

"There is the cauldron. What now Morty?"

"We is throwin' in the leaves." he said.

"Here." Frances rummaged in her pocked and produced the handful of leaves.

"Throw thems in," said Morty. Frances did as she was told. "Gets your little squiggly paws and look in my pocket for my magic silver box." Verity put her hand in Morty's pocket and felt a cuboid metallic box. She pulled it out to see it was a cigarette lighter. "Ah, waits till you sees the magic box, it is a mystical object from far away lands. It has powers what your little bundle of brains cannot dream of!" Morty said proudly. The girls gave each other a puzzled look. "Behold the magic of fire!" Morty announced. He flicked open the lid and pushed the wheel round with his thumb. The lighter sparked into life and produced a tiny flame. Frances started to snigger. "Why is she titterin'?" Morty sounded confused.

"No idea," said Verity who was also trying hard not to laugh at this lovely little moleman.

"Right, light the leaves!" he said.

Verity took the lighter and leaned into the large cauldron and set light to one of the dry brown leaves. The rest soon followed in a little crackling blaze. She stepped back. A plume of smoke rose vertically from the pot. It was thick and changed colour every few seconds, red, yellow, blue, orange. It eventually settled and stayed black. The smoke thinned and became wispy and if Verity didn't know better she could have sworn she saw the image of a forest in the misty blackness. "Right missy and missy, time to go, yes yes yes. Breathe deep, breathe in deep," Morty said pointing to the smoke.

Verity and Frances looked at each other. Verity could see Frances was nervous. "I'll go first," Verity said squeezing Frances' hand gently. She stood by the cauldron and put her face into the smoke. She breathed in deeply. It smelt beautiful, not at all what she imagined. It made her feel dizzy and happy. She felt as though she was in a meadow, the grass was long and the flowers were brightly coloured. The sun felt warm on her skin. A woman was calling to her. A beautiful woman with long dark hair. The room and the cauldron disappeared. She felt as if she was floating in a wonderful happy bubble. Then, blackness came as she lost consciousness.

Chapter 4
Scarlet

'I'm not afraid of storms, for I'm learning to sail my ship.'
Louisa May Alcott

A small girl appeared at the little stone cottage door. Her curly red hair flowed and bounced over her shoulders. She wore a pretty red dress with a black bow and ribbon tied round her waist. She was smiling and her bright ruby eyes smiled with her. She looked out at the scene. She could see her mother in the distance working on the beach. She was painting the fishing boat ready for the spring. The landscape was bare. Green and brown peat bogs, the ground, peppered with grey lumpy rocks. It would soon be time to cut the peat to make fuel for the winter fires. Some sheep were grazing the land while others lay in small groups resting. The only other house nearby was a similar stone cottage. The red headed girl skipped and ran in its direction. When she got there she knocked on the door. She was looking for her best and only friend, Grace. She and Grace were thick as thieves and felt as if they had known each other forever. A thin bony woman wearing a brown apron answered the door. "Morning Mrs McFarlane, is Grace coming out to play?" the redhead chirped.

Grace's mother looked a little uncomfortable. "Grace won't be playing today," she said quickly.

"Oh, will she be able to play tomorrow?" the redhead asked cheerily.

"No, nor the next day, in fact, she won't be playing again. Goodbye Scarlet," the woman said awkwardly as she closed the door. Tears welled but did not fall from Scarlet's eyes as she ran back home.

"What on earth is the matter?" asked Scarlet's mother when she eventually found her sobbing behind the barn.

"Nothing," sniffed Scarlet.

"Ah, I see," her mother said softly, "you know sometimes when I'm upset I like to play a little game to help."

"Oh, what is it?" Scarlet said. She was curious.

"Well I close my eyes and think about the thing that's making me upset, then I imagine myself putting it in a little red bag and then I tie the string tightly and put it away for later."

"Sounds silly," said Scarlet.

"Try it," said her mother. Scarlet closed her eyes. "Shut them tight," her mother said. Scarlet shut her eyes as tightly as she could. "Now imagine putting your worries in the little red bag," she continued. "Now, pull the string and tie it tight," she said. Scarlet opened her eyes.

"Do you feel better?" her mother asked.

"A little," Scarlet smiled. She hugged her mother tightly.

Scarlet's mother made her way over to the McFarlane place. She knocked on the door. Mrs McFarlane answered. "Ah, Martha, come in."

"I can't stay, I have mince in the pan. Scarlet has been upset all day and I wondered if the girls had fallen out or had some kind of problem?"

Mrs McFarlane looked uncomfortable again. "Well Martha, you see, it's, well, it's…" she was cut short by her husband's voice from inside the house.

"Grace won't be seeing that girl any more. Scarlet's not, well she's not right. I'm sorry," he said sternly.

"I don't understand. We have known each other for so long. The girls adore each other," said Martha.

"Folks are talking, Scarlet's not right!" he replied.

"She's my little girl!" Martha said.

"Ah, but she's not YOURS is she?" he sneered from inside. Mrs McFarlane shuffled nervously by the door.

"Well I think we are done here," Martha said. She was trying to sound dignified but was clearly upset. "Goodbye," she said before heading back over the fields.

Scarlet couldn't sleep that night. She could hear her mother sobbing in the next room. She opened the door a little and crept through. "Mummy, what's wrong mummy?" she asked softly. Scarlet stood in her red nightdress and was about to speak again when there was a loud thump at the door.

"Martha, open the door! We need to talk!"

Martha quickly looked out of the corner of the curtains. A large group of men and women had gathered at the door. Some of them carried rifles and some were carrying lit torches which burned brightly in the blackness. The thumps came again.

"Martha, be sensible, the girl can't stay. The crops are failing and the sheep are ill. Come on Martha, nobody is saying she's a witch, but she's not right, we just need to speak with her."

"You can't have her and if you come in that door you will find trouble!" Martha shouted back. She was a lioness, ready for the mob. Scarlet held on to her mother tightly.

"We have to come in Martha. Lets make this easy."

Something started hammering on the door making it shake on its hinges. Suddenly, the door burst open and a small wave of bodies gushed in. Scarlet and her mother held each other tightly at the opposite side of the room. Scarlet started to feel dizzy, a powerful mixture of fear and an anger. Something deep inside her, a fire in her belly.

A big man stepped forward. Scarlet recognised him as James Warner the butcher. "Hand her over," he said.

"What are you doing?" wailed Martha as she held Scarlet as tightly as she could.

"I wish it didn't have to be like this," he said. He nodded to two men behind him. They moved forward and grabbed at Martha and started trying to pull and wrench the two bodies apart. Martha screamed and struggled as their horrible hands forced her to let go of little Scarlet. Their dirty hands bruised and scratched her as they dragged her across the floor. Scarlet could see they were hurting her. The fire inside her roared into life.

Scarlet's ruby eyes started to burn, she felt something taking over. The men backed away as she slowly rose into the air, her arms outstretched to the sides, her hands ablaze.

"GET AWAY FROM HER!" Scarlet screamed.

Her voice was deep and loud. The crowd was terrified. She swept her arms together and as her burning hands touched, the room filled with blinding red light. Scarlet fell and crumpled on the ground, sobbing. Her eyes and hands had stopped burning, and the strange feeling had left her. Wisps of smoke rose from her little body. The crowd had vanished into thin air. Her mother got up and pulled her near. "Oh my little one," she said as she kissed her head, "you will always be my little bee."

"We have to go away, somewhere where nobody will know us, somewhere to start again and be happy. Somewhere really beautiful where it can be just you and me," her voice was reassuring.

"Never leave me," Scarlet said as she clung to her mother.

"I will never leave you, little bee," said Martha as she kissed Scarlet gently on the head.

Time's hands turned the earth and Scarlet had grown to become a young woman. Her hair and eyes were now an elegant deep velvety ruby colour and she had become quite beautiful. She had moved away with her mother years ago to escape the local townsfolk. They had settled near a long golden beach that had a little stream at the end that ran into the sea. When Scarlet was still little she had loved building dams to try and block the stream although no matter how hard she worked, they always overflowed. Scarlet and her mother had looked after each other. The only thing Scarlet had feared was the day her mother might die and leave her. That day came in the autumn. The trees elegantly displayed their golden leaves and although it was cool, the sun shone brightly. Scarlet wetted a towel and took it to her mother's bedside. Martha had become suddenly ill. She had been well only the day before when she sold a woollen scarf to the strange lady in grey who happened by. She had woken with a terrible fever. Scarlet placed the towel gently on her mother's head. "My little bee," Martha's voice was weak.

"Don't talk mother, just rest," soothed Scarlet.

"Little bee, you have been my light."

"Just rest now," said Scarlet.

"I have to tell you the truth before it's time," her voice was a whisper now.

"You don't need to say anything," said Scarlet.

"I have kept a terrible truth from you. I am not your mother. I found you as a baby, wrapped in rags and lying on the beach. I was never blessed with children and from the second I saw you I knew I would never want to let you go. I'm so sorry little bee."

Tears started to roll down Scarlet's face.

"Truth? Lets talk about truth. You are my mother. I love you as you love me. That will be true till time ends. It's is the only thing that matters."

Martha smiled and closed her eyes. Scarlet kissed her forehead and held her as she passed away.

Scarlet felt the sadness of her mother passing as keenly as a blade. Happiness no longer looked for her and her nights came with dark thoughts. A strange figure troubled her dreams. A mysterious grey figure with a pale face.

She spent years travelling from place to place, searching but never really knowing what for. When she turned eighteen, she had settled in a large fishing village called Kergord. There was plenty of work for men at the docks and fishing boats heaved and creaked with plentiful catches. The townsfolk were happy as their pockets were full of coins. One of the popular places for young people to spend these coins was The Devil's Rest, a tavern by the pier. Scarlet had been working as a barmaid there for several weeks. She was very popular with the locals, especially the young fishermen who were enchanted by her mystery and beauty. One particular evening a stranger came in. He ordered a drink and sat at a small table in the corner. He did not touch his drink.

"Here, Scarlet, who's that strange lookin' fellow in the corner?" said Sandy, one of the other barmaids. Scarlet looked over at him. He was young, no more than twenty, slim, and although his face was pale. His eyes were deep navy blue. He was dressed in black and his hair was neatly parted to the side.

"Never seen him before," Scarlet replied.

"He keeps lookin' your way, I reckon he likes you," Sandy teased. Scarlet blushed.

"Don't be silly," she said and took another look at him before carrying on with her work. The next time she looked at that corner only the man's untouched drink remained. The Devil's Rest was busy that night and the two girls worked hard keeping the fishermen and locals happy and full of ale.

It was getting near to closing time. "I think you should be the one dealing with admirers now," Scarlet winked at Sandy. She pointed to the end of the bar. A young man stood wobbling a little on his feet. "Zander is on his fourth mug of Devil's Buttermilk and I think he is ready for home," Scarlet said. Zander was a local lad. He worked as an apprentice for his uncle, a local boatbuilder. He was a strong lad with a mop of messy blonde hair. His face was kind and his smile was warm. He had an athletic frame and many local girls were keen on him. It was the worst kept secret in Kergord that he was hopelessly smitten with Sandy. She was very fond of him and the pair were very good friends. She went over to speak with him.

"I'll take another Devil's Mutterbilk," he said proudly.

"You mean Buttermilk and I think it might be time for you to head to bed," Sandy said.

"I want to tell you something, Sandy," he mumbled very seriously all of a sudden, "I think, well I really think... What I think is, that you..., you are..."

40

"I think it's home time for you, goodnight Zander," Sandy said curtly and walked away to wipe some tables.

"You are mean to him," Scarlet said, "He is sweet."

"I know," said Sandy. She looked at him and smiled. "I think I will let him court me one day," she blushed.

"That's so great! I'm so pleased for you," Scarlet said and gave her friend a big hug.

Scarlet lay in bed that night feeling happy that her friend was happy. Her room was lit by the moonlight streaming in through the window. Suddenly, there was a loud bash on the window. Scarlet was startled. Seconds later there was another bash. Scarlet felt a little frightened but had never been one to be scared of being brave so she crept to the window and looked out. A figure stood below and threw something at her. It bounced off the window. She opened it and called down, "Get lost! Or I will come down to give you a sore chin!"

"Don't come down, I will come up!" a voice called back. The figure started climbing the thick green ivy which covered most of the front of the house. Scarlet watched as he slipped and stumbled but slowly clambered up the wall. She decided that this intruder was a little too clumsy to be dangerous so watched on with interest. As he hauled himself closer to Scarlet's window she could see the face of the pale handsome man who had been in the tavern. His hair was not quite so neat now as he struggled through the ivy. He pulled himself up and sat on her window ledge.

"How can I help you?" Scarlet said with playful suspicion.

"I simply came to tell you that you are the luckiest girl in Kergord!" he declared.

"Really," Scarlet said, deliberately sounding unimpressed, "and why would that be?"

"Because my dear," he said grandly, "earlier today I saw the most amazing creature that there has surely ever been. She made my mind freeze and my heart ache just looking at her. My every thought has been about her from that moment. Do you believe in one true love?"

"I believe in lots of things that I will not share with strangers at my window." She allowed him a small smile, "You still haven't told me why I am so lucky."

"Ah," his charming grin faded and he looked deeply at her as he spoke, "the creature that has made me feel this way is you."

Scarlet smiled and blushed a little but didn't want to show him quite how brilliant those words were to hear. She composed herself, "Well in that case I think it is you who are the luckiest in all Kergord as you will meet me tomorrow at the mermaid fountain by the clock tower at twelve and you shall take me to lunch." With that she closed the window sharply and pulled the curtains.

There was a gentle knock at the window. She opened it. "I don't know your name," he said.

"Scarlet," she replied, "and you are?"

He leant over towards her slowly and whispered in her ear then kissed her gently on the cheek.

"Goodnight, Blake," she said softly. She couldn't help smiling.

She fell onto her bed feeling dizzy and sick and excited all at once as if she might burst! Happiness found her that night and she slept deeply for the first time since her mother had died.

The summer that followed was the happiest time Scarlet could recall. She had fallen deeply in love with Blake, as he had with her. He had found work on one of the local boats and the two had spent every moment they could with each other. The sun had been warm, the sea sparkled and the sky was blue and beautiful. Scarlet and Blake lay side by side in the top meadow overlooking the town.

"So beautiful," said Blake.

"It really is," Scarlet replied looking down over the glistening sea and the happy, busy village of Kergord below.

"I was looking at you," said Blake softly.

Scarlet brushed her hand gently through his jet black hair and rolled over and kissed him slowly. "I hope nothing will ever keep me apart from you," she said.

"I love you," he replied and held her tightly as the warm summer breeze made the corn sway gently and in that moment, their universe was perfect.

The next night was very busy in the Devil's Rest. Sandy and Scarlet were worn out after filling countless mugs of ale but the end of the night was near. Zander stood at the end of the bar trying hard to pluck up the courage to tell Sandy how he felt. "Why don't you put him out of his misery?" Scarlet said to Sandy, "You are both meant for each other."

Sandy looked at him. "I am waiting for him to tell me so," she said.

"You are too stubborn for your own good," replied Scarlet.

Blake was waiting on the pier. Scarlet's shift would finish soon and they had planned to take a walk along the shore. The evenings were still warm and the moon gently laid a blanket of beautiful silvery light across the town. A stranger stopped and stood next to him. It wasn't until she spoke that Blake realised it was a woman. She was dressed in a long grey hooded robe. The hood hid most of her face. She looked up at him.

Blake studied her. "Your eyes are very black," he said.

"Would you like something to eat?" she said, holding out a small bag filled with small black objects.

"Thank you," he said as he popped one into his mouth.

"The moon is low in the sky," she said.

"Is it?" replied Blake a little curious as to what the stranger wanted.

"Yes," she said, "it's preparing to die, the new moon will appear in a few days."

"What do you mean, preparing to die?" he asked.

"Oh yes," she said, "it has the same story as all things. It must die."

"Not all things must die," said Blake with a smile.

"What is it that you think of?" said the mysterious grey woman.

"True love lasts forever. That is why it's so hard to find because it's so precious," Blake said passionately.

"Bless you, my child," said the woman. "I envy you. I was once like you and believed such things, until I learned that even true love must die."

"I'm sorry to hear your tale," said Blake, "but I have found a bond that cannot be broken."

"All bonds can be broken. I fear your true love is more fragile than you think. It is Scarlet that you think of, yes?" The woman's tone changed.

"Yes, but how do you... who are you?" Blake shuffled uneasily.

"Yes, I'm afraid young Scarlet has another whom she loves."

"You are lying," Blake said angrily.

"No I am not, she loves a young man called Zander who visits the Devil's Rest to see her," the woman said.

"No! We have a special love, a true love that cannot be broken. I don't know who you are or what your business is but I am done with you and you best be on your way," Blake said. He could feel the anger inside him growing. An anger for this woman who had poison on her tongue. An anger for himself for thinking this poison could be true.

"I'm sorry to have brought this to you," the woman said. "I will leave you with one last piece of information that you can use as you wish. Scarlet is planning to meet Zander this very night outside the Devil's Rest. You will see then how strong your true love is." With those words she turned and walked away. Blake couldn't see the wicked smile on her face as she did.

Blake found himself in a cloud of confusion. Who was she? How did she know Scarlet? Why would she say such things? Blake's anger grew and he despised himself for thinking that his Scarlet could ever hurt him like that. Yet, he couldn't ignore the feelings. He knew Zander was often in the Devil's Rest. Could it be? He had to know and started to make his way to the tavern.

The night was drawing to an end and Zander was gulping his fourth Buttermilk. "I am going to ask him to take me out!" Sandy giggled to Scarlet.

"About time!" Scarlet giggled back. Sandy looked over but Zander had disappeared. "Don't worry," Scarlet said, "he'll be back."

Scarlet bagged up the last of the rubbish and slung it over her shoulder to take outside. She tossed it into the large bin behind the tavern and was about to head back in when she heard a quiet sobbing. She followed the sound round to the side of the building. It was Zander. He was sitting with his head in his hands. Scarlet could see the shore from here and she rubbed her tummy as she thought of telling Blake her news during their midnight walk. "What's wrong Zander?" she asked kindly as she sat next to him.

"I am useless," he replied, "I love Sandy so much and I can't even tell her. Even if I did, why would she be interested in an idiot like me," he sobbed.

"Don't be so hard on yourself," Scarlet soothed as she put her arm round him. "You are lovely and I happen to know that Sandy thinks so too."

"Really!" Zander's eyes were as wide as dinner plates as he spoke.

"Really," said Scarlet, "I think that you need to get back in there and ask her to lunch tomorrow." She got up and helped him with both hands to his feet. He stumbled towards her and she caught him in her arms. "No more Buttermilks!" she said. "You need a clear head if you are to court Sandy."

"You are lovely just like she said," Zander muttered.

"Who?" asked Scarlet.

"The woman in the grey hood. She said you would help me if I came outside. Thank you for giving me courage Scarlet," he said still in her arms. He kissed her clumsily and then stood straight. "I'm going to speak to Sandy!" he said proudly. Then wobbled back into the tavern. Scarlet smiled, her best friend would find her true love at last.

Blake stood close to the tree so he wouldn't be seen. He could see the path beside the tavern quite clearly and had been watching Scarlet and Zander. His blood ran cold. His heart was beating so hard it felt it might burst out his chest. How could it be? How could she? It had felt like true love. He was in a spin. Unable to think, unable to think! What to do, how could this be? Blake had been hurt before but not by Scarlet. She was the one person in the world he thought would never hurt him, he trusted her, yet there she was driving a blade into his heart. Jealousy and anger slithered and snaked together inside his head intoxicating him, consuming him. He fell to his knees, face to the ground, both hands clutching his head, covering his eyes. He made a noise that came from deep inside. He slowly raised his body up, standing tall on his knees. His hands came away from his face. How could she?

Scarlet wiped down the last of the tables. The night was nearly done. A loud crash startled everyone as Blake entered and kicked a table over.

"Blake?" said Scarlet.

"It's over!" he said bitterly. He fixed his black gaze on Zander. "You!"

Zander stood, terrified, as Blake rushed towards him.

***

As the years passed Scarlet had become consumed by her dreams. They were always the same.

She would be alone in an empty room. It had no furniture, doors or windows. She was sitting in the middle of the room tied to a chair unable to move. She would close her eyes. When she opened them, a figure stood in front of her. The figure was cloaked in grey. It was human but the face was grey with large black holes where the eyes and mouth should have been. Her eyes would close again and she would feel fear wrap around her chest crushing her, choking her. When she opened her eyes again she was floating in the room, looking down at a little girl with red hair tied to a chair. The figure stood over the girl. It slowly put its hands around the little girls neck. Scarlet would try to scream, 'Stop! Fight back!' But no words would come, just wheezing and gasping from her mouth. The little girl in the chair would look up at Scarlet. A tear would roll down her cheek as the grey figure choked her as her little ruby eyes slowly turned black.

Scarlet would wake up sweating, heart racing. The dream confirmed two things that she had long thought. The first was that the world was cruel. The second was that if someone wanted to survive they would have to be cruel too.

The world had grown old around Scarlet. As a witch she had remained young while time had placed its hands on everything else. She had become very wise and very powerful. Since Blake had left her she had spent many years travelling Ulysses far and wide and had discovered many things. She had learned all she could from these places and waited patiently to play her part in the world's story.

Scarlet had been guarding the weeping stones for longer than she cared to remember. The night sky was beautifully black and the stars blazed like rebel diamonds cut out of the sun. Scarlet gazed up at the moon. It was full. She turned and spoke to the gore.

"She is coming."

"Wraaaag," grunted the gore softly.

"Perfidy," she replied.

Chapter 5
Perfidy

'In order for light to shine so brightly, the darkness must be present.'
Francis Bacon

Perfidy woke from her sleep. The room was dark and the air was cool. She swung her legs over the side of the bed and rubbed her eyes. Everything seemed peaceful. Then she heard the old familiar voice, "Where are you?" it called from somewhere far away. She rose to her feet quickly. The wooden floor boards felt cold as she stood on them. "Where are you?" came the voice again. Perfidy opened her door and stepped into a corridor that she could not see the end of. Shut doors lined the corridor left and right as far as she could see. "Where are you?" it came again. She followed the voice down the corridor. It grew louder, "Where are you Perfidy?"

"I'm coming!" she shouted. Perfidy was running down the corridor now.

"I need you Perfidy, where are you?" the voice was close now. Perfidy frantically rattled the handles of as many doors as she could. They were all locked. Perfidy was sweating and breathing hard. "I'm coming!" she cried. She tried the handle of the last door. It was locked. She fell to her knees in despair. The silence engulfed her until all she could hear was her own breathing. Suddenly, she could hear a door creaking open behind her. She turned around. It was only open a fraction and the room was too dark to see into. She slowly pulled herself up onto her feet and walked cautiously through the door. It slammed shut behind her and darkness flooded in. Perfidy was breathing heavily. She didn't move.

A voice rang out of the darkness, "I'm here Perfidy, come and see me." Perfidy squinted as her eyes were dazzled by silver light. She put her arm up to shield her eyes and moved towards it. As she got closer she realised the silver light was a mirror. She stopped in front of it and looked at herself. For a few seconds everything was still then suddenly tears started to run down her reflection's face, then it spoke, "I need you Perfidy, where are you?"

Perfidy sat bolt upright in her bed. She was sweating and breathing hard. She had had this dream many times but her reflection had never cried before.

Perfidy had been keeping a close eye over the forest for a long time. She stood looking out from the top of a round green hill. Her home, Calden Castle lay far off in the distance. The night sky was dominated by the dazzling full moon which shone deeply and brightly. Perfidy knew the moon wouldn't be there for long. She had large piercing blue eyes. Her raven black hair shimmered in the moonlight. Her time before Blake, had taught her that life was difficult and unfair, that some things hurt and didn't get better. She had learned to fear the dark, when it came it brought dark thoughts with it. Perfidy felt no peace with herself. She was a warrior, a lioness. She had needed to fight hard just to survive. Blake had watched her for a long time before he took her in. Perfidy had never questioned Blake. He looked after her when nobody else would. She felt he understood her and helped her manage the fear. He had made her strong. He had given her the skills to protect herself. It made her feel better to know that Blake was there to keep her safe.

Blake carried the ghosts of his past with him. He was tall and slim. His jet black hair was neatly parted to the side. He was deathly pale and always wore a long black leather coat that seemed to cling to his frame as he moved. His eyes were black and empty. His ghosts followed him wherever he went. They hung over him like a curse and they were always just out of his reach.

He looked at the black skies and the moon dazzling in the sky over the forest. It was time for Perfidy to visit the weeping stones. The Grey Witch was growing stronger and they would need their magic.

Perfidy had been waiting for this task for a long time and had prepared herself. She slung her shot bow over her shoulder and checked her arrows. Each one would fly straight and true not only because Perfidy had a dead aim but they had Silver Terpin feathers attached as flights. Each arrowhead had been dipped in gore blood that was highly poisonous to almost everything. She clipped on her dagger belt. Her dagger was slightly serrated down one side of the blade. The hilt was black and smooth. It had been given to her by Blake. She adjusted her tunic. It was a deep red colour and was covered by her brown leather armour. Someone else can feel the fear tonight she thought. I will make sure they do. With that thought, she set off. The forest path was long and she wanted to be back before sunrise.

The weeping stones were hidden deep within the forest. Six rocks that were set in a circle. Nobody really knew who put them there but there were lots of tales that they came from a far away land. Once every hundred years when the moon was about to die the stones produced a liquid which was said to have healing powers beyond that of any medicine. Very few were ever able to take any of the magical liquid as the stones were protected by Scarlet and her gore. Perfidy was one of the few who was skilful enough or brave enough to try. She had no quarrel with the witch but Blake had trusted her to steal the magic of healing from the stones and she wouldn't let him down. The first problem she would face was the gore. Gores were large worker beasts, twice the height of a normal man and twice as wide. Entirely grey and with skin as tough as stone, they were simple creatures that had been bred by the ancients to work and build. They didn't have many feelings other than hunger. They were easily trained to suit their master's needs as long as the master fed them, which made them very useful. Scarlet's gore was particularly dangerous but Perfidy had dealt with gores before and had no concerns about this one, though she knew she would have to be careful.

Blake looked out at the night filled sky. The moon had risen fully and charmed his eyes. It was time to instruct the messenger again. The most important task ever performed he thought. Yet he would send the smallest of creatures to deliver it. He had considered sending Perfidy but decided he couldn't risk her meeting Verity. His boots made no sound as he walked down the long corridor that joined the North Tower to the main hallway. He made his way into his study. The room was home to a large stone table upon which sat a small black cauldron. A large bookcase lay against the nearest wall. All the books were bound in black leather. The titles of the books were written in shimmering silver and were composed in a strange language. Blake sat down and struck a match before throwing it into the cauldron. "The time has come Verity," he whispered under his breath.

Perfidy crawled on her belly between several large bushes and plants. She knew the clearing was close and didn't want to be seen yet. These were the moments she loved. The fear was gone while the whole world melted away because her focus was so intense. She normally delivered the fear to others in these moments but she had never matched up to a witch before. She didn't know whether she could even make her afraid. It didn't matter, even witches would feel the blade. She was close now, inching further towards the clearing where the stones were. She could see them now. Six oddly shaped stones standing in a circle, each one had strange rune like carvings on the sides. She stopped still, waiting, listening, nothing. Perhaps this will be easy after all she thought. Suddenly, the forest came alive and two huge grey hands grabbed her and pinned her arms to her side. She struggled but couldn't reach her dagger. The gore lifted her out of her hiding place. "Of course, I'm sad to see he sent a child," Scarlet said as she stepped out into the open. "No matter, I'm afraid I'm going to make you very sorry you came," she said coolly. Scarlet was hooded in ruby velvet. Her eyes burned fiercely as did her hair. Her lips were crimson, she looked surprisingly young for a witch. She walked to Perfidy and pushed a foul smelling rag in her face. Perfidy struggled then felt sick and then felt nothing.

Perfidy woke to find her hands and feet stuck together as if tied but there were no ropes to see. She was lying on her side on top of a large flat stone. She struggled but could not move. "I wouldn't worry about going anywhere my child. My magic will keep you quite still." Perfidy could hear but not see the witch. "I am upset child," she continued, "upset that Blake would send you to do his dirty work. I wish he had come himself. I would have enjoyed making him suffer. Such a shame."

"Listen to me, please." Perfidy started, "He told me to come here. I don't even know why. I am afraid of him." Scarlet eyed her carefully. "I am so sorry. I had no idea. You have to believe me." A crocodile tear slid down Perfidy's cheek. "I want to help you stop him. I can take you to him. We can help each other." Perfidy's voice was small and weak.

"How old are you child?" asked the witch.

"I just want to be free from him," Perfidy continued. "I need you to help me, maybe that's why I came," she pleaded with her eyes.

"Some say this world is complicated," the witch started, "full of mysterious magic and creatures. Full of things people can't explain. The ancients longed to understand the world. They believed everything must make sense. They developed a magic called science, which they used to try to understand everything. Everyone was happy because they believed they could see the true way of things." Scarlet had not taken her eyes away from Perfidy yet.

"I don't understand," sobbed Perfidy.

The witch continued, "I have seen the truth. Science is strong but the world is failing. We are busy creating our own destruction. We build special tools like the gun to pull and tear our hearts and bodies apart. Vanity, greed and ignorance lie with us in the darkness. Our world, Ulysses, is in danger. The darkness grows stronger with every wave of greed that laps at our shore. It will envelop Ulysses as the Grey Witch wishes. She won't be stopped. I have looked into the smoke and foreseen it."

"Tell me how I can help, anything, please! This can't happen!" Perfidy wailed.

Scarlet waved her hand and the invisible bonds that held Perfidy let go. Perfidy sat up and rubbed her wrists. "We need to make a plan." she said, "Where is the gore?"

"The gore sleeps now, you need not worry about him. I have waited a long time for you Perfidy," said the witch. She was facing away from Perfidy looking through the trees.

"How did you know my name?" Perfidy said, a little puzzled.

"There is much to come. You must follow your path," said Scarlet.

Perfidy looked at her properly for the first time. She was tall and elegant and her red robes flowed around her. Her face was looking out through the trees but her ruby eyes did not see them. Perfidy held her tight as the blade cut deep. As Scarlet gurgled, crimson flowed from her neck like a silken stream down her red robes. "That's the problem with trusting people," Perfidy whispered in her ear, "they always let you down in the end. Didn't your mother ever teach you that?" she pulled the dagger sharply towards her. Scarlet gurgled two last words.

"Find Verity."

Perfidy let the witch's body fall to the ground. She had blood on her hands and on her leather armour but she would have to clean herself later. She filled her gourd with the liquid from the stones. She took one look back over her shoulder. The witch's body had disappeared. The gore wasn't asleep after all, why didn't it attack her? She shook the thought away because she didn't have time for the gore. Perfidy left quickly and vanished back into the darkness from where she came.

Verity, Frances and Morty crouched low among the bushes so as not to be seen. They had been able to hear the events between Perfidy and Scarlet but were not been able to see what had happened. "I'll go and take a look, wait here," whispered Verity. She waited a few moments till it seemed to be safe to come out. She looked around. She could see the stone circle and kept scanning the woods for the owners of the voices they had heard. There was nobody there. Verity felt strange. She couldn't quite understand it but something inside felt different. It was a strange but not unpleasant feeling. She could almost swear there was a whispering in her head that she couldn't make out. Suddenly, a crack tore through the silence. Verity was moving before she was able to think. Her feet stayed where they were but her upper body twisted and leant back. It seemed to happen in slow motion to Verity but she had reacted in a fraction of a second. There was a thud as an arrow sank into the tree next to her. It had passed so close she felt the moving air as it went by. It would have sunk into Verity's chest had she not moved. Another crack. Verity spun the other way as another arrow whistled by and disappeared into the forest. Verity looked desperately to see where they were coming from. *Crack*! Verity twisted as another arrow missed her and hit the tree. She moved gracefully but at an incredible speed. She saw a figure darting between two trees ahead of her around twenty metres away. It was loading another arrow as it ran. Verity started moving without thinking. She used the trees as cover as she made her way towards the figure. Three more arrows flew her way but each time she avoided them with ease. The figure was behind a large tree. Verity ran to it and pinned herself to the opposite side. "You are a slippery one!" Perfidy called out.

Verity was breathing hard.

"Why don't you give yourself up and I promise to let you go." Perfidy slowly pulled out her dagger as she spoke. "Just come out and I won't hurt you."

Verity was feeling very strange. The whispering was loud now. "Come out so I can kill you," it hissed. "How did you escape my arrows?" it continued.

"I don't trust you!" shouted Verity. "And I don't know how I escaped your arrows!" she called.

Perfidy could hear a voice too. "Where have you been? I need you," it said. She shook herself. This was some magic she thought, to try and trick me. Perfidy tightened her grip on the dagger and sprung out from her side of the tree. She was in front of the other girl in a second and her hand was raised ready to strike. The girl didn't move and didn't try to defend herself. Perfidy froze like a statue as she stared at herself. Her dagger dropped to the ground. Verity looked at Perfidy; the reflection was beautiful.

Everything changed in a second.

They finally understood that they had spent their whole lives missing each other.

Chapter 6
Geminus

'All who would win joy, must share it; happiness was born a twin.'
Lord Byron

The twins had taken little time to get over the shock of each other. They were so alike, the only way to tell them apart was their clothes.

"This is creeping me out," was all that Frances could say.

Morty seemed to be the only one who didn't think the twins meeting was particularly amazing. He lay on the ground still sore from his wound. "If I is having a twin you is not seeing me get all squiggly eyed and tongue twiddled," he muttered. They sat in a small clearing in the forest not quite sure what to say.

"How could I not know about this?" said Perfidy, "Why didn't Blake tell me?" She was talking as much to herself than anyone. "How could he hide this? He must have known."

Verity had been looking at Perfidy for quite a while. She was struck with how beautiful she was. She still didn't think herself to share that beauty despite the fact they seemed to be identical. Perfidy seemed so strong and full of life. "What's your name?" she asked.

"You don't know?" replied Perfidy, "It's Perfidy."

"And I am…" Verity started.

"Verity, I know," Perfidy butted in.

"But how did you, how do you know…" Verity stuttered.

"The witch said it and then you show up," Perfidy said. She was feeling a mixture of emotions and she didn't know how to deal with them. The shock of Verity, Blake's apparent deception and what on earth should happen next?

Verity was clouded in confusion. The day's events were catching up with her. A hundred questions spun her head round. Out of nowhere had come a feeling that she thought she might never have. A feeling that she had hidden away and not used for a long time. A feeling as if she wasn't alone. She started to laugh! A chuckle at first that quickly became louder and soon she was giggling uncontrollably, Frances was stunned. She had never seen Verity laugh and now hardly seemed like the best time to start. "Oh great, Verity has lost it." she moaned, "Verity has finally gone cuckoo. That's great, just great."

"I'm sorry!" Verity said through the chuckles. "So far today I have been locked in a cellar, made friends with a moleman, escaped death, TWICE! and now I am in a strange forest with the twin sister I never knew about. If I didn't laugh, I really do think I would go cuckoo!"

Perfidy was pacing now. She was trying to calculate her next move. She thought about Blake and how she might confront him about Verity. She couldn't get out of her head why he would hide Verity from her. Perfidy looked at her sister. Verity was like a piece of jigsaw that clicked into her soul. It felt good, yet she was so muddled.

"We is needing to be tiddlin' away me thinks," came Morty's voice.

Perfidy eyed him carefully. "And just where is it that you want to 'tiddle' away to Mr Mole?" she said.

"It's Morty, Miss Perfidy my lovely and there is someone Verity needs to be meetin'," he replied with a little smile.

"I don't know anyone here?" said Verity.

"Ah but they is knowin' you my little lovely pop," Morty said.

"Who?" inquired Perfidy.

"All in soon time my deary, all in soon time. We must make our way to the East. The wise one is waiting."

Morty led the small band through the woods towards the east. He saddled himself on Verity's back and she was able to carry him quite comfortably. Frances babbled about her hair needing a wash and her dress needing a clean as well as several other things that nobody was listening to. Perfidy followed a little behind. "In case anything unfriendly jumps out," she said. She was deep in thought as they wound their way through the trees. The forest floor was damp and the trees were thick enough overhead to block out most of the daylight. It gave the forest an eerie feel as their feet crunched over leaves and twigs. Perfidy was still trying to figure out what to do. They were headed in the same direction as Calden Castle which worried her. It wouldn't be hard for her to disappear and head back to Blake. Would he be angry she didn't bring Verity? If she brought her, would he be angry then? Did she want to see him after his lies? She couldn't think straight so decided that the best thing to do was to stick with Verity. At a time when nothing seemed to make sense it seemed the most sensible thing to do. The bond Perfidy already felt between them was growing.

As they began to reach the edge of the forest, light started to filter through the trees. Large slices cut through the gloom and created beautiful shapes. Morty was growing weak from his wound and had begun to sleep in between directing the way for Verity.

"Have we long to go?" groaned Frances.

"We is just needing to squinkle a little further Miss Frances," Morty replied wearily.

The scene took Verity's breath away as they emerged from the forest. She waded through the long grass and squinted at the sun as it blazed in a sky that was so beautiful, it looked as though an artist had brushed it on. The air was crisp and clean; Verity gulped it in deeply. In front of her lay a patchwork quilt of fields in every shade of green, green waves in a green sea. In the distance, further to the East lay the Dakx Mountain range where Calden Castle lay. Off to the west Verity could see a small village made up of several bunches of little thatched cottages. The village lay at the bottom of a large mountain, down which gushed a huge green waterfall.

"Where now Morty?" Verity asked, "Morty?"

Morty was very groggy now. He was starting his reply when a blood curdling shriek filled the air! It was followed by a whistling sound and then an arrow thumped into Morty's side sending both he and Verity falling to the ground. Verity looked at him, eyes closed and not breathing. Her heart sank. Perfidy had taken no more than a few seconds to sprint over and pull Frances to the ground. She held her hand over her mouth. The long grass covered them. *Thud, thud, thud.* Three arrows hit the ground nearby.

"Stay still and quiet," ordered Perfidy, "I will come back for you." Keeping low, she disappeared into the long grass. Verity had not moved. Perfidy appeared out of nowhere beside her. "Are you hit?" she said. "Are you hurt?"

"I'm ok but," Verity looked at Morty's little body, "Morty." She was fighting tears back.

Screeches were ringing out all around now and the thuds of arrows hitting the ground were too close for comfort. "Nightwalkers," Perfidy said. "I have never seen them out in the day before? Something's not right," she continued. "I might be able to buy you some time depending on how many there are. They always hunt in packs. Try to make it back to the woods with Frances when I give the signal." Perfidy grabbed her shot bow with one hand and grasped her dagger in the other. A second later she was gone. Verity tried to stay calm and waited for the signal.

Perfidy popped her head above the grass. She immediately saw the group of around twelve nightwalkers that was beginning to form a circle round them. The skin around their heads was thinly stretched revealing their skulls. They had been human once but these creatures had sold their souls long ago and now roamed the darkness feeding on any flesh they could find. They were dressed in various states of disrepair, odd pieces of armour and weaponry that had been harvested from victims. They looked human but had no eyes or mouths, only black holes where they should have been.

A dash for the woods would be hopeless, Perfidy quickly realised. That only left one option. It's good old fashioned us or them, she thought to herself. She rose to her full height and fixed her aim on a nightwalker in front of her. Quick as a flash she squeezed the trigger. The arrow flew straight and true before sinking into the nightwalker's neck. It gurgled and fell to the ground. The closest nightwalker started running towards her. It was clutching a rusty blade.

Still crouching with Morty in the long grass, Verity closed her eyes tightly. In her head she could see everything as if she was high above, she looked at Perfidy and the nightwalker running towards her. She imagined herself making the twisting movement Perfidy would need to make to dodge the creature.

Perfidy found herself closing her eyes. Despite the danger, she felt a deep sense of calm. The walker was close enough to lunge now. She twisted as the walker approached. Its lunge missed her and she sliced twice with her blade as it went by. She spun back round as the walker fell to the ground clutching its stomach.

It was as if Verity was watching in slow motion hidden in the long grass. Two arrows were winging their way towards Perfidy. In her mind Verity twisted and spun as if she were in the arrows' path herself. Perfidy found herself moving and turning one way then the next as the arrows shot by. One of them found its way into the chest of a nearby walker. Perfidy was moving with a speed and accuracy that she had never felt before. Verity continued to watch the events unfold around Perfidy and guided her thoughts to help her. The group rounded on Perfidy. She made lightning quick movements as she dodged and twisted to stay clear of the swinging blades. Her blade found its mark again and again. Blood sprayed into the air and settled on the long grass as it flew from throats, chests and limbs. The last nightwalker started to flee from the battle. Perfidy cooly loaded her last arrow and raised the shot bow. The arrow whistled across the beautiful meadow. She had already turned round when it struck the walker's back and sent him diving face first into the grass. The wind blew gently as Verity stood up. Perfidy went back and found Frances who was shaking in a ball. "It's done," said Perfidy gently.

She helped Frances to her feet who then grabbed her and hugged her tightly as she sobbed, "I was so scared, so scared."

"It's over," Perfidy said and eventually started to hug her back, "it's over."

The three girls gathered round Morty. With tears forming in her eyes Verity said, "He's gone, there is nothing we can do. He's gone."

Perfidy thought about the gourd of potion she had taken from the stones. She didn't know how strong it was but it was strong enough for Scarlet to guard it and for Blake to want it so badly. Could she waste it on this silly little creature she thought? She looked at Verity. She could feel the ache of loss that seemed to flow from Verity. She had known Verity for a matter of hours but felt as though she had known her all her life. She didn't want Verity to hurt. "There might be something," she said a little reluctantly.

"What are you talking about?" asked Frances.

"I might have a way of helping him," said Perfidy.

"But he's, he's..." Frances couldn't bring herself to say it.

"Yes, he's dead," Perfidy replied, "he's dead and we are in Ulysses. Sometimes people don't stay dead here."

Verity was listening very carefully. "What can be done?" she asked.

"Well, I have a medicine that might and it is only a 'might' bring him back," said Perfidy.

"That's great!" Frances said excitedly, "Get it! Use it! Do it!"

"It's not that simple," Perfidy said.

"Why?" asked Frances.

"Well to my knowledge there is only one person who knows how to use this medicine properly and I, well I, killed her," Perfidy said a little sheepishly.

"We have to try!" said Frances. Her big green eyes stared at Perfidy and Perfidy couldn't help but feel she had to look after this girl, even if she was as soppy as a rag. There was just something about her.

"Ok," said Perfidy. She rummaged in her tunic and produced a small leather gourd that had a little nozzle at one end plugged with a stopper. She pulled the stopper and it made a satisfying *plunk* as it came out. She leant over Morty and pinched his cheeks with her hand to open his mouth. She let three or four drops fall down his throat. She stepped back and they all waited. Nothing happened. Perfidy looked at Verity and shrugged her shoulders. "I'm going to see if I can retrieve any arrows, I'll be back," she said before heading through the grass.

Frances sank into Verity's arms. "It's just not fair!" she sobbed. A tear rolled down Verity's cheek. Frances looked at her and sobbed a little laugh. "Big day for you Verity, first a laugh and now tears. I have never seen you like this," she said as she cuddled back in.

"I have never felt like this," Verity said quietly.

The two friends sat holding each other as the gentle breeze made the grass sway around them.

"PICKLE ME WALNUTS AND SLAP ME CHEEKS!" erupted a voice from the grass. "Stay in bed, Mother Morty used to say. Nothing bad happens in your snuggle bunker! Oh how right she is! I steps out for a mouse's minute and I is stabbed and pricked with arrows. Tiddle my toddle!"

The girls looked at each other in amazement then in joy. They rushed over to where he lay. "Morty, you're alive!" cried Frances.

"Be I alive, or be I dead, pickle my bones to make your bread!" he replied. "Of course I'm alive, alive and kickin' but I am twitchy and tired." He groaned and Verity noticed he was breathing heavily.

"We need to get you help," Verity said. "Where were you taking us? How do we get there?"

Morty was struggling to speak now. "Twitchy tired," he mumbled, "so twitchy tired. The Wise One you must meet. The Wise One will show you the way. Shadows and secrets, yes, yes, secrets and shadows." His voice was becoming weak. "It's Blake!" he muttered. "Blake's not safe! Not safe!" with that his eyes closed.

Verity listened to his chest. "He's still breathing," she said, "but he will need some proper help."

Just then Perfidy appeared as if from nowhere. "How do you do that?" said Frances. "It gives me the creeps!"

"Practice," Perfidy replied. "What's happening?"

Verity explained what Morty had just said. "Blake is not safe," Perfidy said to herself. Perfidy couldn't think clearly. Last night she would have done anything for Blake. He had been the only family she had ever known. Now, Verity was here and her world was upside down. The only thing she knew for sure right now was that she wouldn't let anyone hurt her sister, while she had breath in her lungs. She needed more time to think and she needed to speak to Blake. At that moment, she knew she would get neither. She looked at the village, then at the mountains where Calden lay. "If Blake is not safe then we must make our way to Jarlton. We will find shelter and medicine there." She felt as if she was betraying the only one who truly cared for her. Nothing made sense. With the sickly Morty on Perfidy's back they headed for the busy little village of Jarlton.

A figure stood at the edge of the trees, so as not to be seen. She had watched all the events that had unfolded in the meadow. Cloaked in crimson, Scarlet smiled as she waited for the quartet to vanish over the hill before slowly following their path.

Chapter 7
Jarlton

*'We learn more by looking for the answer to a question and
not finding it than we do from learning the answer itself.'*
Lloyd Alexander

Blake stood looking out from the North Tower. Perfidy
had not returned. That could mean one of two things. Either
Scarlet had her, or she had decided not to come back and
there was only one reason why she would do that, Verity.
He cursed himself. I should never have sent her he thought.
Scarlet was too strong. Feelings for her fought to break the
surface but the ghosts of the past would not let them out.
He had not been able to contact the messenger so didn't
know where Verity was. The plan was starting to unravel.
He paced and cursed himself again. It was the last thing he
wanted to do but he knew it was time to act. He would have
to go himself to find Scarlet and deal with everything that
would bring. Everything depended on it. He pulled on a
tight fitting, long black coat and adjusted his dagger belt
before making his way to the woods, to the stones, to
Scarlet.

The travellers made good time and reached Jarlton as
the sun started setting. Perfidy went on ahead to find
somewhere to stay for the night. "It's best we don't draw
attention to ourselves," she said. A little later she
reappeared with a brown rusty key and led them through
several winding cobbled lanes and alleyways that made up
Jarlton, some of which were so tight it felt as if they were
in a maze. They reached a small cottage and Perfidy let
them in. Verity found a bed and some blankets in the

second room and lay Morty down and covered him to keep him warm.

"We need to get him help soon," she said to Perfidy.

"I have spoken with an old friend of mine who owes me a favour. He said he could help. I need to go and meet him before sundown," she replied. "You should get some rest," she said to Frances before vanishing out the door.

Scarlet had been watching the small group of travellers from a distance. She had seen them disappear into the cottage and seen Perfidy emerge again and head for the centre of the village. She could feel that Verity was close. It sent shivers down her body. She was close now. She had to wait for the right time; she had to be patient.

Perfidy approached a rough looking man with a dirty beard who was standing opposite the baker's shop. The baker was busy closing down his shop for the day. "Did you find someone?" Perfidy asked.

"At such short notice, it's a miracle but I did," replied a husky voice. "I hope you're grateful."

"Yes I am, and you just make sure you remember that next time you need to escape from Braxen's dungeon," Perfidy said sharply.

"Yes, yes let's not go through all that again," said the man.

"Can I trust him?" Perfidy said.

"The Shaman is a little odd but if anyone can help your friend, he can," the voice said. "He will meet you at the bridge."

"You better hope you are right. I don't want to have to find you again. Stay away from trouble." Perfidy turned and was quickly gone.

The light was fading as Perfidy saw an odd man sitting by the bridge. He was quite short and looked very old. He had a long floaty white beard and a pair of metal spectacles sat on top of his blotchy nose. Perfidy approached him. "I was told you could help me," she said.

The small man looked up slowly. "Yes, I believe I can, Benedict Fairfax, at your service." There was something about his brown smile that Perfidy didn't like, she couldn't think why. She started to lead him to the house.

Not more than a minute after they had left, another man arrived at the bridge. He sat down. One of the town guards came to move him on. "What's your business here?" the guard growled.

"I was told to wait here for a girl. Raven said I was going to help her," the Shaman said.

"Don't stay long," said the guard before walking away.

A woman cloaked in grey approached the Shaman. "Your friend is no longer in need," she said. "Take this and forget you were ever troubled," she handed him a small pouch that jingled with coins. He pocketed it and hobbled off. The woman hidden in the hood was smiling.

Back at the cottage Fairfax stood over Morty and muttered, "Yes, yes, tricky, tricky." He poked and prodded him and waved his hands over him theatrically. "Your friend is in bad shape," he announced.

Verity had little time for this strange small man. "Well you must be a master of medicine indeed!" she said sarcastically.

Fairfax took offence. "If my help isn't appreciated, then I shall take it elsewhere," he said dramatically.

Perfidy decided to butt in, "Your help is appreciated and if you do take it elsewhere I will make sure even your great skills won't bring your arms back." She stared hard at him. "Fix him!"

"Err yes well," stuttered Fairfax, "I was just about to. Now where did I put my bag?" He picked up his small brown leather bag and rummaged around. He pulled out several coloured bottles and some sponges before he said, "Ah there it is!" Out came a large purple pill. "This should do the trick!" he sounded very pleased with himself. He gently opened Morty's mouth and dropped it in. Morty stirred a little as it made its way down his throat. The others watched on with nervous anticipation. They waited for what seemed like an age, nobody spoke until Frances broke the silence.

"Will he be better soon?" she said.

"Are you in a hurry dear?" he enquired with a false innocence.

"We are on a journey!" Frances blurted out. "Morty is taking us to see someone wise!"

Perfidy scowled at her.

"Very indeed," Fairfax sneered.

"Yes," continued Frances, "but we don't know the way, only Morty does!"

Perfidy looked angrily at her. She didn't like this Shaman and didn't want him knowing their business.

"My, my, my, that is a pickle," he said trying to sound concerned but still wore his little smile. "You must be very worried, eh. You don't know where to go, that is a pickle indeed." He was packing the bottles slowly back into his bag. "I suppose, I could tell you how to find the wise one, for a small fee, just to cover costs you understand." His voice was sounding sickly.

"No," said Perfidy, "thank you for your help and you can be on your way."

"As you wish," said Fairfax and made his way to the door.

"Wait!" called Verity. "How do you know where Morty meant to take us?"

"There are things in this world that you need not understand young pretty," he said.

Perfidy flashed her a look.

"Morty said we must see the wise one and everything would become clear. I need to make some kind of sense of all this mess. Morty can't help us right now and we have little time to lose. Fairfax is the best chance we have."

Perfidy sighed. She knew Verity was right and if she was going to continue with this strange journey, Fairfax was their only option. "Fine," Perfidy said reluctantly.

Fairfax was grinning. "Ah how lovely. You may cross my palm with silver now," he delivered with a smile that revealed several brown teeth missing.

Perfidy rummaged in her tunic and produced some coins which she pushed into his hand. He looked pleased.

"Where are we headed?" asked Frances.

"The way you seek, is through the Staxcian Door and it is hidden underneath the Green Amber Falls. The Staxcian Door is locked and bound with magic, only those who are worthy may enter. The path up to the falls is dangerous and a favourite place for nightwalkers to rest, so one would want to be careful." He pulled a small piece of paper and charcoal pencil out of his cloak and started to draw a surprisingly detailed map. He handed this to Perfidy and grinned. "There you are pretty," he made a small bow as he did so, "and remember, the light will show the way." With that he disappeared out the door.

He turned round the first corner and saw the grey cloaked figure up ahead. He walked towards her. They stood in a narrow lane. The light was poor. She lowered her grey hood but he couldn't make out her face. "Did you do as I asked?" she said.

"Yes. I made sure they are headed for the Staxcian Door just as you said." He was nervous now.

"Good, the twins will find their way. It will be difficult for their union to stop me once they have been torn apart by my rock troll," she said smiling.

"I can't help but remember the mention of a small payment for my services?" he said anxiously.

"You have done well, you shall certainly get what you deserve," she said menacingly. She raised her hand that held a small round, glowing stone. Fairfax grabbed his throat as he started to choke. The skin on his face began to peel and smoke started pouring out of his ears and nose. He fell to his knees then he hit the ground wriggling and squirming. He slowly stopped moving and twitching. His body was still. His eyes were wide. The woman cocked her head as she looked at him one last time. Her lips curled into a wicked smile then she pulled her grey hood up and walked away. A few moments later a gore appeared and picked up the body before vanishing into the darkness.

Blake had forgotten how far the forest was from Calden Castle. Nevertheless, he was nearly there. He had thought about what he should say to Scarlet but he found no answer. He had not seen her since the terrible events that night in Kergord. The woman in grey had planted a seed in his mind and he had seen with his own eyes how Scarlet felt. The jealousy and rage soaked his soul as if a terrible storm had sent waves to crash into him and break him. He was powerless to resist. It was as if she had poisoned him. It was that night he first learned of his powers. Abilities that made him very dangerous indeed. He knew now that he was always the match of his enemies because he could turn their own strength and magic against them. He let some memories play in his mind as he walked. He remembered standing on the hill in the meadow where he and Scarlet had been so happy, or so he thought. He remembered Zander's body, lifeless and Scarlet bending over it, her eyes, full of fire and hurt. He had been desperate to make her feel his pain. He remembered watching from the beach as Kergord burned in the darkness, Scarlet lay at his feet. The air smelled of burnt wood and smoke billowed into the sky. The power he felt that night was intoxicating. It kept him safe from the pain. The ghosts found him that night for the first time.

He made his way swiftly through the forest to the Weeping Stones. He moved carefully, his eyes darting around for any small glimpse of her. If she was going to attack, he would have to be very quick indeed. Moments passed and nothing moved or stirred around him. He heard a small rustle behind him, he spun round just in time to see a huge grey fist smash him in the face. It sent him flying into a tree. He was groggy and tried to get up as the gore wrapped a huge hand round his throat and started to squeeze. Blake was crippled. He tried to speak but only gasps came out. He was feeling dizzy. He tried to reach out to the gore with his mind. "Stop, I am not a danger!" his voice echoed in the gore's head. It was confused and loosened its grip slightly. "I am not danger. I need to see Scarlet. She is in trouble, she needs me," The gore let go. Blake held his throat and gasped for breath.

"Wraa mm wruu," the gore grumbled.

"Yes I am Blake," he replied.

"Gruu muun caag," the gore continued.

"Where did they go?"

"Ruug Haa kuul," grunted the gore.

"Perfidy left with two girls and a mole. Why didn't they come to me?" Blake muttered to himself. "The messenger knew to bring them to me, why didn't Morty bring them to me?"

"Grre daar reeg," came another grunt.

"He said I wasn't safe?" Blake's black eyes widened, "Why would he betray me?" With that he disappeared into the forest in the direction of Jarlton.

Verity lifted little Morty carefully onto her back like a rucksack, as the group got ready to leave. Perfidy was busy checking her arrows and dagger belt. Frances was happily chewing a large mouthful of bread which Perfidy had brought back for breakfast. "This is very good Perfidy," Frances said, "but next time maybe you could pick up a few fat sausages and some juicy bacon, maybe an egg or two?"

Perfidy smiled at her. "Of course madam Frances," she said grandly. Frances giggled.

"This is going to be very dangerous," Verity said. "You could stay here Frances, until we get back."

"You won't last five minutes without me." Frances declared. Verity looked surprised. "Who was it that saved you from the evil clutches of Krankle? Little old me! We are together to the end Verity, I'm coming!" Frances said.

Verity smiled. "Together to the end," she said.

The small group gathered the few supplies they had and headed out into the town. The sun was strong and the warmth made Verity tingle. She looked up at the huge mountain that the Green Amber Falls tumbled down. Looking at it now, it seemed impossible that anyone could get up there, let alone with a moleman stuck to their back. She looked at her sister and felt strong again. Perfidy was so brave. Nothing seemed to frighten her.

Perfidy was already tired. She had not slept all night. She couldn't stop worrying about the journey up the mountain. She knew how dangerous it could be and the thought of anything happening to Verity or Frances gnawed at her stomach. She looked at her sister and felt strong again. Verity was so brave. Nothing seemed to frighten her.

They wound their way through the cobbled streets and lanes, making their way out of town to the mountain. The Shaman had marked a path on his map and Perfidy was leading them to it. It wasn't an unpleasant journey despite the fact it took all morning. They had reached the base of the mountain and it hadn't taken Perfidy long to find the small path that led upwards. "I wouldn't have found this without the map," she said. The path was tucked away from sight behind a crop of large rocks. "We will sit and eat before starting up the track."

The group made themselves comfortable and Perfidy pulled out a loaf of bread and a lump of cheese which she broke into pieces and handed round. She kept the smallest pieces for herself. "Make it last," she said, "there won't be more for a while." The three girls sat in the sunshine and filled their hungry tummies. They talked and laughed and for a little while it felt exciting as they were getting ready for their adventure.

They didn't know the hooded woman waited patiently for them at the Staxcian Door.

Blake had reached Jarlton and made his way to the middle of town. If anyone wanted to know anything in this town, they could find out at the Skeleton's Locker. He pushed the door open and walked in. The day was bright and warm outside but it was dark and smoky inside the tavern. It smelt musty and his leather boots stuck to the wooden floor as he walked. The place was busy and full of chattering noise. It was full of strange looking characters. Nobody noticed him as he sat down at the bar. "A Devil's Buttermilk my love?" called the large barmaid from the other side of the bar. "Sommin' to eat? I got a lovely horse and rabbit pie."

Blake stared at her. "You is a pretty one," she said as she looked at him carefully, "but you is full of sadness. What happened my petal?"

"I need some information," Blake said, "I am looking for three girls and a moleman."

"I am sure I would have remembered them my lovely. They ain't not been in 'ere. I think love has hurt you my petal?" She seemed very interested in him now, "Yes love has burnt you, has it not? Don't worry, a pretty thing like you will find it again. True love can't be broken," she chirped.

"True love has the same story as all things," Blake replied, "All things must die."

"Maybe so," she said thoughtfully, "but I think I would rather take the chance that you are wrong than to never find out if I could have been right. Just shout when you decide what you want my lovely." With that she headed to serve someone else.

Blake was trying to dismiss the woman but her words troubled him. His thoughts were broken by a voice, "I couldn't help but overhearin', that you are looking for information. I might be able to help you, for a coin or two of course." The voice belonged to a strange looking little man.

"If you can tell me what I need to know, you will have your coins," said Blake.

"Well I have this friend, you see, who I sorts of does favours for every now and then. Well he came to me just yesterday and said he needed me to do something."

"What's his name?" asked Blake.

"His name is Raven. Anyway he comes to me and says I have to go to the bridge and wait for a girl. He says I will know her because she has black hair and real blue eyes. He says she has a creature friend what needs some special medical attention. That's my specialty you see."

"So you saw them, where were they? Where are they now?" Blake was getting animated.

"Ah now, there's the strange thing. I never did meet the girl."

"What happened?"

"A woman came to me and told me I wasn't to meet the girl and gave me a little bag of monies for me troubles."

"What did she look like?" asked Blake.

"Ah, I couldn't rightly say, she was wrapped up in a grey cloak and a hood hid her face, alls I could see was she had long white hair."

Blake's head started to spin back to Kergord. Could it be her, he thought, have I finally found her?

Blake tried to think what to do next. He got up and started to walk away. "Ahem," coughed the little man, "coins?"

Blake walked back to him and grabbed his throat tightly. "Let's have a think. You have told me the girls were here, which I already knew. You don't know where they were or where they are. You met someone who you didn't see and don't know. What exactly am I going to be paying for?" Blake snarled.

"I think I would love for you to not give me anything!" the little man gurgled. Blake let him go. "Fair do's," said the man, "I thought I might have been able to bag a few coins earlier as well, guess it's not my day."

"Go on," said Blake.

"Yes, I thought I saw the grey woman and I followed her for a little bit, thought I might be able to get more from her you see."

"And?" said Blake.

"And, it wasn't her. This woman pulled down her hood and had a shock of bright red hair." he said.

Scarlet! Thought Blake. "Where did she go?"

"She was headed to the foot of Green Amber Falls Mountain," said the little man. Blake pushed some coins into his hand and quickly left the Skeleton's Locker.

Chapter 8
Let The Dark Light The Way

'It cannot be seen, cannot be felt,
Cannot be heard, cannot be smelt.
It lies behind stars and under hills,
And empty holes it fills.
It comes first and follows after,
Ends life, kills laughter.'
Gollum - The Hobbit, Riddles in the Dark.

The three girls made their way up the small broken track. Other than tiredness nothing much bothered them as they slowly made their way. Perfidy was twitchy. "I thought we would have run into something by now," she said while scanning the path ahead. The path was steep in most places and rocky underfoot. Frances was struggling and had fallen a little behind the twins. "We will rest here a while," announced Perfidy. She pulled out three red apples and a large chunk of cheese from her knapsack. The three ate hungrily and were glad of the break.

"How far are we, do you think?" Verity asked Perfidy.

"Not even halfway," she replied. The light was beginning to fade. "Verity, you fetch whatever you can find for a fire. I will scout ahead just to make sure there are no nasty surprises in the night," Perfidy said.

"I will come with you," piped up Frances. Verity smiled.

"You are a brave one Frances, but we need you here to look after Morty. Try to keep him warm and comfortable."

Perfidy disappeared up the track while Verity hunted around for anything that might burn. Frances pulled a thick cloak over Morty and gently stroked his head. "Oh little Morty, what will happen to us all?" she whispered.

Perfidy had made her way about two hundred metres up the track. She moved silently, just as Blake had taught her. She stopped by a large rock. She could see the twinkling lights of Jarlton far below. The night had settled now and the stars looked as though they had been sprayed across the sky. Everything was still. It made her feel uneasy. She knew the dangers that lay in the mountains. Stories of ancient creatures that had lived there for centuries, feeding on the nightwalkers who made their rest there. Her mind was taken back to the battle in the field. She still couldn't figure out why they had been out in daylight. It was unheard of. She laid three trip wires attached to which were small bells, then she turned and headed back down the track. Just as she did she thought she caught a glimpse of a small light disappearing further down the path. It was so quick she dismissed it as her eyes playing tricks on her. She returned to find Verity had collected a pile of dry moss and some branches and twigs. "Not much," said Verity, "but it will give us a small fire."

"Small is good," replied Perfidy, "we don't want the whole mountain knowing we are here."

"Can I light it?" chirped Frances.

"I think you should leave this to me," Perfidy replied.

"But I could just..." tried Frances.

"I think I know how to start a fire," said Perfidy.

"But..."

"Watch and you might just learn something," Perfidy said as she grabbed two sticks and started rubbing them together. She was trying for a while before the sticks started to smoke but no fire appeared. Perfidy started sweating a little. A short while later she gave up. "The wood must be damp," she puffed, "It isn't going to light."

Frances got up and leant over. "May I?" she said politely. With a cheeky grin, she flicked open Morty's lighter and sparked it into flame. Seconds later the fire was burning.

"You, you let me..." started Perfidy crossly.

"I tried to tell you," Frances giggled. Perfidy broke into a smile. She had never met anyone like Frances before, so much good in her, it was impossible to be mad at her for long. The three girls lay near the fire and slept under the black sparkling sky. Even Perfidy managed to find sleep for a little while.

The morning sun was dazzling. Verity woke and sleepily looked around. Frances was cuddled up to Morty but Perfidy was nowhere to be seen. She appeared from behind a nearby rock dangling a creature from each hand. "Breakfast!" she said smiling.

"What are they?" Verity asked cautiously.

"Mountain Rats!" replied Perfidy. Verity's appetite disappeared all of a sudden. A short while later Perfidy had skinned the rats and they sizzled over a small fire. As they ate breakfast Verity decided not to tell Frances what it was, although they tasted remarkably good, for mountain rats. The morning was spent trudging up the small track. It still bothered Perfidy that they had not seen anything or anyone and she couldn't shake the feeling they were being followed.

"Are we there yet?" whined Frances.

"The map says we are close. Another couple of hours and we should nearly be there," said Perfidy. The rushing of the waterfall was growing louder the further up the mountain they went. The air was getting colder and Morty seemed to get heavier on Verity's back with every step but she wouldn't let anyone else carry him. Daylight was just beginning to fade when Verity spotted the path was coming to an end. A huge vertical rock face lay ahead.

"Are we there?" asked a puzzled Frances.

"The map says it's beyond that rock face," replied Perfidy.

"But that's impossible to climb!" moaned Frances. The group carried on till they could go no further. "No gate, no door, no point!" grumbled Frances.

"I knew we shouldn't have trusted that little toad," said Perfidy. "He took our money and led us up a dead end path. He better hope he never meets me again!"

"Just wait," said Verity, "he said that it would be difficult. He said that only the worthy would gain access."

"So?" snapped Perfidy.

"So... so maybe this is some kind of test, some kind of puzzle to solve?" she said hopefully.

Perfidy sat down on a rock with a face like thunder. "I'll wring his neck!" she grumped.

Frances could see the desperation in Verity's face. "Maybe Verity is right?" she said positively. "I mean we have dealt with a lot lately, surely a silly little wall won't beat us?"

Perfidy scowled.

"Is there anything else on that map? Let me have a look," said Frances. Perfidy crumpled it up and threw it at her feet.

"There!"

"Thank you," Frances said deliberately. She unscrewed the paper. It was a small piece with a neatly drawn map. The map did point them up this path and did show the gate to be just beyond the rock face. There was nothing else written.

"It will take two days to get back down, and we are out of food," said Perfidy as she got up and started to head back down the path. Verity slowly rose and trudged behind her. Frances was thinking, something was bugging her; she didn't want to give up.

The twins were about to walk out of sight when Frances cried out as loud as she could, "WHY!"

Perfidy came darting towards her, blade in hand. "What's wrong? Are you OK?" she said franticly. Verity appeared after her.

"Why?" said Frances excitedly.

"Why what? What's the question?" asked Verity.

"Why is the answer, not the question!" said Frances.

"You sound like Morty now." Verity said. "He didn't make much sense either."

"No, don't you see? Why is the answer. Something has been bugging me all the way up this stupid mountain. Why?" Frances said.

"If you don't tell us what you are on about soon you will be wondering why I made you eat mountain rat for a month!" Perfidy scowled.

"The answer is the question, why is this path here? Nobody seems to know about it, nobody uses it, it goes nowhere, so why? Why would there be such a clear path to nowhere, that nobody knows about! Unless it really is the path to the gate!" Frances was so excited she was out of breath.

Perfidy looked at Verity. "It kinda makes sense? So, Mrs Brains, how do we carry on?"

"Well I haven't figured out that bit yet," said Frances, a little deflated. "I can't do all the work you know!"

Verity started looking around for any way through. "Let me see that map again," said Frances. She opened up the piece of paper. "The light will show the way," she whispered. She stretched the paper out and held it up towards the sun. The light made her squint as she saw letters appearing in the middle of the paper. The letters were small and neatly written .

"Let the dark light the way," she read out.

"Light you mean? Let the light show the way," puzzled Verity.

"No it's dark, look," Frances handed the paper to her.

"It doesn't make sense," said Verity glumly.

"It might," piped up Perfidy. "There was a saying Blake used to tell me when I was little. 'Darkness can hide the truth but light can also be blinding.'"

"What does it mean?" asked Verity.

"I'm not sure, maybe we just can't see the answer yet. I don't really know," Perfidy said. "It's getting dark now anyway so travelling would be too dangerous. Let's set up camp and get moving in the morning."

The sun didn't take long to dip beneath the horizon. The sky was cloudy and the moon fought to be seen. "We came so close," said Frances. "How are we going to find out why we are here, what's going on?"

Perfidy had searched the rock face top to bottom for any clues but found nothing. She sat down cross legged next to the others. "Perhaps Morty will help when he gets better," she said hopefully. The clouds drifted apart and the large pale moon shone through.

"What's that?" asked Frances.

"What?" said Verity. She looked where Frances was staring and sure enough something seemed to be glinting in the moonlight etched in the rock face. She went over to look. There was a small Jewel embedded in the rock.

"I am telling you now, I checked every inch of the face," said Perfidy, "that wasn't there before!"

The jewel gleamed in the moonlight until clouds drifted back in front of the moon and the jewel was gone. "This is giving me the creeps," said Frances. The twins looked at each other not quite sure what to think.

"Let the dark light the way?" Perfidy muttered to herself. "Quick! Put out the fire," she said excitedly. "The dark will show the way! We need it to be dark!"

Verity reluctantly kicked stones and dirt over the flames putting them out. The clouds parted and the shimmering moonlight gently lit the rock face. The Jewel glinted again. "Look!" said Perfidy. The clouds rolled over and the moon's light was gone. The rock face was very dark now. Verity couldn't really make out much. It didn't take long before the moon's light illuminated them again.

Frances looked around. "Where's Perfidy?" her voice was shaky. Sure enough Perfidy had vanished. Verity looked worried. Perfidy was quiet and quick but the dark had only lasted a few seconds. Not even Perfidy could have passed her to get down the track in that time. A large black cloud blocked out the moon. Total darkness followed, again it took only seconds before the moon's light returned.

There stood Perfidy as if by magic. She was grinning from ear to ear.

"Where have you been?" blurted Frances.

"Oh, I just took a little stroll to the other side of the rocks," Perfidy said, still grinning. "Gather your things. I want to show you how beautiful it is."

They quickly packed and prepared to leave. Verity and Frances were puzzled while Perfidy was very pleased with herself. "Right come over here." Perfidy stood in front of the rock where the Jewel was glinting. "I will take Morty. We need to hold hands," she said, "like a chain. When I start to move just follow me, ok?"

"Ok," said Verity.

"Err, ok?" said Frances.

Perfidy looked up to the sky and waited. It wasn't long before the clouds drifted in front of the moon. Darkness fell. "NOW!" called Perfidy. She tugged Verity's hand and plunged forward. Verity was as good as blind but the trust in her sister was already solid so she shut her eyes and followed. Frances was behind her and gripped her hand tightly as they lurched forward together. Verity waited for the crunch and bump of the rock. One step, two, three... The crunch didn't come, four, five, six, on they went. A little blind train bundling through the dark. Eventually Verity stumbled and fell. Frances tumbled on top of her. She looked up at the moonlight. Behind them was a huge rock face with a little glinting jewel embedded in it. The sound of the soft rush of water was behind her.

"Let the dark light the way," said Perfidy. "The passage is only open in the darkness! Only those who know about it would ever find a way through. The jewels mark the spot!"

Frances sat up and rubbed her head. "A little warning is always nice," she grumbled.

Verity stood and looked around properly. Perfidy had been right, it was beautiful. They stood at the edge of a huge circular clearing that seemed to be carved out of the mountain. The Green Amber Falls, although huge, seemed to tumble gently into a large pool of emerald green water.

Small trees were dotted around everywhere and they were bursting with green, yellow and blue leaves. The ground was covered in lush green grass and unlike the other side of the rock, the light was soft and pleasant and the air was warm. Small birds flitted from tree to tree. Several stone paths led up and out of the basin in three different places round the circle. "It's beautiful," Verity said.

"Yeah," said Frances, "shame my knees aren't! Look at them! Those bruises will take ages to go away. I will have to wear tights forever!"

"The Shaman said the Gate was hidden behind the waterfall," Perfidy nodded to it as she spoke. They started to make their way to the falls when Perfidy stopped. "Wait!" She put her arm out to signal the others to stop while simultaneously pulling out her shot bow. The group froze. Verity soon saw why. A tall hooded figure cloaked in grey emerged and walked out from behind the falls. It moved quickly but elegantly across the ground. It made its way towards them. "Be ready for anything," said Perfidy. The figure stopped a little way in front of them and pulled back its hood. Verity stared at a grey faced woman. She had long white hair that hung down either side of her face. She had grey lips and black eyes.

"You won't need that for me," she said to Perfidy. "I won't do you any harm." Her voice was soft and Verity couldn't shake the feeling it was familiar, just like the woman.

"I prefer to make my own mind up about such things," replied Perfidy.

"I know you do child," replied the white haired woman.

"You know nothing about me," said Perfidy.

"I know everything about you child, you too Verity," she smiled.

"Step closer and you will know how good my aim is," said Perfidy.

"I told you not to worry about me," said the woman, wearing a sinister smile.

Verity could hear her sister in her head. 'I don't trust her. She makes me nervous. Do I know her?'

Verity felt uneasy.

"I am glad you came my sweetness. I have waited a long time to see you," the woman said. Perfidy's aim was locked solid but it didn't seem to bother her. "I worried that Blake would find you Verity."

Perfidy felt Morty stirring on her back. "Blake's not safe," he mumbled weakly.

"I thought that he would find you and you would not be able to fulfil your destiny."

"Are you the one Morty wanted us to meet?" Verity asked.

The woman started to laugh. "No child. I am not," she laughed again.

"Blake's not safe," mumbled Morty.

Perfidy's finger twitched on the trigger.

"What is our destiny?" Verity pleaded.

"You should have fulfilled your destiny a long time ago," the woman continued. "You have grown so much from the little girls I remember."

"You have met us before?" said Verity, her head was spinning.

"Met you!" The woman laughed again, "Yes I 'met' you! You were taken before your destiny could be fulfilled."

"Taken by who? Did you know our parents?" Verity was desperate now.

"I knew your mother but it was Blake who took you child. He stopped everything; he ruined everything!" The woman sounded angry now.

"Not safe," croaked Morty.

"We know," whispered Perfidy, "that's why we didn't go back to him."

"You is not understandin', HE is not safe! She will kill him! She is the Witchfinder! She will kill us all! He thinks he can stop her, but he can't!" Morty passed out with the effort of talking.

"Now children," the Witchfinder said, "it's time we put things right and do what should already be done."

"What do you need us to do?" asked Verity.

The Witchfinder flashed her evil grin.

"I need you to die my sweetness!"

Chapter 9
The Witchfinder

'The world is a dangerous place to live; not because of the people who are evil, but because of the people who don't do anything about it.'
Albert Einstein

Verity shuddered as the Witchfinder's words echoed in her head. Perfidy stood like a statue, her aim fixed on the Witchfinder's chest. She squeezed the trigger. The arrow flew but fell away as soon as the Witchfinder raised her hand and waved it to the side. Her gaze turned to Perfidy. She held out both hands and clenched her fists. Perfidy felt a searing pain erupting from her stomach. She was lifted into the air and couldn't breathe; her insides felt as though they were being crushed. "Such a disappointment Perfidy," said the Witchfinder. "I thought you would have at least put up a fight."

Perfidy couldn't resist any longer. She saw nothing but blinding white light. This is it she thought. She tried to scream but could only gasp.

Verity started to run to the Witchfinder but stopped almost immediately. The Witchfinder bent down and clutched her own stomach then was suddenly lifted into the air, struggling to breathe. Perfidy fell back to the ground as if she had been let go by some invisible hand, gulping and gasping for air. Verity ran to her. The Witchfinder screamed and fell to the ground. Blake stepped into view. "How lovely to see you again," he said sarcastically. The Witchfinder stood up clutching her stomach. "What's the matter? Don't you like your own magic being used against you?" Blake asked.

"I knew you would appear again one day," said the Witchfinder. "This is going to be a very good day. The twins, you and … wait," she stopped and looked slowly around. "There is another waiting to join us. Witch, why do you hide? You won't escape me my sweetness, come out. I will be happy to add another to my list!"

Scarlet! Thought Blake. He looked around frantically but she was nowhere to be seen. "You know you can't use your magic on me witch!" Blake snarled. "You know I can use your own magic to destroy you!"

"Ah yes, the great Blake, blessed with the gift to turn an enemy's strength against them. Where did you get that power I wonder? The more fearsome the enemy the greater Blake becomes," said the Witchfinder. "Well, perhaps magic won't kill you but I am sure a blade will do the job just as well!" She raised both hands and the sky darkened. Screams and screeches filled the air. Each of the three paths flooded with dozens of nightwalkers. They poured down the hillside.

Perfidy drew her dagger. "Take cover with Frances and guide me like you did in the field!" she said as she shoved Verity hard towards Frances. They scurried behind some large rocks. Verity closed her eyes and concentrated hard.

Blake rushed to the bottom of the eastern path and met the stream of walkers head on. He smashed the first one in the face with a black leather fist, sending it flying backwards. Blake closed his eyes for a second as he felt the walker's physical strength pour into him. He grabbed the next crawler with his right hand and hammered it against a rock on his left. The walker's head cracked open. He hit the rock again with the beast and its skull burst. A walker leapt towards him. He grabbed it with both hands as it jumped. He hurled it into the rock face. Its body broke on impact. Another walker latched on to him and tore at his chest. Pieces of leather flew away as his jacket was shredded. Blake lifted it away and tore the creature in two. He dumped the pieces on the ground.

Verity could see him now in her head as if she was above everyone. She watched Blake pounding the rush of walkers that streamed down the path. She focused in on Perfidy. Perfidy had made her way to the western path and stood at the bottom, ready for the fight. Verity focused on the walkers who were coming towards her. She imagined how she would move to dodge them. Perfidy could feel Verity. The walkers screamed towards her. She spun just as the first one reached for her and sliced it down. She spun again and again, her dagger cutting down walkers with each swipe. Another lunged for her, she twisted out of the way and caught the beast in the chest with her elbow. It stunned him which gave her just enough time to swipe her blade. Its throat opened sending a shower of blood into the air.

Blake glanced over his shoulder at the third path. Perfidy was holding the western path and he was holding the eastern path but the walkers from the southern pass had now made it to the ground and were hunting for Verity. Blake knew they couldn't beat them, there were just too many.

Frances froze with fear as an ugly walker's head appeared from in front of the rock. The holes where its eyes should have been stared through her. It wore thick leather shoulder armour and its gloved hands clutched a large blade that seemed to be stained with something dark. It raised the blade and licked its lips. Frances could see the few teeth it had were covered in black saliva. He was ready to strike. Frances closed her eyes tightly. She waited. She felt Verity pulling her close. She heard the walker scream. She opened her eyes and saw the beast clutching its throat and then flames burst from its eyes before it fell to the ground screaming. A woman moved into view. "Don't be scared," she said, "I will keep you safe." The woman's ruby eyes burned fiercely. Scarlet turned and walked through the basin. Walkers were hurled this way and that as their bodies burned, tore and exploded as she neared them. She soon made it to Perfidy who was still cutting down walkers.

Scarlet moved gracefully and quickly in front of her and sent a river of fire snaking up the path. Everything in its way was torn apart by the flames.

Perfidy looked at her in disbelief. "You? But I, I killed you?" she stuttered.

"Well, you can't have done a very good job my child," Scarlet said.

Perfidy caught sight of Blake out the corner of her eye. He was still struggling with walkers. "Blake! We have to help him!" Perfidy rushed in his direction.

Scarlet looked over. She had not seen Blake for such a long time. It felt like someone else's life now. The girl who had been so in love with him was gone. Her mind drifted back to that terrible night in Kergord.

She had gone back into The Devil's Rest to clear up and was wiping down tables when Blake burst in. She smiled at first but soon stopped when she saw the anger in his face. He stormed across the floor pushing her aside and grabbing Zander. She could see it so clearly now, Sandy screaming, Zander's lifeless eyes. An innocent life taken. Emotion burned Scarlet's heart, she lost control. Into the air she rose, hands bursting into flame. The tavern erupted in panic with people scattered this way and that, trying to get out. Hurt, rage, confusion and fire poured out of her.

Blake was like a black mirror, he wanted Scarlet to feel the pain he did. He felt Scarlet's fire and returned it, she started to feel terrible burning. It wasn't long before the Tavern was ablaze and the couple spilled out into the street. As the lovers' anger spread so did the flames and Kergord burned. Scarlet's last memory was being consumed by the fire.

A day later Scarlet had woken up on the beach. The sea lapped at her toes. She saw the skeleton of Kergord, burned to its bones, the air thick with black smoke as the last of the glowing embers faded.

She hadn't seen Blake till now.

She walked slowly over to where Blake and Perfidy were frantically holding back the wave of walkers. She raised her hand and closed her eyes. Each walker stopped in their tracks and clutched their throats as chunks of skin and bits of bodies flew away. An eruption of wails and screams was followed by a strange silence.

Verity and Frances cautiously came out from their hiding place. Perfidy and Blake looked at each other but said nothing. Blake could see she was upset. She went to find Verity. Scarlet sat cloaked in wine coloured velvet on a rock. Small tufts of her red hair poked out from under her hood. Blake had forgotten how beautiful she was. "Scarlet…" he said. "Scarlet?" he didn't know what else to say.

"My heart doesn't beat the way it used to. And my eyes don't recognise you anymore," she replied. Her ruby eyes glowed as she spoke to him.

Blake thought he had wanted to be angry with her, that he still wanted her to feel the betrayal that he had felt but looking at her now he wasn't so sure anymore. "Scarlet I…"

The Witchfinder looked carefully at Scarlet. "Now then my sweetness, you look so much like your mother. Or at least you did. Your mother was missing a few pieces when I finished with her," she said. "Ahh, this is special. Two lovers reunited," she sneered. She stood a little way up the western path. "Their true love never to be broken. Isn't that right Blake?" she laughed.

Blake cast his mind back to the strange grey woman on the pier. "The story of all things is that they must die," Blake whispered to himself.

"Did you enjoy your sweet on the pier that night? Intoxicating, wasn't it!" she said. "I knew Scarlet was powerful; the plan was brilliant! I was going to mother her and gain her trust, after you were gone, I would be there to pick up the pieces."

"Why?" Scarlet pleaded.

"So I could get close enough to kill you my dear. You and the others are the only ones left to stop me."

"The others?" Scarlet said.

"The Witches Circle," she replied.

"The story of all things is that everything must die. Darkness is banished by light, in turn light is extinguished by dark and so the cycle goes on and the world is balanced. But what if someone could break the cycle? Take power away from those disgusting witches? Such a being could create a new world! The end of the Witches Circle!" she spoke manically.

"The Circle protected the balance of the world," said Scarlet.

"The Circle was poisonous. It started to infect everything. I have worked hard to cleanse things."

"You mean, murder people!" Scarlet said.

"Yes quite right my sweetness. I have been busy for a very long time. I had to break the Witches Circle first, with that ugliness gone, who would have the power to stop me? One by one I found ways of ending their disgusting little existences. The Amber Witch, the Summer Witch, the Mountain Witch, they all begged me for their pathetic lives in the end. Only a few remained. The circle was smashed and I was nearly ready."

Scarlet felt uneasy.

"You and Blake are important pieces of the puzzle. I had you driven from your homes and I gave those weaklings who took you in, the illness that took them away from you. You were broken! I would have had you there and then but you disappeared! It took a long time to find you, then there you were, waiting for me in Kergord. Only there was a problem," she hissed, "your souls were new, healed! Blake's 'True Love' had restored you. It had to end. With just a little magic, it was easier than I thought to tap into Blake's darkness and let him believe that his precious Scarlet could love another," she said.

Zander! Thought Scarlet.

"Of course, nobody could have known how destructive you would be together! Where did you get that power Blake?"

Verity had been listening intently. She was trying to see the whole picture as the Witchfinder revealed her story. Scarlet, Blake, were they the key to it all?

"You lied to me! You destroyed my world!" Blake shouted angrily.

"You destroyed your own world my sweetness, I only planted a seed. You did the rest," she snarled back. "You were so weak, your jealousy and anger crushed you."

Scarlet was reeling, she was thinking of her mother and Kergord and who she really was.

"This is over!" shouted Blake. "It's time for you to pay for your actions. In the end, we all pay!"

Verity was clouded in confusion. "WAIT!" she cried. "Why me? I'm just Verity. Why am I here?" Her cry silenced the basin.

The Witchfinder produced an evil smile. "You are so special Verity. I can honestly say I enjoyed tearing out your mother's Heart Stone more than all the others. You are the daughter of a witch Verity! A most powerful witch, the Grand Matriarch Arabella. The stars say the Witches Circle will be complete again, united by a powerful truth, united by you Verity. That's why you were hidden but now I finally have you."

"What about me? Why was I left behind?" demanded Perfidy.

"Twin witches. It's never been known. My dear Perfidy don't feel left out. You will cry and beg for your worthless life as well."

"Never!" cried Perfidy.

"I command an army of walkers, trained to fight in daylight, gores who crave flesh. Ulysses is on the edge, the people have made the darkness strong with greed, and hatred. I will finish what they started and create a new world, my world!" the Witchfinder shrieked. The sky was darkened and the clouds rumbled loudly with thunder. "You are right Blake, this is over. Don't feel bad, your story is the story of all things! They all must die!" She held her hands high and entered a trance. The clouds rumbled again, lightning snapped and flashed into the rock. All at once the earth shook. It knocked everyone off their feet. Perfidy looked up and saw the eastern face of the basin crumbling. It felt like the whole world was shaking. A huge shape started to appear in the rock, a huge human shaped figure. Stones and rock tumbled down as a beast rose from within the mountain.

"Rock Troll!" shouted Blake as he grabbed Verity to her feet. Perfidy ran to Frances and slung Morty over her shoulder. "This way!" Blake shouted again, pointing at the Green Amber Falls. The Rock Troll stopped rising. It stood as tall as two trees. Its roar was deafening. It swung a massive fist slowly at the mountainside and smashed out a huge grey hole, spraying rock everywhere. The group ran and stumbled towards the falls. All except Scarlet. She faced the troll and sent a river of fire towards the beast. It roared loudly but didn't stop. She hurled fireballs and rained flame down but it still lurched forward. Scarlet turned and ran. The whole ground shook as its huge stone clad foot thumped into the ground. The group had reached the falls. They saw Scarlet running to them.

"What now!" panted Perfidy.

Blake quickly looked around. The Witchfinder had gone, the Rock Troll had destroyed two of the paths and to get to the last one they would have to run past it. "I can't see a way out!" he said desperately. Scarlet was nearly with them.

"What about the Staxcian Door?" piped up a terrified Frances. Blake looked over his shoulder. There it was, the Staxcian Door. He knew it took strong magic to open and once inside they would be the prey of the Black Witch. The Beast roared again and smashed a fist into the ground knocking everyone off their feet.

Scarlet arrived. "We don't have long. The Gate is our only chance!" she gasped. Verity, Perfidy, Blake and

Scarlet ran to the huge door to try to find a way in. Another footstep thundered as the Rock Troll moved closer.

"It's no use," said Blake, "only the strongest magic can open it!"

Frances was shaking with fear while watching the others. Morty started to mumble next to her. "Only the worthy shall pass," he croaked. "You can open the door." Then, he drifted away again. Frances took a deep breath and rose to her feet. Another footstep crashed down. The troll was bending down to try to swipe at them.

"Can I help?" came a little voice.

Everyone turned and looked at Frances. She walked to the door and placed her left hand on it and closed her eyes. Please! She thought. A huge rock fist swiped in and sent the group flying in all directions as they dodged it. PLEASE! Thought Frances.

"We won't get away from another one, it's too close!" cried Blake.

"PLEASE!" Frances called out loud.

The door started to crack and groan as the ancient hinges creaked into life. "You did it!" cried Perfidy. The troll started its huge swing.

"MOVE!" shouted Blake as he grabbed Morty. He shoved and pushed Perfidy then Verity and Frances through the gap in the door. Scarlet's face paused in front of his for a second as she passed. He had just enough time to remember how beautiful her eyes were, then she was gone. The fist swung towards the door. Blake barged through into blackness, then there was nothing but falling. The roars of the troll quickly faded away.

Chapter 10
Alone in the dark

'I knew nothing but shadows and I thought them to be real.'
Oscar Wilde

Blake opened his eyes. He didn't remember hitting the ground. He stared into the blinding darkness. "Scarlet! Perfidy! Anyone there?" his voice echoed into the blackness. He thought of Morty then blindly felt the cold dusty ground around him with his hands. Nothing. "Anyone there?" he called again. Nothing. He slowly made his way to his feet. He didn't seem to be hurt by the fall.

He had heard of the Black Caves. The prison of the Black Witch. He had heard the stories, as everyone had, of the great terrors that lay within. Legend had it that the Black Witch had been one of the Witches Circle. The tales told of her dark heart, black magic and the dark arts. The Witches Circle became worried and after a long battle they imprisoned her deep in the mountain. She was rumoured to have taken a sacred treasure which the Witches Circle had fiercely protected, The Book of Veritas. A huge reward was promised to anyone who could retrieve it. Blake knew better than to believe in tales, but there was no doubt the Black Witch was waiting. Many had gone in. Few ever came back. Brave warriors came from all around seeking fame and riches but only one was ever known to have made it out of the caves alive. A traveller from the Eastern lands. He told stories of broken bodies and broken minds. He said the Black Witch brought despair to the hearts and souls of her victims till they begged to die. That she made them face their worst fears until they simply didn't want to live. Blake knew he could turn her against herself to make his escape but what of the others? He wondered if his world without

Perfidy, without Scarlet, would be any different to the suffocating blindness he was in right now. He heard a scuffling somewhere close by but couldn't be sure where. "Come out of hiding!" he said boldly. "Come out and meet your match!"

There was a small scraping noise followed by a small but dazzling flame as a lighter sparked into life. The flame illuminated a small whiskery face. "You is full of mumbles and grumbles today Mr Master. Old Morty has been in all sorts of pains and aches, oh yes, yes, yes, you don't see him rumble and grumble, no, no, no. Where is we Mr Blakey sir?"

Perfidy opened her eyes. She didn't remember hitting the ground. She stared into the blinding darkness. "Verity! Frances! Anyone there?" her voice echoed into the blackness. She slowly rose to her feet. She didn't seem to be hurt after the fall. "Anyone there?" she called again. This time a small voice came out of the darkness. It was so faint that Perfidy couldn't work out who or what it was but it was definitely there. She fumbled around feeling for her weapons. No shot bow but her dagger was secure in her belt. She blindly swiped her arms around trying to find a point of reference.

Nothing. She heard the voice calling for help again. She was almost sure which direction it was coming from. "I'm coming!" she shouted. With her arms outstretched in front of her, she very cautiously shuffled forward into the black. Her tiny steps meant progress was slow. The ground was uneven and she nearly fell several times.

The voice grew louder. She could make it out more clearly now. "Hurry!" it said. "Please hurry, she's coming back!" Perfidy's heart started thumping, it was Frances.

"I'm coming!" she shouted, "I'm coming!" she started stumbling forward as quickly as she dared. Her foot caught something and sent her toppling to the ground.

"She's coming back, hurry Perfidy, I need you!" came the little voice again. Perfidy clumsily got back to her feet. She rubbed her sore arm.

"I'm coming Frances, just hold on!" She bundled blindly forward again. The blackness was thick. Her eyes saw nothing. Her heart raced. She had to get to Frances, she could hear how frightened she was.

"Perfidy, I need you! Please don't let me down!" came the voice again.

"I'm coming, please hold on!" Perfidy cried desperately. Suddenly, Perfidy could see two dim lights in the distance, one to her right and one to her left. Another voice came out of the black.

"Perfidy, is that you?" it sounded like Verity.

"Verity! It's me, where are you? Is Frances with you?" Perfidy replied.

"Frances isn't with me. I need your help Perfidy. Hurry, she's coming back!" Verity's voice rang out. Perfidy stopped moving.

"Perfidy!" called Frances. "I need you, she's nearly here!"

Perfidy could hear Verity's voice was coming from the direction of the light on her left and Frances was to her right.

"The Black Witch is coming Perfidy. Help me!" cried out Verity.

Perfidy's limbs were frozen. The lights were so far apart. At her speed, she couldn't reach them both quickly. Her heart was torn in two. Verity was strong, she was brave. Frances needed looking after. Verity was her sister. Frances was her friend. She stood helpless, not knowing what to do.

"She's here!" screamed Frances.

"She's here!" screamed Verity.

Perfidy shut her eyes tight. Her heart broke as she made her choice and started running. The ground seemed smoother now and she could run quite quickly since she had the light to concentrate on. As it grew brighter, she could see the rough outline of a figure ahead. It was Frances. She was standing still, facing away. Perfidy reached the light, which seemed to come from nowhere. "Frances!" she called as she stopped a short distance from her. She put her hands on her knees and was trying to catch her breath. "Frances. It's me. I came to save you!" she blurted out. Frances didn't move. She was as still as a statue. "Frances?" said Perfidy. She walked over to her and put her hand on her shoulder. Frances crumpled to the floor. "Frances!" cried Perfidy. She quickly bent down and picked up her head. A thin crimson line was drawn across her throat.

"You let me down," was all Frances could gurgle before her head flopped down. Perfidy cried out as she held her friend's body. She shook herself, Verity! She thought.

She rose and started running towards the second light. When she got there Verity was standing still, facing away. Perfidy slowed as she approached. "Verity," came her shaky voice. Verity didn't answer. Perfidy felt sick in her stomach. She slowly walked up and put a hand on Verity's shoulder. Verity turned, a thin crimson line drawn across her throat.

"Why wouldn't you come for me? I'm your sister," she said before flopping to the floor.

"You are strong," Perfidy wept, "you are brave. I thought you had a better chance of saving yourself. I'm so sorry!" She was sobbing while holding Verity's body.

"It seems you have let everyone down," came a sickly dark voice. The Black Witch stood in front of Perfidy. "You betrayed your own blood," she hissed.

"No, I tried to do the best thing," wept Perfidy.

"You killed her. You killed them both because you were slow and disloyal."

"No," sobbed Perfidy weakly.

"Yes child, and now you have to choose your own fate. I will help you," the Black Witch sneered as the blackness closed in.

Frances opened her eyes. She didn't remember hitting the ground. She stared into the blinding darkness. "Verity! Perfidy! Anyone there?" her voice echoed into the blackness. She slowly rose to her feet. She didn't seem to be hurt after the fall. "Anyone there?" she called again.

"I'm in here," came a voice. It sounded like Verity.

"I can't see anything! Where are you?" Frances called back.

"Here in the next room, come through," the voice came back. Frances fumbled around in the dark. The voice didn't sound very far away. She scuffled around on her hands and knees and it wasn't long before she gently bumped into a wall. She placed both hands against it and slowly rose to her feet. The wall felt like stone, it was cold and wet. "I'm in here," Verity's voice came again.

"I'm coming!" replied Frances. She followed the sound of the voice. Moving her hands across the wall, she side stepped until the wall stopped. She ran her hand over what felt like something wooden.

"I'm in here," came Verity's voice again.

"I think I'm at the door!" Frances squeaked excitedly. She scrabbled around for a handle. It was solid, cold and round. It clunked as it turned, light poured into the darkness as she opened it.

Verity opened her eyes. She didn't remember hitting the ground. She stared into the blinding darkness. "Frances! Perfidy! Anyone there?" her voice echoed into the blackness. She slowly rose to her feet. She didn't seem to be hurt after the fall. "Anyone there?" she called again. A small glowing light floated through the air towards her. It stopped just in front of her then floated away before stopping again. Verity fixed her gaze and slowly moved towards it. The way she was walking made her feel like an old woman. Each step was shaky as she made her way through the inky blackness. Each time she neared the light it would float away a little further and stop. It wants me to follow it, Verity thought. This went on for what seemed like a very long time, yet Verity had no idea exactly how long, or how far she had come. She was so disorientated that she could have walked a mile or just a few metres, she couldn't tell. A woman's voice faintly cut through the darkness. Verity didn't know who the voice belonged to but it did sound familiar, somehow.

Verity continued plunging into the dark, following the light.

The voice became clearer. "Verity," it called. Verity still could not place it, although she could hear it very clearly now. It called out again and again. It carried the sound of sadness with it. Suddenly, the light disappeared and Verity was left, alone in the dark. She looked around but the darkness was blinding. Panic crept in and she breathed deeply. After a few moments, the darkness thinned. Verity started to think she could make out shapes in the gloom. She slowly began to see walls nearby and what might be a door. Blocky shapes started to form into chairs and a table, as more light seeped in. Verity couldn't tell where the light was coming from. Soon, she found herself squinting as she looked around. She was in a room. Yellow floral wallpaper covered the walls. In the middle of the room sat a fine oak table on top of which sat a large bunch of colourful flowers in a jug of water. There were three places set for a meal. Pots bubbled on a stove in the corner. Verity smelt something delicious, she sniffed and closed her eyes as she recognised the beautiful scent of fresh bread baking. Logs smouldered and crackled on a small fire, which made Verity's toes tingle as its warmth breathed into her bones. There was a photograph hanging on the wall. Verity looked at it. There was a man and a dark haired woman in front of whom stood a little girl. Verity took a step back and gasped. The girl was her.

Frances found herself in a corridor. It was well lit and stretched out a little way before it turned off to the right. There was a door a few yards from her to the left. The floor was wooden and the walls were painted in a deep dark green. There was nothing else in the corridor except a picture hanging crookedly on the wall. "I'm in here," came Verity's voice.

"I'm coming!" Frances called. She made her way to the door on the left and turned the handle. It was locked. She knocked hard. "Are you in there?" she shouted. There was no reply.

"This is giving me the creeps," she muttered under her breath. Her heart beat quickly and she was sweating a little though she felt quite cold. She moved further down the corridor and stopped at the picture. She straightened it as she looked at it. A family posing together. Two parents and two children. Their faces were cut out of the picture. "Double creeps," muttered Frances. She headed to the end of the corridor and turned the corner. Another corridor lay before her. Two doors this time. One to her right and one directly ahead at the end of the corridor. "Verity?" she called. No reply. She tried the door to her right which was locked.

"I'm in here," came Verity's voice from behind the door at the end of the corridor. Frances rushed towards it and turned the handle, it opened and she hurried through. She found herself in what looked like the same corridor as the first one. A door to the left, green walls and a crooked picture hanging. The corridor turned off to the right at the end. Frances shivered. She tried the door on the left, it was locked. She walked up to the picture and straightened it. The same four people were there with their faces cut out. She thought she could hear the faint sound of a child crying. She ran to the end of the corridor and turned the corner to see the same thing she'd seen before. A door to her right and a door at the end. The door to her right wouldn't budge. She walked slowly to the door at the end and turned the handle. It opened and she crept through.

Verity was shaken out of her shock by a voice behind her.

"Nice, isn't it?"

Verity spun round. The Black Witch sat at the table. She wore a long black skirt and a black blouse. Her eyes looked like two pools of black ink that blazed out from her pale face. A large scar snaked down her left cheek. Her face was also streaked in what looked like black mascara tear stains. She wore black gloves. Her legs were neatly crossed and she sipped tea from a small blue patterned china cup. "Nice picture, don't you think?" she said.

"Who are you? Where am I, where are my friends?" Verity blurted out. The Black Witch smiled and took another sip from her cup.

"Why don't you come and sit down and have some tea my sweetness," she said.

Verity slowly went to the table and sat down. "I don't want tea, where are my friends and Perfidy?" she said.

"Don't fret child, they are safe, for now." There was an edge of danger in her voice.

"Who are you, the Black Witch?" Verity asked.

"I am not important child. What is important is that you are here. Let's stand by the stove." She rose to her feet and moved gracefully across the floor. She beckoned Verity to follow her. Verity reluctantly obliged. "Now watch," she said. The door handle clicked and clunked and a small bright blue eyed girl barged into the room. Verity was stunned. It was her, younger, but her. She was followed by a black haired woman and a man.

"Mummy is lunch ready yet?" squeaked the little girl.

"Patience my darling, it will be ready soon, go and wash your hands first," said the woman. Verity stared at her. She was taken by the woman's beauty and her warmth.

"Mum?" Verity called. The woman ignored her and carried on cutting bread. "MUM?" Verity called again.

"She can't hear you my dear," the Black Witch said, "she can't see or hear us. This isn't really happening."

Verity was so confused. She watched the little family getting ready for lunch. They sat down and ate and laughed together. "They are so happy," Verity said as if to herself.

"Of course they are dear, they have everything they ever wanted. A loving family and a happy home. Isn't that something you want Verity?" The Black Witch's mouth curled into an evil grin.

Verity's heart ached. Since she could understand the world, all she had ever craved was to be loved in a family. To have that feeling only a mother can give.

"This isn't real Verity, but I can make it real."

"You are the Black Witch," said Verity.

"Yes and I can give you what your heart longs for. I can make this fantasy your reality. You wouldn't remember the orphanage or this place or even me. You would just be a normal happy girl in a loving family. Doesn't that sound nice?" The Black Witch's tone was sinister. Verity was caught in the dream. She looked at the little girl eating with her parents. They were so happy.

"Wait," she said, "what about Perfidy, and Frances. Where are they?"

"You won't need to worry about them my dear. I will make sure you won't even remember them," the Black Witch sneered.

"I don't want to forget them!" Verity exclaimed.

The Black Witch's face became angry. She clapped her hands and the family vanished. They were in a small empty room. "I am offering you everything child. I can make your dreams come true. All you have to do is walk through that door and tell your friends that you are not coming with them. Then, you can have the life you deserve," she snapped.

"What will happen to them?" Verity asked.

"Their sacrifice will make your dreams come true. You won't even remember them. They would want it this way," said the witch. "Just go through and tell them you are staying and I will do the rest," she grinned evilly. Verity was lost. She couldn't get the image of the family out of her head. She was on the edge of getting everything she ever wanted.

"Ok," she said with a heavy heart, "I'll do it."

Frances didn't move as the door clicked shut behind her. She was back in the first corridor, green walls and a crooked picture. She stood deathly still, this time the door on the left was open. She could see that the room inside was pitch black but there was a flicker of dazzling light that strobed randomly every few seconds. Frances crept towards the door. "Verity?" she said shakily. Her voice was small and frightened. Closer and closer she inched to the door. She could hear someone weeping inside. She was nearly at the door. She stopped and tried to pluck up the courage to look in. The weeping grew louder. She took a deep breath and looked through the door. The light hurt her eyes as it flickered. She squinted and could just make out a girl standing in the room facing her. Her face was in her hands. Frances was shaking. "Verity?" she whimpered. The strobe lighting continued to flicker. The girl lowered her hands. Frances gasped.

"IT WAS YOUR FAULT!" screamed the girl.

Suddenly, the door slammed shut and Frances toppled backwards onto her bottom. She was breathing so hard her lungs felt as if they were going to burst. Had she just seen her sister? She shook herself and rushed to the door. The handle wouldn't budge. "Abigail!" she cried. "Abigail!" She thumped her fist on the door, but there was no response. She crumpled to the floor in despair and was about to sob when a door slammed further down the corridor. She slowly picked herself up and headed towards it. She stopped at the crooked picture. She straightened it before clamping her hand over her mouth. It was the same family but this time one face had not been cut out. It was her face. She turned and ran in panic. She quickly rounded the corner and reached the door but it was locked. The sound of another door slamming came from back down the corridor.

"IT WAS YOUR FAULT!" came a scream followed by the clump of slow deliberate footsteps. "YOUR FAULT!" it screamed.

Frances was in a blind panic. She rushed to the door at the end of the corridor and barged through. She fell in a heap on the floor. She was gasping for air as she looked around. She was in a familiar room, her old bedroom. The green fluffy carpet, her little wooden bookcase, her old toy box in the corner. Her little old bed with her little old duvet covered in stars. Her old teddy, Sir Lancelot, sat on the pillow. Frances couldn't take it all in. This was her room while her parents were alive.

Frances didn't notice the Black Witch sitting in the corner until she spoke. She was looking at a picture. "Such a happy family," she said. Frances spun round and looked at her. "Such a shame, such a waste," the witch continued. She turned the picture round to reveal Frances, Abigail and their mum and dad together. The same picture Frances had seen in the corridor with no faces cut out.

"I, I..." croaked Frances, "I don't understand?"

"Such a shame," the witch went on, "do you ever think about them? Do you ever wonder what could have been?" sneered the evil woman. Frances felt sick. She had thought about nothing else every single moment since the accident. She couldn't speak.

"Such a lot for a little girl, to take all the blame," the witch said.

"W, wh, what do you mean?" sniffed Frances.

"Didn't they tell you? They thought they were protecting you I expect. It was all your fault child. Don't feel bad," the words dripped from her mouth.

"No, it, it wasn't, it was an accident," whimpered Frances.

"No sweetness. It was you. Your father was tired that day wasn't he? He had been up in the night seeing to you."

"I had a cough, I couldn't sleep," pleaded Frances.

"You were arguing with your sister in the car, weren't you?" shrieked the witch. "Your mother was worried about you at school, wasn't she?"

"I had fallen out with my friend, that's all," Frances replied weakly.

"She was trying to talk to your father about your troubles at school, you were squabbling with your sister in the back. He was tired, he couldn't concentrate! Instead of seeing the lorry and slowing down he was busy dealing with all your problems until..." the Black Witch was clearly enjoying herself.

"I didn't realise," sobbed Frances, "I shouldn't have caused so many problems. It's my fault!" she wailed.

The Black Witch cracked her knuckles and smiled, "Yes child but your sacrifice will make things right."

Blake and Morty made their way through the dark caverns easily once they had been able to light an old torch which they had prised from the skeletal fingers of a dead man. They had not seen or heard anyone since arriving. "I is not thinkin' too fondly of this place Mr Blakey sir," Morty piped up.

"We must find the others," replied Blake, "they will need us. The Black Witch will destroy their minds before breaking their bodies."

"How is she nobblin' their noodles Mr Blakey sir?" asked Morty.

"Her magic forces people to face their worst fears. She makes them believe that their fears are real and it makes them feel so terrible they don't want to carry on. It's like a game to her," Blake said.

"Are you not afraid Mr Blakey sir, that she would jibble your giblets?" asked Morty.

"She can't get to me that way. I will use her own magic against her and make her feel her own despair," Blake replied.

"We is needin' to find the little girly peeps!" announced Morty. "They needs us to make thems safe!"

"You are brave my furry friend, we will find them," said Blake as they continued deep into the belly of the mountain. The pair followed a long path of winding corridors that seemed to trail endlessly downward. Eventually, they reached a large oak door. It was made from several oak panels and hung on huge black iron hinges. There was no handle. "Be ready," said Blake. He placed his hand flat against the door and pushed. He had to apply considerable weight before the door yielded. The room he entered was large and cold. There were no windows and the walls were made of stone as was the floor. The outline of the room made the shape of an equilateral triangle, one of the corners was bathed in darkness. There were four chairs placed in the centre of the room. They backed on to each other. There was a body tied to each chair, Verity, Perfidy, Frances and Scarlet. Each asleep, each head bowed. Blake walked cautiously towards them. The door shut behind him. He turned to see Morty was not there. Instead, the Black Witch stared at him with icy black eyes.

"They are all broken," she said. "They are all ready."

"Ready for what?" Blake replied.

"Ready to die," she said coldly. "It was very easy. They all broke quickly, even the witch. A simple story about her mother brought her to her knees. Love is such a weakness."

"Love is a great strength," Blake protested.

The Black Witch walked around the edges of the room, eyeing Blake carefully. "What of you, my child? I see you are out of reach. This is strange indeed. Your eyes are very black," she said suspiciously.

"So are yours," Blake said. "I can turn your power against you," he declared.

"Your magic is quite useless here my dear, please believe me. There is something else! I see your ghosts. How long do you think they can keep you safe?" she said.

"Perhaps I have conquered my fear, I keep it under control," Blake replied.

"No my child, I don't think so. One without fear cares for nothing," she said. She was still moving round the room and still hadn't taken her eyes from him. "Is it true? Can a man care for nothing?"

Blake didn't take his eyes from her. He knew how she might try to deceive him. The Black Witch stopped her perimeter walk and headed to him. She stopped in front of him. "I don't quite know what to do with you, my dear?" she said.

"Where is Morty?" Blake demanded. "Open that door, let him in."

The Black Witch thought for a second before turning and raising her hand to the door. It creaked open. All at once Morty burst in. "Mr Blakey sir! Show me where is she and I shall smite her, fight her, bite her bottom!"

The Black Witch's eyes widened. "What did you say?" she said.

"I is saying, I will bite your bottom Mrs Witch!" Morty declared proudly.

"What did you call him?" the Black Witch's eyes grew.

"My name is Blake and it's time for you to pay! We all pay in the end!" he said boldly.

The witches voice trailed off as she spoke, "Blake..." she seemed to be in a daze. "Blake..." she said again, "Do you know who gave you that name?"

"I have no mother. The past is irrelevant. I only look forward."

"The past chases you like a wolf. You have run far and it has exhausted you my child."

"I am strong," Blake said.

"You should be dead. You are strong indeed," the witch said.

"I will not be seduced by you, witch!"

"That is true my child. Fate won't always be so kind. She rummaged inside her cloak and produced a small, perfectly round, gleaming black pearl. "Blake..." she said staring at the pearl as she crumpled to her knees. "I hid you deeply in the darkness, I had to."

Blake watched her carefully. Morty flashed him a confused look. Blake remained vigilant while the witch sobbed into her hands.

"What is this witch? A trick? I am ready for you!" he said.

She lifted her head. Black streaks ran down her face where her black tears ran. "I have done terrible things. They took my baby, what did they expect? You are my miracle, I kept you safe. I named you my child."

"Are you my mother?" he asked.

"No child."

"But you knew her?"

"Know her child, I know her."

"The glorious Witches Circle showed their true colours. They planned murder to protect the status quo of the world. I found you, a baby. I took your Heart Stone. I'm so sorry. I couldn't see any other way. It's yours." The pearl gleamed in her palm, Blake walked cautiously towards her and picked it up out of her outstretched hand. She stood up, black tear tracks snaked down her face.

"Help us and we will help you," Blake said.

"I am beyond help," she said.

She waved her arm and the ties that held everyone to their chairs fell away. Slowly they started to wake.

"Head back through the door. You will find your way out," she said. The others rubbed their eyes and gently moved their tired limbs. The Black Witch shuffled into the dark corner of the triangle. She reappeared with a small, brown, leather-bound book. "Take this, she will know what to do," she said, pointing at Scarlet. Blake took the book. The Black Witch raised one hand and gently brushed Blake's fringe to one side before turning and disappearing into the dark corner. Blake and Morty helped the others to the door. One by one they stumbled through, heading towards a dazzling bright green light.

Chapter 11
The Book of Veritas

'You forgave and I won't forget.'
Mumford and Sons - Nothing is written.

Everyone sat round the camp fire except Scarlet, who said she needed to scout the area. From the looks her and Blake had been giving each other Verity guessed that she wanted to be alone. The fire snapped and crackled as it sent thin wisps of smoke into the starry night sky. Nobody spoke. Blake broke the silence. "Morty and I will look for something to eat. Sometimes when you have feelings that hurt inside it's best to let them be felt, then they can leave," he said. The three girls shuffled and wriggled anxiously. Blake rose to his feet. "Morty!" he beckoned.

"Oh and woe! I has found a comfy snuggle spot, I was thinkin' I is havin' forty blinks, oh lovely master," Morty pleaded.

"Morty!" said Blake again raising his eyebrows.

"Food and eats, yes, yes, yes, splendid plan!" replied Morty hastily as he rose to his feet. "Poor little Moley peeps. Keeps away from bubbles and troubles Mother Morty said, stay in your moley hole. Blakey sir doesn't have creaky knees and a tricky bladder, does he?" Morty grumbled quietly.

"Did you say something?" Blake said smiling, pretending not to hear.

"Coming oh great one, I is just saying how much I is lookin' forward to trampin' through the woods now," grouched Morty.

"Excellent," said Blake sarcastically, "come on then, let's leave these girls to talk." He turned and Morty followed him into the wood.

Perfidy looked at the ground while Verity stared into the fire. It was Frances who spoke first, "I never thought I would see my sister again. But then I never really did, did I? The Black Witch made me feel like I hated myself, I just couldn't think straight. I'm so sorry." Tears started to trickle as she spoke.

Perfidy went next, "Don't you dare feel that way! Nobody blames you. You did what you thought you had to do, for your family! Not like me." She looked at the ground in despair.

Verity snapped out of her trance, "Don't YOU dare feel that way! You made a really brave choice. You risked your life for a friend. I hope I would have been brave enough to do the same." Her eyes were full of kindness. "Most people would have chosen to do nothing. Too busy thinking about themselves but that's not you," she said.

"You wanted to save me," Frances sobbed and fell into Perfidy's arms. Her embrace poured into Perfidy and started to fill the emptiness.

"It was me who would have betrayed everyone, for what?" Verity said sadly.

"A family," replied Perfidy sympathetically.

"You are my family!" Tears streamed down Verity's face. "You and Frances are the only family I have ever known and I... I love you both."

The three girls reached for each other and held tightly. "The Black Witch was powerful, but we are still here together, aren't we?" said Perfidy. Eventually, they let go and leaned back. Perfidy put her hand into the middle, "Forgiven?" she said. The other two each placed a hand on top.

"Forgiven!" they said together.

"Sisters," said Verity looking at Frances then Perfidy.

"Sisters!" they echoed. They all smiled and then laughed as they hugged again.

Blake emerged from the shadows. "Excellent," he said, holding up two large woodland pheasants, "who wants dinner?"

The morning breathed sunshine into weary bones. Frances woke to find the others already sitting eating breakfast. "I should have ordered an alarm call," she mumbled sleepily.

"Are you well rested?" Perfidy asked.

"Rested and hungry!" grinned Frances. She joined the others and tucked into a large handful of red berries and freshly roasted pheasant meat.

"What are we to do now?" asked Perfidy.

Scarlet spoke for the first time that morning, "Your escape from the caves has slowed the Witchfinder down but she will already be formulating a new plan."

"If she commands an army, all is lost," said Blake. "Ulysses will fall to her and the balance of the world will shift to darkness. She will be free to create a new world and the balance might never be restored."

"Let me get this straight," Frances said through a mouthful of berries, "the Witchfinder wants to create a new world of darkness, destroying Ulysses in the process?"

"Yes," replied Blake.

"And she has been busy destroying her opposition, the Witches Circle?"

"Yes," said Blake wearily.

"And she wants to release an army of nightwalkers to do her bidding?" Frances said.

"Could we hurry the brain cells along please?" said Blake sarcastically.

"And Verity and Perfidy are daughters of a Witch and she thinks they can stop her?" Frances carried on.

"She believes they can form a new circle, one powerful enough to destroy her," Scarlet said.

"We have to stop her!" chirped Frances.

"Excellent young Frances, and how do you propose we do that exactly?" sighed Blake.

"I can't do all the work!" Frances replied grumpily, "You are the ones who can disappear, reappear and pull rabbits out of hats!"

"Pull what out of where?" asked Perfidy.

"Never mind," said Frances.

"We have the Book of Veritas, it will show us how to keep the balance of light and dark," said Scarlet. She pulled the small leather bound book from her robe. "You should open it Verity."

"But I'm just Verity?" she said nervously.

"Yes, never forget that," Scarlet said.

Verity held out a trembling hand and took the book. She looked at Perfidy. Perfidy nodded. She held the book carefully with both hands. It was quite an unremarkable looking object. She took a short breath and opened it. She gasped at what she saw. Two creamy blank pages. She turned the pages, slowly at first then quickly. Everyone like the last, blank. She looked at Scarlet. Scarlet said nothing.

"Beggin your pardons Miss, but is it not going to be difficult to read a book with no wiggly little words?" Morty said.

"Yes, it is," Blake sighed.

"We still have the book," Scarlet said.

"Yes but it's all blank! What use is it?" moaned Perfidy.

"There is one who might be able to read it," said Scarlet.

"Who?" asked Verity.

"The Witch of the Seas," she replied.

"I thought all the witches were dead?" said Frances.

"No my dear, the Witchfinder smashed the Witches Circle but she didn't kill them all. Those who were left fled and took refuge in dark, hidden places, guarding magic and waiting," said Scarlet.

"Like you?" asked Perfidy.

"Yes my child, like me," Scarlet replied.

"So where is this Witch of the Seas?" asked Blake.

"She lives in the belly of the beast that roams in the deepest darkest parts of the Soulless Sea," Scarlet answered.

"Great," groaned Blake, "just great. It could take years to find her! We have days if we are lucky! The Witchfinder won't stay idle for long."

Scarlet looked thoughtful. "We must strike the Witchfinder before it's too late. None of us will be able to defeat her. We will need help. We must seek out the last remaining witches from the Circle, together we might have a chance. If the Witchfinder falls then her army will fall with her."

"Do you know where the witches are?" Blake asked.

"I know where the Green Witch waits. She watches the Hanging Tree. She has become distrustful and dangerous," she said.

"If the Green Witch is dangerous, what makes you think she will help us?" asked Blake.

"I have something to show her," Scarlet said.

"This is all giving me the creeps," Frances groaned.

"What about us?" asked Verity.

"Your search is for something far greater. You must find the Witch of the Seas to try to learn the secrets of The Book of Veritas. The Witches Circle was smashed but the story of light and dark says that it is inevitable that all things must come round again. The Witches Circle can be restored. The book can show us the truth that will save us all. Blake, Frances and I will seek out the Green Witch. Verity, Perfidy and Morty, you must find the Witch of the Seas," she said.

"I'm not going without Verity!" announced Frances.

"You must come with us," said Scarlet.

"I'm not leaving Verity and Perfidy!" Frances said.

"They will have Morty to keep them right, we will need you before we are done," Scarlet said. She flashed Verity a knowing look over Frances shoulder. Verity thought she understood.

"It's ok," said Verity, "they will look after you. It won't be long before we are back together to share our adventures and have a giggle." Even Verity sounded a little unconvinced by her words.

"Ok," Frances said reluctantly.

The group gathered their things and started to say their goodbyes. Frances cried while Verity held back her tears. Perfidy stood a little way back from the group. Scarlet joined her. "Head for the fishing village of Hamnavoe. Seek out a man known as Dead Fred. He is someone I used to know. He can be found in the tavern. He will help you find the Witch of the Seas."

"How do you know he will help us?" Perfidy asked.

"It is his destiny," Scarlet replied.

Perfidy looked into Scarlet's deep ruby eyes, "But after what I tried to do to you? How can you..."

"The things that will destroy your soul are not swords and arrows my dear. Nothing can truly harm you unless you let them. The soul is locked tight and kept safe by the bonds of family, truth and love. These bonds can be fragile and delicate, easily broken, but they can also be strong as iron. Without them, the soul will surely perish. Remember, family, truth and love my dear, if you need me, keep this close to your heart." Scarlet pushed a small, glistening ruby into Perfidy's hand.

"Thank you," replied Perfidy. A single tear rolled down her cheek.

Verity's heart felt heavy as the group walked off on their separate paths. She felt the weight of everyone's expectations sitting firmly on her shoulders. It was too heavy.

"Mother Morty said strangers is dangers! Stay in your hidey hole! Nothin' bad happens under a cosy snuggle blanket in a lovely dark mole hole! I is not a fishy beast lover, no, no, no, I does likes to be under... underground! Not under water!" moaned Morty.

Perfidy could feel her sister's heavy burden. "Find a witch inside a terrible sea beast, how hard can it be?" she smiled. Morty grumbled as Perfidy and Verity chuckled down the long dusty track to the sea.

Chapter 12
Dead Fred

'The only difference between me and a madman is that I'm not mad.'
Salvador Dali

Hamnavoe brimmed and bustled with life. The market in the town square was awash with colour, noise and smell. Verity looked around in wonder. She had never seen anything like it. They had to squeeze and squash their way through the chattering crowds. Traders were shouting and bawling, trying to entice customers. Stall after stall boasted everything and anything, spices in rainbows of colours, piled high, delivering intriguing scents into the air. Beautiful silks and leathers adorned brightly decorated stalls. Glassware and metal work to the left and right. The buyers and sellers argued and haggled noisily. The trio slowly filed through the crowds. The last few stalls lay ahead. The smell of fish hit Verity like a wet slap in the face, it made her feel queasy. Buckets of ice were being poured over their slimy, scaly bodies as they waited to be bought. All kinds of shapes and sizes of fish were laid out. Verity had never seen such creatures before. Some of them flipped and flapped helplessly on their trays. Morty slowly approached a rather large fish sitting on a pile of ice. He curiously reached out a paw to poke it. Just as his hand was near the beast it opened its eyes and snapped its jaws at him. He jumped back like a little bolt of furry lightning. "Mother of all my saints reserve me!" he cried. "Is you seein' that beasty trying to end old Morty!"

"Twenty silver gotts," came the gruff voice of the fish seller.

Morty nearly imploded. "Twenty gotts! Twenty gotts! Your monster beast is nearly endin' all my days and you wants twenty gotts!" he ranted.

"All right, fifteen," the seller said.

"Come on now Morty," Perfidy chipped in, smiling, "Let's leave this nice fellow and his fish to their business." She chuckled as she took his hand and led him away, still grumbling about his near death experience.

They left the hustle and bustle of the market and headed down a quiet cobbled lane. Empty shops and houses lined the street left to right. Perfidy saw a sign hanging up ahead. "There it is," she said. "The World's End!"

The World's End was the last tavern before the docks. It never closed and was the kind of place people went to forget or be forgotten. Perfidy led the others in. The gloom was thick and although there were several people sitting drinking, it was strangely quiet. The roof was quite low and large sturdy oak beams ran along the ceiling. Faces appeared out of the smoke as they walked past before disappearing back into the gloom. A man, sitting on a stool, lay slumped over the bar snoring. "Are you lost me pretties?" said the barmaid. She was a large woman and wore a tight blue apron. Her hair was messily tied behind her head and her nails were panted bright red which matched her lipstick.

"We need to find someone," Perfidy said.

"Find someone, ha ha, everyone is lookin' to find somebody but they ain't not never findin' 'em in here my dear!" replied the woman.

"We were told this is a place he has spent time in," said Perfidy.

"Lots spend time here, they come and go dear. They don't want to be found," the barmaid said.

"He goes by the name of Dead Fred," continued Perfidy, ignoring the barmaid's attempts to put her off.

The woman shuffled awkwardly for a second. "I ain't never heard of him, now I fink it's time you pretty things left and forgot about whatever it is you fink you is lookin' for," she said sharply. She walked away and started drying glasses behind the bar.

Verity looked at Perfidy. "What now?" she said.

"I don't know," Perfidy replied. The sleeping man grunted and sicked up a little on the bar before laying his head back down in it. A voice came from over Perfidy's shoulder.

"Hello, I couldn't help but overhear you are looking for someone." Perfidy turned to see a small man with a hunch. He wore a slightly torn cloak and brown boots which reached his knees. His head was bowed and his hands were clasped together. "Cyril Snake, at your service."

"How can you help us?" asked Perfidy.

"I have information, oh gracious one, I live to give," his words were as slimy as his name.

"I don't trust him," Verity whispered.

"What do you know Mr Snake?" demanded Perfidy.

"Ah, now, before we strike an accord I would have to ask for a small token in return, your grace." He lifted his head to reveal a leathery face dotted with pimples. His nose was large and squashed and small amounts of black spit collected at the corner of his mouth.

"What do you ask?" said Perfidy.

"I ask only that you part with your dirty animal servant," he sneered, "he will fetch a good price at market."

Morty looked round in confusion. "Where is this animal servant?" he said.

"He means you," said Verity.

"Heavens blast us and save us! You sir, is as cheeky as a chestnut and as nutty!" snapped Morty.

"Your beast speaks out of turn! I warn you, he will be sorry if he does it again!" the little man sneered.

"What are we going to do?" whispered Verity anxiously. "He might be able to help us."

"Don't worry," whispered Perfidy, "tact and delicacy are required here."

Perfidy winked then turned and grabbed a handful of the man's collar. She drew his face close to hers. His breath smelt of mackerel. "I would love to strike an accord with you," she said sternly. "How about this? If you don't tell me what you know, I will kill you. If you lie to me, I will kill you. If your information is no good to me, I will kill you! In fact, you are going to have to work very hard right now to stay alive!" she growled. Snake shuddered and shook as he eyed her dagger.

"Now then, what an interesting proposition," he squeaked. "I would love to help you, of course I would! Did you like my little joke about the rat?" he said trembling.

"He is a mole, and I didn't." Perfidy eyeballed him as she spoke. "Now let's get to the bit where you tell us what you know about Dead Fred," she said, letting him go.

"Ah thank you my grace," he said bowing and clasping his hands together. "Dead Fred is a tricky one," he said, "Dead Fred is well known for wicked deeds round these parts, I am a little surprised you would want to find him, he hasn't got a reputation for kindness."

"Neither have I," said Perfidy.

"Yes my sweetness, that was the impression I got from you! He is not normally a man who wants to be found and those that do are often sorry," continued Snake.

"My patience is running out," Perfidy said. "Where is he, how do we find him?"

"I see you are not someone who is easily put off. I can help you but there is one big problem with Dead Fred," he said.

"Which is?" said Perfidy impatiently.

"Well," said Snake, "the problem with Fred is... he's dead!"

The town clock chimed midnight. Four shadowy figures made their way through the graveyard illuminated by the light of the moon. Cyril Snake led the way. "Not far now, oh gracious ones," he grovelled. The graveyard was situated just outside the town boundaries. A higgledy piggeldy stone wall ran round its edges. Although it was dark, the sky was clear and the moon lit the gravestones. Most were crumbling and in need of repair. Some had fallen and some lay broken in pieces. They waded through the grass. "This way," Snake said.

He led them to the far end of the graveyard and stopped in front of a small stone. "Give me your lighter," Perfidy said to Morty. She flipped it open and sparked it into flame. Bending down, she held it in front of the stone and read out the inscription.

'Here lies Frederick Bonniger.
May the Devil take his soul.'

"Nice," said Verity.

"I is feelin' ills and chills! Let's go," said Morty.

"What's the story?" Perfidy asked Snake.

"Well you see my grace, Dead Fred was not a well-liked man. An orphan boy, he upset three rich local merchants years ago when he stole some sheep from them. The merchants got together to decide what was to be done with Frederick Bonniger. They put a price on his head and before long he was brought before them. They put him on trial and decided to make an example of him so they had a large bonfire built in the town square."

"Go on," said Perfidy.

"Well, they left a nice space in the middle and put him in it. His hands and feet were bound and his mouth was gagged. The gag was removed before they lit it so the crowd would hear him scream," Snake said.

"How could they be so horrible?" Verity gasped.

"They were greedy men and wanted to show everyone how powerful they were. A large crowd gathered and watched in shock as the fire was lit and the flames climbed into the sky. Fred could be seen in the middle but he made no sound as the flames engulfed him. Finally his body collapsed. The next morning, once the bonfire was nothing more than ash, there was no trace of Fred. No human remains to be seen at all. The locals were scared and reports of sightings of Fred started to spread. A week later

119

the three merchants were found dead in the square, burned alive."

"How terrible!" said Verity.

"So where does that leave us?" asked Perfidy.

"Well he became known as Dead Fred and appeared and disappeared through the years. Until yesterday," he said.

"What is happenin' yesterday?" asked Morty.

"Dead Fred died! I was in The Worlds End having me usual morning tipple when he came in. He drank quietly in a corner. A woman approached him, dressed in grey she was."

"The Witchfinder!" Perfidy said.

"Well whoever she was, he didn't like her. He shouted at her and told her to leave, which she did. The next thing you know, Dead Fred is dead. Again! Body left in the middle of the square, not a mark on it! The locals buried him here last night," Snake said.

Perfidy's mind was whizzing. "She must have known we would try to find him. She must have tried to find the Witch of the Seas herself and he wouldn't tell her. The Witchfinder beat us to him!" she said in frustration.

"How are we going to find her now?" groaned Verity, "We can't give up."

"He is dead in the cold, black earth," said Perfidy. "There is only one thing we can do."

"What?" asked Verity.

There was a look of determination in Perfidy's eyes.

"We dig!"

Despite Morty's protests, he found himself shifting large lumps of earth underneath the headstone. "After all, you are a mole," Perfidy had said. The grave was fresh so the earth wasn't difficult for Morty to dig.

"They is sinkin' him deep!" he said.

"Yes, as I said, there was no love for him. I expect they buried him as far down as they could," added Snake.

Morty stopped. "What is it Morty? Have you found something?" asked Verity.

"I is thinkin'," said Morty, "is they boxin' him up or is they just throwin' him in a hole? I don't want to be putting my lovely little paws all over his flaky flesh!"

Snake looked puzzled. "I don't know," he said, "I didn't watch."

"Carry on!" demanded Perfidy. Morty grumbled but obliged. It didn't take long before he had his answer. Morty yelped and jumped back. A dirty, cold hand stuck out of the earth. Perfidy jumped into the hole and started clawing at the earth. First came an arm, then a shoulder. Perfidy scraped and dug franticly. She began to uncover his forehead and then started to brush the earth away to reveal his cold pale face. "Good evening, Mr Bonniger!" grinned Perfidy. Verity peeked over Perfidy's shoulder. She could see the face clearly. His eyes were open wide as was his mouth which was full of dirt. A large scar trailed down his left cheek. Perfidy took two fingers and started to scoop the earth out of his mouth. "I will need some help to get him out," she said. The others looked at each other. "Don't all jump at once!" said Perfidy sarcastically. Verity reluctantly moved nearer. "Grab his arm," Perfidy said. Taking an arm each, Perfidy and Verity freed the body from the remaining earth and hauled it out of the grave. "There!" announced Perfidy proudly, "That wasn't as difficult as you thought, was it!"

"Forgive me, your grace, but what do you intend to do now?" enquired Snake.

"Yes, I has been meanin' to ask why you is thinkin' him out the ground is any better than him in the ground, cause it isn't!" Morty said.

"It is going to be a little difficult for a dead man to help us," Verity added kindly.

Perfidy rummaged around in her tunic. "You are, of course, right. Dead men don't talk and many would say that's an improvement on live ones, but I have a feeling that Dead Fred won't be dead for long!" She held out the small gourd with the stopper on top.

"Let's see what those weeping stones can really do!" Perfidy grinned.

The others stood back while Perfidy tilted Fred's head back. She squeezed his muddy cheeks with one hand and poured in the last few drops of liquid. She let him go and stood back. Nothing happened. Perfidy turned to the others. "Well it was worth a try," she said. "I really thought it might work."

"Erm, Perfidy..." Verity started to speak.

"I know, it was a long shot but I really thought it might work," Perfidy replied.

"Perfidy!" Verity said wide eyed, this time pointing a slightly shaky finger over Perfidy's shoulder. Perfidy could hear breathing behind her. Wheezing and gasping. She slowly turned around.

"'Ello darlin'!" Fred wheezed before punching her hard in the mouth. She was sent reeling to the ground. "Eeeeee," said Fred as he turned his neck till it cracked loudly, "being murdered and buried doesn't half make the arthritis flare!" He flashed a manic look at Verity, "It's the damp ya see!"

Perfidy rose to her feet rubbing her jaw. She could taste iron as she swallowed some blood. Fred was fidgeting around mumbling to himself. He spun and stared at Verity. "What a pretty little thing!" He looked at Perfidy, "Not sure about her though! Ooooo, me knee." He proceeded to hop around on one leg till he fell over clutching it. He pulled at it till it crunched. "AAAAAhhhhhhh, that's the spot!" he shouted then got back up.

"He's as dotty as a doorbell," Morty whispered to Verity.

Fred looked back at Perfidy. "Now where was I, oh yes, I was in the middle of beatin' you blue girly!" he said.

"I'm afraid you will have to wait," said Perfidy, "I have something for you."

"Pray tell, girly, what does a little pixie such as yourself, have to interest Dead Fred, except your pretty little face of course!" Fred said.

"I want to give you something. Come over here," she said coolly.

Fred hopped and twirled theatrically as he made his way to her. "I'm ready child!" he said manically while making a gesture to kiss her. Perfidy punched him square in the middle of the face. Verity winced as she heard his nose crack. Fred landed in a heap howling. Perfidy took a handful of his collar and dragged him across the ground, and dumped him back into the grave they dug him out of. She put her boot on his chest.

"Now, we are even. If you ever touch me again, you will be even deader, Fred! Now tell me, are we going to go to The World's End to talk about witches, or am I going to cut your throat and bury you in the cold black earth?" she stared hard into his eyes.

Fred started to laugh. "HAAAaaaaa Ahhhhhhaaaaaa." He stopped suddenly and looked at Perfidy very sternly. "I like you!" he said with crazed eyes. "AAAAAAAhhhhhh HHHHAAaaaaaa, the girl's got style!" he roared. Perfidy lifted her boot cautiously. She held out a hand and helped Fred out of the grave. He made a large theatrical bow, "Frederick Bonniger, at your service!"

"Do my duster! What in blazes are you doing here?" Fred said as he spied Morty.

"Morty, do you know him?" Verity asked.

"We has not seen each other for a long time," Morty replied sheepishly.

"I would love to accompany you to dinner, ma lady," he grinned.

"Good," said Perfidy, "but first, we need to find you some clothes!"

Snake had snuck away easily once Fred had appeared. He walked through the cold midnight streets of Hamnavoe. He made his way to the docks and approached the Witchfinder who was standing looking out to sea. The moon hung low in the sky. "It is done, majesty," he said in a grovelling tone.

The Witchfinder spoke without turning round. She was wrapped in her grey cloak and hood. "Is Bonniger alive?" she inquired coldly.

"Yes majesty," Snake snivelled.

"Good, he will lead them to the Witch of the Seas. It won't be long before we have her and the rest," she said. "Be gone! But be ready. I shall call for you soon."

"Yes majesty," Snake said then slithered off into the darkness.

Verity was glad Snake had disappeared but she wasn't so glad to be walking through Hamnavoe with someone, who she couldn't be sure was dead or not, dressed in a large flowery frock!

"I'm a lady!" Fred called out loudly in a ridiculously high pitched voice. "Pay no heed! Just a lady, doing lady things!" he shouted in the same silly voice.

Perfidy scowled at Morty. "Were they really the only clothes you could find?" she snapped.

"Poor old Morty, I is the miracle makin' mole and I still gets no thanks. I'd like to see you snufflin' up some clothes in the middle of night. Lucky I found that washing line!" Morty protested.

"Lucky!" Perfidy said, "Lucky! Look at him! He's got a beard!"

"Helloooo, just a normal lady, coming through, pay no heed!" sang Fred. They gathered several strange looks before they reached The World's End.

"Get in!" said Perfidy as she grabbed Fred and pushed him towards the door.

"You mustn't man handle me, I'm a lady!" squealed Fred. Perfidy but her boot on his bottom and shoved him in.

Thankfully the tavern was quiet. They sat at a table in one of the dark corners. Fred was swigging from a large mug of Gutrot, a particularly strong ale.

"AAHHHHHHHH! That's the stuff, sure you don't want some girly?" he asked pushing the mug under Verity's nose. The sulphurous smell made her gag.

"Awfully kind, but no," Verity answered. "Can you tell us about the Witch of the Seas?"

Fred took another large slug of ale then belched loudly. "Better out than in!" he roared and slapped Morty's back, much to Morty's displeasure.

"Be you alive, or be you dead, Mr Fred, I is not caring for happy slaps at all!" Morty said.

To Perfidy and Verity's surprise Fred answered calmly, "Quite right, quite right, furry one, I'm sorry! Now then, witches you say? Why would a couple of pretties, like your good selves, be lookin' for witches?" Fred asked. His eyes wildly darted around every time he spoke.

"It's very important that we find her," Verity said.

"If you already know about the Sea Witch then you also know where she is. Deep in the belly of The Beast. What makes you think you won't certainly die trying to get to her, eh?" Fred said before he drained his mug and belched again. He looked sheepishly at Morty, "Er, pardon," he said. Morty gave him an approving look.

"We have to find her!" said Perfidy forcefully.

"Listen girly, I like you, any girl who breaks my nose is alright with me! Now, all this has been fun and I am ever so grateful for the lovely dress, oh and reviving me from the dead. But I think it's time we part ways." He smiled, bowed then started to walk away.

"What now Verity?" groaned Perfidy.

Fred stopped dead. He turned and walked back to the table. He looked very serious. "What did you say girly?"

"Nothing?" answered Perfidy.

"Not nothing my pretty," said Fred, "what did you call her?" His voice was nearly a whisper.

"Who? Verity?" Perfidy replied.

Fred started spinning round and dancing as if an electric current had just been passed through his body. All at once he stopped, put his hands on Verity's shoulders and stared hard at her.

"Verity! The truth is savin' us all!"

Chapter 13
The Green Witch

'The idea of an afterlife where you can be reunited with loved ones can be immensely consoling - though not to me.'
Richard Dawkins

Frances, Blake and Scarlet made their way east through fields and woods, nobody had spoken for a long time. Frances felt as if she would burst and had to break the silence. "This is great, isn't it. I love a good walk," she said enthusiastically. Blake gave her a strange look. "I mean, it must be great meeting again after all this time. So much to catch up on, so much to talk about?" Frances said hopefully. Nobody answered. "I guess it's just one of those things, I mean, I remember when I met Gemma Brown after a whole two weeks and we had so much to say, well, she had been to the hairdressers and had her hair cut short, and I thought it was too short but I didn't say that of course, I just..." she stopped because Blake had stopped dead and held his finger to his lips. "What is it?" whispered Frances, "Danger?"

"No," Blake whispered back, "I just wanted you to stop talking!"

Frances frowned at him. "We will camp here tonight. I'll check the area," he said before disappearing into the trees.

Scarlet didn't take long to gather some wood and dry moss for the fire. She touched it with the tip of her finger and it burst into life. Frances sat near it, hugging her knees. Scarlet sat opposite. She looked beautiful as the shadows from the fire danced over her face. "You are a very brave young lady," Scarlet said gently.

"Huh, I don't feel it. Most of the time I'm scared stiff!" Frances replied. "I'm not really overly keen on the idea of hunting the Green Witch to be honest."

"You mustn't worry about the Green Witch," Scarlet replied. "Not many people would be able to cope with things the way you have. That takes courage and strength, even if you don't always feel it," Scarlet said. Her words were kind and soft. "It must be so hard not to remember your mother. Tell me about the crash," Scarlet said.

Frances was a little taken aback. "I don't remember it," she said.

"Tell me what you remember from before the crash," Scarlet said.

"I don't remember much from before. Mainly what people told me afterwards," Frances replied.

"How would you feel if I told you there was no crash?" Scarlet said kindly.

"What are you saying?" Frances asked.

Scarlet continued, "Have you ever wondered if you are special, Frances?"

"What do you mean?" Frances said.

"How did you open the Staxcian Door, Frances?" Scarlet's words were warm and soft as she gently led Frances closer to her truth.

"I...I don't know! It just opened! I don't like this. Why are you saying these things?" Frances said anxiously.

"The parents you think you had didn't exist, they were invented to keep you safe," Scarlet said.

"Keep me safe! They died to keep me safe!" Frances said.

"They didn't die; they were never real," Scarlet replied.

"I don't believe you! Why are you saying this to me?" whimpered Frances.

"The crash never happened, your memory was hidden from you so you wouldn't see the truth."

"What is the truth?" Frances said forcefully.

Scarlet looked at her carefully before she spoke, "You are a witch's daughter Frances, the Green Witch's daughter and when we find her the new Witches Circle can begin to form!"

Frances didn't sleep that night. Her head was reeling with everything Scarlet had told her. She still mourned her dead mother, who never existed, and didn't want to believe in the one that all of a sudden did. It was all too confusing. Did she have a sister? Scarlet had evaded that question. She didn't know what she was supposed to feel. The fire crackled and slowly died as the night wore on. As always the moon shone like a beacon above. It was awe inspiring as it sliced through the darkness. Frances looked at Blake who slept opposite. She thought that this was the only time she had seen him at peace. His black hair glistened in the moonlight. Frances had sensed the ghosts that followed Blake. She had felt them when she first saw him at Green Amber Falls. They followed him and engulfed him yet at the same time he would not let them go. She rolled over and looked for Scarlet but the space she had lain down in was empty. Frances had seen how strong Scarlet was but she could also feel how lost Scarlet felt. It was as if she was constantly searching for something, like a garden or a room or a dream that she kept on trying to find. She began to wonder if these senses were a witch thing, was she even a witch? There was so much to figure out. Although she thought about nothing else all night she was no nearer to any sensible thoughts when she finally fell asleep just as the sun's red light started to bleed through the trees.

Blake awoke to see two dazzling ruby eyes staring at him. "Scarlet?" he said. He slowly sat up and stretched. "We will need to wake Frances."

"She didn't sleep well, leave her a while," she said.

Blake looked at her carefully. He was determined to loath her for everything that he had become but his heart warmed every time he saw her. The ghosts of the past eagerly beat the feeling away. "Why did you follow them?" he asked. "For so many years you have guarded the weeping stones, why choose to leave now?"

Scarlet looked at him. "I saw someone I didn't expect to," she said.

"Who, Perfidy?" asked Blake.

"I saw a young girl, full of anger and fear. A young lioness, afraid of nothing except for the day she might look in a mirror and see more than just her skin. Terrified that she might see who she really was. I saw myself in her, when I was young. While she thought she was killing me, my heart told me to help her. I wanted to remember what it is like to do something good, not because it benefits me, but because it's the right thing to do, come what may," Scarlet said, as she gazed at the rising sun. She turned and stared sharply at Blake, "Can you remember when you last sacrificed yourself for another?" This question was uncomfortable, as she knew it would be.

"My heart doesn't beat like it used to Scarlet," he said. "I learned a long time ago that sacrifice for another is a fool's game." He rose to his feet. "We need to move if we are to reach the Hanging Tree before dusk, the path is long." He brushed past Scarlet and lifted Frances over his shoulder. She snored loudly. He set off into the trees. Scarlet watched him for a few seconds, his words had hurt her. It bothered her that he could still make her feel like that. She gathered the rest of their things and followed Blake's path.

The woods grew thicker and thicker. The beautiful sunlight that had streamed through the gaps in the trees had been blotted out and replaced with thick greeny gloom. They had been tramping through the undergrowth for a few hours before Blake stopped and put the still sleeping Frances down. "How far to go?" he asked.

"Not far to the Hanging Tree," Scarlet replied. "Frances mustn't see." She had been dreading reaching the Hanging Tree. It was a truly majestic thick oak tree. It had grown and stood for centuries. Every year, shiny brown acorns showered down on the forest floor, harvested by various creatures to enjoy in the winter. No acorns had fallen for years. Its leaves had once been a brilliant patchwork of dazzling greens but now they remained a brilliant deep red all year round.

Frances started to stir. "Where are we?" she said groggily.

"We are near the Hanging Tree," said Blake.

"Hanging Tree, that sounds nice," mumbled Frances. Scarlet shivered. The trio carried on until they came to a small clearing. An old tree trunk lay on its side in the middle and a few large rocks were scattered around. The air felt cool and crisp. The clearing didn't fit with the rest of its surroundings.

"You need to wait here," Blake said to Frances.

"Where are you going?" Frances asked nervously.

He pointed to two tree trunks that appeared to have fallen into one another propping each other up, making a kind of archway. Scarlet said nothing and stared at the archway. "We won't be long," he said. "Whatever happens, don't leave this clearing. Do you understand?" he said sternly.

"All right, calm down, I get it, go and do whatever witchy magic you have to, just don't be too long," she answered cheekily.

Scarlet looked at Blake. He looked back at her and nodded. They walked together and disappeared through the arch of trees.

Blake and Scarlet walked on, following a small path which was peppered with small brown twigs that snapped and crunched beneath their feet. They hadn't gone far before Scarlet stopped. "It's just through the next gap in the trees," she said. She bowed her head sorrowfully.

"I have never seen you afraid of anything," Blake said. "What magic does this Green Witch have over us?" he asked.

"No magic that will harm us," she replied, struggling to speak the words.

"Then why are you so afraid?" Blake pleaded. She continued staring at the ground wishing she could cry.

"Because..." she started and raised her eyes to meet Blake's. There were no tears but sadness still poured out of them. "Because... I know what we are about to see."

Frances sat on the log. The other two hadn't been gone long but it felt like an age. She was getting fidgety and less happy about being on her own by the second. She hopped off the log and looked around. The clearing was small and she couldn't quite tell where all the light was coming from. She stood and listened. Nothing. Can you hear silence? She thought to herself. She closed her eyes for a second to soak up the stillness. Suddenly, she heard the loud crack of a branch from somewhere outside the clearing. She opened her eyes wide and looked around. Nothing. No movement, no noise. "Blake?" she called out in a whisper. No reply. Another crack came from somewhere behind her. She spun around and looked. Still nothing. "Blake if that's you, this isn't funny," she whispered out again. She slowly turned on the spot, looking for any sign of movement. Her heart was pounding and small beads of sweat started to appear on her brow. Still nothing. She fixed her gaze on the archway, praying that either Blake or Scarlet would appear. She heard something sniff then grunt. Whatever it was, was right behind her. She froze solid. Another sniff and this time she felt its warm breath on her neck. Her legs were planted with fear. Next came a small growl followed by another sniff. She could feel it breathing behind her. Nothing happened for a few seconds. She slowly started turning round. Bit by bit, trying not to make any sudden movements. She could hear it snuffling. Her stomach was frozen with sickness as she forced herself round. She couldn't see it all at first; it was big. She saw lumpy dark green skin which her gaze followed until she met two large yellow diamond eyes blazing at her. The beast was human shaped but was far too big to have ever been human. It did have two arms and two hands. Frances gaped at a gloved hand that boasted long glinting blades on each finger. The beast grunted, raised its arm and readied itself to cut her to ribbons. Fear locked Frances solid. She wasn't even able to scream.

Blake was troubled. "Why does the Witchfinder burn with so much desire for the dark?" he asked.

Scarlet told him a story.

The Witches Circle had lived in harmony with Ulysses for centuries. A unique group of women who bonded together for the greater good. Thirteen in number, presided over by Adrianna, the Witch Mother. She was followed loyally by the Green Witch, the Red Witch, the Blue Witch, the Witch of the Seas, the Black Witch, the Summer Witch, the Mountain Witch, the Amber Witch, the Sky Witch, the Witch of Light, the Night Witch and the Grey Witch. Together they became much more than the sum of their parts. They controlled the balance between the darkness and the light thus ensuring that Ulysses prospered. Like the world they protected, the circle grew old. New blood was needed to pass the burden of the Witches Circle on. Each witch was to bear their one and only daughter. The thirteen daughters would learn the world's secrets and renew the Circle. At least, that was the plan but fate was waiting to lay down its cards. The first two witches bore sons. Eleven members of the Circle met to discuss this dramatic happening. Witches were not supposed to be able to create sons. Thirteen witches were needed to form the new Circle and as a witch was only granted the gift of child but once, a huge problem lay before them. Adrianna struggled to find the right way forward as the Witches Circle struggled to find the answer. Five decided that the two witches must be banished and the children disposed of as punishment for breaking the new Circle. Another five believed that fate was showing them the way, no matter how strange it might be and that the sons were special. It was with a heavy heart that Adrianna decided the only course of action was to expel the two witches from the Circle and form a new bond of eleven and that their sons should be taken from them as a witch bearing a boy child could not be accepted. The Grey Witch and the Black Witch anxiously waited to hear their fate. At first, they had been horrified that they had created sons, witches surely couldn't, but soon, mother's love could not be ignored and they cherished their children. They were brought before the Witches Circle. Some looked away, unable to meet their gaze. Some looked down upon them with an air of superiority that had not been there before. The Black Witch put her head in her hands after the sentence was issued. The boys were to be destroyed and the witches condemned to the belly of the Amber Mountain. They did not go quietly and escaped after a bloody battle. The Black Witch escaped with the children. She was later captured but the boys had vanished. The Grey Witch had been left weak and her magic was gone but she vowed to spend every last breath destroying the Witches Circle, the Witchfinder was born. She took her time, learned new witchcraft. She preyed on the members of the Circle, one at a time. They started to perish at her hand. The last remaining few witches fled and hid in the cracks of the world, praying for Verity. The one the Book of Veritas foretold would renew the Circle. The Grey Witch became a huntress, a blackness that extinguished the light of life, her thirst for revenge couldn't be quenched. She knew killing the Witches Circle wouldn't be enough punishment. She had to kill their children.

Blake couldn't help but be agitated by Scarlet's apparent fear. He had never seen her like this. He steeled himself and pressed on through the trees. Scarlet's head hung low as she followed him. The undergrowth was thicker here and Blake found himself pushing armfuls of leaves and branches aside. All at once he stumbled forward and fell to his hands and knees as he pushed unexpectedly through into a clearing. He slowly raised his head. His gaze travelled up the huge majestic oak that stood in the middle of the clearing.

Then, he saw them.

He needed a double take to be sure it was true. He cocked his head to the side in amazement. For what might as well have been eternity, he didn't move, didn't blink. His jet black pupils grew large as they soaked up the scene. The oak boasted a large collage of dark wine red leaves. Its trunk was thick and gnarled. Its great branches stretched out like the graceful limbs of a ballerina displaying her pretty leaves.

The lowest branch had no leaves.

Blake looked at the ground and then back up again. He started to gag. The lowest branch was about head height for an average man. Eleven thick ropes hung equal distances apart along the branch. Blake swallowed the sick that rose to his throat. Eight of the ropes dangled little objects by the neck. Eight little girls. Eight beautiful little witches, each head covered with a sack cloth.

Frances was frozen. The creature seemed to be taking an age to strike her. She squinted one eye open. The creature was gone. In its place stood the Witchfinder. "Hello my sweetness," she sneered, "how strange to see you here."

Frances opened her mouth, ready to scream for help when the Witchfinder raised her hand and all that came out of Frances' mouth was silence. "I don't think that's a good idea, sweetness," she said. "Sorry if my little pet scared you, he's quite friendly really." She gently moved towards Frances and leant in to whisper in her ear, "Now, tell me where they are and I promise, I will kill you quickly."

Frances was terrified yet she would not betray Blake and Scarlet. She stared at the Witchfinder, she could sense a blackness inside her, not evil but an emptiness. The emptiness filled her.

"Why do you feel so empty?" Frances mustered with a trembling voice. The Witchfinder stood sharply upright. She looked at this small child in front of her with her two empty black eyes.

"What an odd thing to say, sweetness!" she said suspiciously. "What an odd thing to say indeed. Now shall we take a look for your friends at the hanging tree?" Her smile was sickly. She clicked her fingers and the large beast that Frances had seen, lumbered out of the trees, followed by two others. She pointed and they trudged towards the tree archway.

It took Blake a long time to get to his feet. He felt shaky when he did. Scarlet stood next to him. "These are the daughters of the Witches Circle," she said sadly. "They were going to form a new Circle and keep the balance of the world safe. The Witchfinder will stop at nothing to find the rest."

"They are just children," Blake said in disbelief.

"They are little witches who would grow up to be very powerful indeed. The Witchfinder wouldn't let that happen," Scarlet replied.

Blake grabbed for his dagger. "For pity's sake, let's get them down," he said heading towards the tree.

"Stop!" cried Scarlet. Blake spun round and looked at her. "The ropes are tied with strong magic. Cutting them would mean cutting away all hope," she said.

"There is hope?" said Blake.

"Every witch possesses a Heart Stone. A magical object that carries their soul. A witch can only truly die if the Heart Stone is destroyed. The Witchfinder has harvested the stones of these poor girls but they cannot be destroyed until all eleven are united. They must remain as they are if they are ever to be saved."

"There are eleven ropes for eleven witches, that leaves three," said Blake thinking out loud. "Verity, Perfidy?"

"Yes, but only one rope hangs for them. They share a Heart Stone," Scarlet said.

"That leaves two. But who?" Blake's mind spun quickly round.

"The Green Witch's daughter," Scarlet said.

"What about the other?" he asked urgently, "We must help her, we must keep her safe."

Suddenly, Scarlet looked up to the treetops.

"What's wrong?" said Blake.

"It's too late," she said, "One of the ropes hangs for me, the Red Witch's daughter."

"Why did you bring me here? You could have told me all of this before," he asked, turning away, feeling frustrated.

Scarlet's reply was slow and calm. "You had to see," she said.

"See what?" Blake replied.

"She how black the darkness really is."

Blake turned back to look at the tree.

"What do we do now?" he said.

"Don't let her get Frances. You need to..."

No sooner had she started her words, than Scarlet was lifted into the air. Five sharp blades shone out of her stomach. The creature behind her lifted her like a rag doll. It grunted. Blood dribbled out of her mouth. Blake roared and ran towards the creature drawing his dagger. It happened so quickly he didn't even feel the second creature swipe and slash his legs from under him.

Dirt.

Eyes.

Fist.

Black.

Blake opened his eyes groggily. He was lying on the ground. Everything was blurry. He became suddenly aware of the tremendous pain in his legs. His head hurt and he couldn't move. He could see he was still at the Hanging Tree. He had no idea how long he had been unconscious. Slowly, memories returned to him through a fog. The little witches, Frances and... He closed his eyes tightly as he remembered the last time he had seen Scarlet.

"Such a shame," came the Witchfinder's voice. She sounded smug. "I always thought things would work out for you two. Such a shame."

Blake tried to reply but couldn't speak.

"Save your energy my sweetness, you will need it later. I'm glad you woke up. I wouldn't want you to miss me finding Scarlet's Heart Stone. Where do you think it will be?" she smiled cruelly. "I nearly had it a long time ago but things always seemed to get in the way, including you! You seem to be making a habit of it my sweetness. We really must fix that."

Blake tried to struggle but was being held tightly by invisible bonds. His legs seared with pain. The Witchfinder motioned to one of the creatures, who moved over and picked Blake up and held him in a standing position. Blake's neck was frozen but his eyes darted round frantically, trying to spot Frances. He couldn't see her. "Looking for someone?" the Witchfinder said, in a sinister tone. Another creature appeared holding Frances perfectly still. She said nothing but her eyes were wide and full of fear. "Now, let's get to the good bit," said the Witchfinder. The third creature dumped Scarlet's body at the Witchfinder's feet. Even now she still looked beautiful to Blake, the pain in his legs was replaced by the pain in his heart. He struggled uselessly.

"We need something to use," the Witchfinder said, "what shall we use? Ah I know, let's try this." She took a few steps and picked up Blake's fallen dagger. "How appropriate!" she sneered. She proceeded to kneel down over Scarlet. She looked deliberately at Blake and didn't take her eyes off him as she sunk the blade into Scarlet's chest. Blake ached, the creature held him fast. The Witchfinder had to use both hands to get through the breastbone. Then, she pulled out the dagger and looked up at Blake again. She flashed him a sickly smile. She plunged her left hand into Scarlet's body. She felt and rummaged for a few seconds, after that her grin disappeared and was replaced with rage. She pulled out a bloody hand and screamed. She strode over to Blake and grabbed his throat with her bloodied hand. "Where is it!" she screeched, "WHERE IS IT!" Her face twisted and contorted as she struggled to hold in her anger. "SPEAK!" she screamed.

Blake coughed and struggled to breathe. The Witchfinder let him go. "Speak!" she said.

Blake gurgled out his words, "Go and die witch!"

She grabbed his throat again. "Where is the Heart Stone?" she said, her black eyes staring into his.

"Even if I knew I wouldn't tell you," he said. "Go on, kill me, you still won't know."

The Witchfinder took a step back. "Well, my sweetness, one of us will meet fate soon." She seemed to compose herself. She muttered something Blake couldn't hear to the creatures and walked out of the clearing. Blake watched as one creature followed her carrying Frances over its shoulder. The second creature lumbered over to Scarlet. The beast picked her up, placed a cloth sack over her head before hanging her body from the tree. Blake shut his eyes tight. The creature holding Blake took him over to the tree and set him up against it. It cocked its head as it wiggled the large fingers inside its bladed glove. Blake stared at its horrible yellow eyes, still unable to move. If this was it, he thought, he would not be afraid. The creature pulled back its arm and thrusted it towards him. He was determined to keep his eyes open.

The blades rushed towards his chest before stopping suddenly, barely touching his leather jacket. Something coiled round its neck, it looked like a vine or a creeper. The creature struggled as it was wrenched backwards. More vines appeared as if from nowhere. They tangled round its limbs and pulled it in all sorts of different directions. It didn't have time to roar before it was torn in two. A fountain of green blood rose and fell. Its yellow eyes stopped glowing as the pieces lay twitching on the forest floor. Blake was stunned. He looked around. The vines snaked back into the trees. A woman walked out into the clearing. She was dressed head to toe in green robes made of cloth. As she lowered her hood Blake realised he had found the Green Witch.

Chapter 14
Dotty

*'You can't call it an adventure unless it's tinged with
danger. The greatest danger in life, though, is not taking
the adventure at all. To have the objective of a life of ease
is death. I think we've all got to go after our own Everest.'*
Brian Blessed

Fred's excitement at finding Verity was matched only by
his excitement about the prospect of finding the Witch of
the Seas. "AAAAAHHHhhh, this is goin' to be great! The
open sea, captain at the helm, the smell of old briney!" he
bellowed.

"Have you ever been to sea?" Perfidy asked.

"NEVER!" cried Fred. "But I did used to put my head
under the water in the bath as a kid," he said very seriously.
Looking at how grubby and scruffy he was it was hard for
Verity to imagine he had ever had a bath.

"If you have never been to sea, how do you know where
to find the Beast?" Verity asked.

"AAAAAAHHHHHHhhhh, good question my girl. One
I wish I had an answer to!" he said, his eyes darting right
and left as he spoke.

Verity rolled her eyes at Perfidy and gave her a look to
say, you deal with him. "How do we find it?" Perfidy said
slowly and deliberately.

"You ever been fishin' missy girl?" asked Fred. Perfidy
was about to answer but he didn't give her the chance. Fred
leaned in close to her and whispered. "I don't mind
admitting to you that I was fishing champion of Ulysses
two years runnin'! It's all I have ever known." He leaned
out again and nodded at her sternly.

Perfidy was less than impressed. "Does that competition actually exist?" she asked, raising her eyebrows.

Fred looked thoughtful. "No!" he said proudly.

"Have you ever been fishing?" Perfidy asked, already guessing the answer.

"No!" said Fred. "But I firmly believe that if I had fished and if the competition had existed, I would have won! HHHHHHHHHAAAAAAAAaaaaaaaa! Take that! All you doubters! Fred ain't lying down on the fishing issue!" he roared at an invisible crowd.

"He's as mad as a box of hedgehogs," moaned Morty.

"RIGHT!" said Fred.

"A captain is what we need and what a captain we are going to have! There is only one man who might be drunk enough or stupid enough or handsome enough to come with us, FOLLOW ME!" and with that he marched grandly out the door. Verity looked helplessly at Perfidy. Perfidy looked helplessly back. They turned and followed him.

Fred led them through narrow winding streets, past shops and houses. They stopped in a small dingy alleyway. Pieces of what looked like dog dirt and rubbish lay on the cobbles. Many windows seemed to be stained brown or green. Fred marched up to a dirty red door and thumped it hard three times with his fist. He turned and grinned proudly at Perfidy. "You are about to meet one of the finest men that ever set sail on the deep ocean green," he said. He thumped on the door three more times and shouted through, "Open up you saggy old piece of seaweed! Open up or I'll break in and tickle yer feet!" He turned to Perfidy smugly and said, "He hates that!"

"BOG OFF!" came the reply.

Fred turned and smiled at Perfidy again. "He is a king among men, a prince among thieves! The most feared and respected seafarer that there ever was. If you cross him you better have your coffin ready!"

Perfidy started feeling a glimmer of hope that they might have found someone fierce enough for their dangerous task. "What's his name?" she asked.

"Dorothy Pinafore!" Fred replied, seeming very pleased with himself. Perfidy looked less than impressed. He banged again. "I've got a lovely bottle of black rum in my pocket," Fred sang through the door. It opened immediately but only a crack. A large grubby hand appeared. Fred placed the bottle of rum in it. He turned and smiled again at Perfidy. The hand disappeared and the door snapped shut.

Audible glugging was followed by a large belch then, "AAAAAAaaaaarrrr, that'll keep the hair on yer bum!" The voice was loud and gruff. The door opened and the empty bottle flew through the air, making a satisfying crunch as it broke in a heap over the cobbles. The door opened again and a long shotgun barrel slid into view and rested on Fred's chest. "Whaddya want?" came the gruff voice.

Fred didn't seem worried. "Dotty!" he said cheerily. "How the devil are you?"

The shotgun was retracted quickly and the gruff voice lightened. "Fred? I thought you were dead...again!"

"Yes, yes, a terrible business but as you can see, I have made a wonderful recovery!" Fred said waving his arms theatrically.

"Come here you salty old dog!" Dotty swept Fred up in his trunk like arms and kissed him. Fred hugged him back. There was something strangely lovely about these two very strange men.

"Listen Dotty, there's a caper afoot!" Fred said in a hushed voice once Dotty had put him down.

"Well what are you waiting for!" cried Dotty. "Come in and tell me everything my love, we haven't a moment to lose!"

Dotty's house was nothing like anyone had expected. It was immaculately clean. A plum coloured carpet ran like a deep soft river along the floor. Floral wallpaper boasted daisies, daffies and tulips in soft pastel colours. There were several watercolour pictures hanging on the walls, presenting peaceful scenes of rivers in summer and gushing waterfalls tumbling down into fresh pools of cool green water. The house was small, much too small for Dotty who

seemed to have to squeeze and stoop at every turn.
Everyone sat in the living room on a pink and yellow floral
three piece suite. Everyone except Morty who had been
dispatched to fetch more rum. The living room was small
and cosy, a little coal fire burned gently and despite his
gruff looks, Dotty's smile also seemed to warm the room.
The walls were cream coloured and a small criss cross
window overlooked a little green garden. A large wooden
cabinet rested against one wall, in which sat delicate
patterned china plates and colourful glassware. Dotty did
not fit these surroundings. He was a large stout fellow, six
foot and more. He sported a huge wild bushy beard that
was clearly bleached blonde. His hands were grubby and
his dark, straggly hair was draped messily over his
shoulders. His arms were thick and hairy as were his legs
that poked out the ends of raggedy trousers that were a bit
too tight and a bit too short. His large tummy stretched his
smart mauve waistcoat to its limits. Verity didn't like to
stare but she was sure he was wearing lipstick, eyeliner and
possibly rouge on the parts of his cheeks that were not
covered by dazzling blonde beard.

"Sure I can't tempt you with some rum?" Dotty asked
the girls, after he had drained his second bottle. He reached
for another and held it up. "It's the good stuff you know,
Granny Arbuckle's Rancid Rum," he said, shoving the
bottle in front of Verity's face. She read the small print on
the label.

*'Temporary blindness, gut rot and constipation
guaranteed! Or your money back!*

*(Terms and conditions apply, Granny Arbuckle Ltd
claim no responsibility for blindness or gut rot,
constipation is however guaranteed. Granny Arbuckle
reserves the right to ignore any and all correspondence. If
death occurs as a direct result of consuming Granny
Arbuckle the deceased may be compensated with a half
price bottle of Granny Arbuckle's Rancid Rum to be served
at the funeral. 0%apr)*

"Awfully kind, but no," Verity smiled politely.

"How long has it been Dotty?" Fred asked while wrenching the cork out of another rum bottle with a *plunk*.

"Too long my dear," Dotty said, "the last time I saw you, you were running naked out of Braxen's Dungeon."

"Sounds familiar," Perfidy whispered to Verity.

"Yes, what fun," said Fred gazing into space, seemingly enjoying the memory. "But listen!" he said, snapping out of the daydream. "Dotty! I need your help."

"Anything for you my dear, it sounds serious. Had I better prepare for the worst?" Dotty replied before dramatically finishing his current bottle of rum.

"It's a bad one Dot," Fred's eyes were darting wildly as he spoke, "the Witches are up to no good."

"Witches?" Dotty said with raised eyebrows. Fred nodded slowly.

"HELL AND BLAST!" Dotty exclaimed before unplugging another bottle and swigging furiously.

"The Witchfinder is up to her tricks and wants to destroy everything!" Fred announced theatrically.

"HELL AND THUNDER!" roared Dotty before more rum disappeared.

Verity and Perfidy looked at each other, not quite knowing what to make of this scene.

"What must be done my love? Tell all! Or so help me, my trousers will explode!" Dotty bellowed.

"We will need to risk life and limb!" said Fred.

"Go on!" replied Dotty.

"We need to stare down the reaper!" Fred said.

"Go on!" Dotty's eyes were growing wider by the second.

"We will almost certainly die!" shouted Fred.

"Then, we shall die HEROES! What must be done?" Dotty shouted back.

"We need to find the Beast in the Soulless Seas, catch it, kill it and liberate the witch from within! Then, a perilous battle of dark and light will ensue with the Witchfinder, during which we shall fight until death!" Fred was so worked up he was slightly out of breath.

Dotty looked thoughtful. "Oh my dear love, is that all? For a moment there I thought you were going to say something terrible!" He leaned over and whispered in Perfidy's ear, "I had heard there were plans afoot to close the Granny Arbuckle distillery!" He leaned back and winked at her. "My dear Fred, if you had brought me a caper where my death was anything less than certain, I would have been very disappointed in you indeed. The Beast of the Seas eh? I'd better bring my coat!"

The docks hummed with busy noises, catches being unloaded, ropes being flung to shore from incoming boats and gathered by those ready on the pier. Sailors and fishermen smoked their strong tobacco and chatted in the pleasant sunshine. Seagulls peppered the sky and those brave enough to venture down waddled around scavenging for any tasty morsel they could find. The twins and Morty stood waiting for their two strange companions who had temporarily disappeared on a mission to locate 'Dotty's crew'. Verity looked out to the horizon. She lost herself for a moment. So much had happened in such a short time. A few days ago she was just a lost little girl in a world that didn't seem to want her. Now everyone she met seemed to think she was some kind of saviour. She gazed deeply into the green sea. It seemed like the sun was raining down on it, as if the sundrops were creating splashes of sparkle and light as they hit the water. Verity thought about how she felt, here and now, on the pier. She closed her eyes and took a deep breath. 'Am I still lost?' She thought. She could feel Perfidy's love for her, keeping her safe. 'I don't know where I am or what will become of me, but I am not lost anymore.' She smiled, still with her eyes closed, she felt an arm around her. Perfidy squeezed her gently and she nestled her head into her shoulder. Morty joined in and hugged both girls' legs. Nobody spoke, nobody needed to.

The moment was shattered by Fred's screaming.

"RRRRRRUN!" followed by what sounded like gunshots. Fred appeared tumbling round the corner, falling as he knocked over several crates of fish.

Dotty appeared a second after him. He comically slipped on some pickled herring and landed flat on his back. Quick as a flash he was back on his feet. Another gunshot went off, and a crate behind him exploded in a shower of splinters. "HA, MISSED! WHY DON'T YOU TRY AIMING AT SOMETHING BIGGER! YOUR MOTHERS BOTTOM SHOULD DO!" Dotty roared as he shook his fist in the air. Another shot came and blasted the wooden post next to Dotty in half. He gave a theatrical bow before starting to sprint towards the twins, Fred was already ahead of him.

"RRRUUN!" Fred shouted as he hurtled straight past them. Morty and the girls stared in shock as Dotty thundered down the pier towards them being chased by several angry looking men who were busy unloading several pistols towards him.

"BOAT'S LEAVING! TIME TO GO!" Dotty shouted as he raced past. Bullets zipped and whistled around him, bursting crates and cracking wood wherever they landed. The twins flashed each other worried looks then turned to run. Verity went first. Perfidy slung Morty onto her back and followed. The air rang with shouting and gunshots. It didn't take long for Verity to realise the pier they were running down was long and was also ending. A small ship lay at anchor at the end. Fred was in it, wildly hauling and pulling ropes. Dotty arrived, leapt on board and disappeared. Verity ran as hard as she could. Perfidy was a little way behind and some of the chasing pack were closing in on her.

"Puts me down Mrs Perfidy, you is quicker without me," Morty pleaded. Perfidy quickly calculated that she would not outrun the mob.

"Together to the end!" she called over her shoulder. She scurried and took shelter behind a large wooden crate. Morty clambered down. The crate cracked and snapped as bullets bit at its wooden skin. Perfidy unsheathed her dagger.

"You is quick Mrs Perfidy, but you is not quicker than a bullet," Morty warned.

Perfidy looked at him, she knew he was right. Knees bent, back pressed against the crate, she tried to think. They were no more than 50 yards from the ship; it was too far to run. By this time Verity had made it on board. "Help her!" she screamed at Fred. As they both sheltered on deck, Fred stared wildly at Verity. The mob were getting close. A few moments more and they would reach her. "PLEASE!" Verity pleaded. Fred nodded and jumped up into view just in time for a bullet to burst through his shoulder. He was sent tumbling onto his back, he lay groaning. Verity felt helpless, she closed her eyes and concentrated. She could see the scene as if from above, Perfidy and Morty crouching behind the crate below. Perfidy could feel her now. 'I will guide you,' Verity's voice appeared in Perfidy's head. Perfidy smiled. She tightened the grip on her dagger and coiled herself, ready to pounce. She was about to strike, when a bellowing voice flooded the pier.

"LADIES AND GENTLEMEN! BOYS AND GIRLS, AND MOLES! SAY GOOD MORNING TO MRS MAY!" Dotty had appeared on the upper deck standing proudly behind a large silver Gatling gun. Its six barrels glinted in the sunlight. It perched on a sturdy tripod. Dotty cranked and turned the handle and in turn the barrels started clanking, spinning and spitting out bullets. *Chug, chug, chug, chug, chug, chug, chug, chug, chug, chug.* Metal rain hammered the pier. Perfidy pulled Morty close. The mob scattered this way and that. Splinters erupted as the bullets landed. Some men turned and fled while others dived off the pier to save themselves.

"HAAAAAAHAAAAAAHAAAA!" Dotty roared as the last of the mob disappeared. Perfidy gingerly poked her head round the corner of the crate, to see the coast was clear. She grabbed Morty and quickly made for the ship. Dotty stood behind the smoking barrels of Mrs May and unplugged a bottle of Granny Arbuckle and took a triumphant swig. Perfidy jumped on as the ship gently started to drift away from the pier, Verity let out a sigh of relief.

Fred groaned behind her. She raced over to him, he looked at her, his shoulder was bloodied. "I'm afraid I won't make it...AGAIN! Please remember me and tell them all that I died a hero. Tell them I dressed well. Tell them I was handsome, that I died a handsome, well dressed hero. Tell them I said something clever at the end. Just make it up," he coughed loudly.

Dotty charged over. "Let me through! Let me through! Let me have one last embrace!" He fell to his knees and looked carefully at Fred, "Fred my darling."

"Yes," Fred croaked.

"You really are..."

"Don't let emotion get the better of you old chum, get it out," Fred said weakly.

"You really are an old QUEEN! I was more hurt the last time I stubbed my toe!" He got up and tossed a rum bottle on Fred's chest.

Fred sat up sheepishly and took a swig. "I feel a little better already," he said.

"Really!" Verity said with raised eyebrows.

Dotty took the helm and barked his orders, he looked as happy as a pig in, a ship! "ALL HANDS ON DECK, SWAB THE RIGGING, HOIST THE MAST, WALK THE PLANK! AAAAA HHHHHAAAAHHHAAAA!"

The small ship gently sailed away from the harbour and headed out onto the dazzling green sea.

It hadn't taken long before Hamnavoe disappeared out of sight. The ship might have been small but it cut through the water with great ease. Morty stood holding the wheel while Dotty and Fred sat in the deck house, claiming they were studying charts and formulating plans, while occasionally shouting for Morty to turn the wheel. The sun beat down on them and the sky shone blue, everything was peaceful. Dotty and Fred had been predictably evasive on the issue of the gun toting mob. Fred shuffled his feet and looked at the ground a lot while Verity quizzed them. Dotty spun a yarn about a misunderstanding over some patterned shag pile carpets. Verity made no bones about her displeasure and disbelief at the whole affair. The pair skulked off like scolded schoolboys. As for the lack of crew, Dotty had mumbled something about mutinous dogs and that he wouldn't widdle on them if they caught fire.

As Verity looked out to sea she couldn't help but think this could be paradise. The shimmering green sea was so calm and peaceful. The sun warmed her shivered bones and all she could hear was the gentle lapping of the water as the ship glided along. Provided that Verity ignored the sporadic belching that echoed from the deck house, she couldn't remember another time when she felt so at peace.

This feeling was quickly shaken away as Fred appeared asking her to come to the deck house. The first thing that hit her as she walked in was the smell. "Boys, would anyone mind if I opened a window?" she said politely. Dotty rose and unscrewed the small circular porthole that looked out to starboard. Perfidy, Fred and Dotty sat round a small rectangular table that was covered in old raggedy maps and charts. Verity joined them and sat down.

Dotty addressed the table, "AAHHHEEMM, listen up shipmates, we are getting closer to our destination." He shuffled a map to the middle of the table and started prodding it wildly as he spoke, "We set sail from here, followed a northerly path before heading south along here."

Perfidy looked at Verity wearily then said, "I can't help but notice, Captain, that the map you are using is in fact just a large piece of blank paper."

"What's that girly? Where was I? Ah yes, the last sighting of the Beast was here." The paper tore a little as he prodded it with his large grubby finger. "Oops a daisy," he said while smoothing it over. "Yes the last sighting was here. The Beast rose and devoured a trading ship, crew of 60, all gone. Nasty business. Several men managed to escape in life rafts from its sister ship before it was turned

to fish and ships! HA HA! Did you see what I did there!"
He chuckled loudly. Fred slapped his thigh and grinned like
an idiot. The girls were unimpressed.

"If two large ships with big crews were destroyed so
easily, what chance does a little ship like this have?"
Perfidy asked.

"Yes my dear, a question of the highest importance. Did
anyone ever tell you the story of David and the Giant?"
Dotty asked.

"No," Perfidy replied curtly.

"Well the only thing that will save us deary, is the fact
that this is a tiddler. Fred could you explain the secret plan
to the girlies here, I need to haul anchor, if you know what
I mean." Dotty got up and left the deck house.

"Right girls, listen in, this is the secret plan. This is why
Scarlet told you to find me, this is what it's all been leading
to!" Fred said, in an excited whisper.

The twins eyes grew and they leaned closer, hanging on
his every word. "It's a little complicated so I will try to
explain slowly," he said.

"Go on," Verity said, in anticipation.

"Right, the secret plan, yes, the plan." He stood up, put
both hands on the table and leaned towards the twins on the
other side of the table. "We find the Beast."

"Get to it," Perfidy said impatiently.

"We find the Beast and… let it eat us!" Fred stood up
triumphantly and put his hands on his hips. Verity slumped
back.

"That's it, that's the secret plan. That's what took you all
this time to come up with! I trusted you but you are just a
fool!" Perfidy snapped as she picked up a half finished rum
bottle and lifted it in anger at Fred.

"Now, now missy, keep calm," Fred stammered, "that
bottle's still got rum in it, here, use this empty one."
Perfidy lowered the bottle as he held out the empty one
towards her. Verity scowled at her.

"Sorry," she said to Fred, reluctantly.

"I am sorry, me lady," he replied, "I know I am a fool but make no mistake; I would move hell and earth if it would help you. You take me as I am, you see. You're the closest thing to family I ever had."

Verity looked at Perfidy again. Perfidy felt a huge wave of immediate guilt. She reached over and patted Fred on the shoulder. "You might well be a fool," she said, "but you're our fool and we will be together to the end."

Fred started to well up and turned away a little embarrassed. Verity glanced pleasingly at Perfidy.

"You can stop that now," Perfidy said.

"Stop what?" Verity asked innocently.

"Looking at me and doing that, that, thing!" Perfidy replied.

"I never said a word," smiled Verity.

"That was the problem," Perfidy replied.

"ALL HANDS ON DECK!" Dotty roared. The three companions made their way hastily outside.

Out on deck, Dotty was peering through a small copper telescope. "There she lies!" he called out.

Verity could see a small blob of land in the distance. "What is it?" she asked.

"That, right there my dear, is Spider Island," Dotty answered.

"Never heard of it," Perfidy said.

"You is not wantin' to Mrs Perfidy," piped up Morty. "I heard the tales but I is never thinkin' it existed."

"Oh it exists my furry companion and whatever tales you were told were lies. The truth is probably much worse." Dotty grinned as he spoke, "Only a ship of fools would ever venture near."

Morty stood at the wheel. "Shall I steer us a wide path around Mr Dotty?" he said.

"Captain, if you please," Dotty replied.

"Shall I steer us a wide path around Mr Dotty Captain sir?" Morty said again. "Only ships of fools go near, right?"

"Right, yes, right, a ship of fools. SECOND MATE FRED REPORT!" he bellowed. Fred was standing right next to him.

"Yes sa!" he replied.

"Instruct our furry little sea dog, err, sea mole, regarding our course," Dotty said then plonked the telescope back to his eye.

"YES SA! THIRD MATE MORTY, SET SAIL EAST, TO SPIDER ISLAND!" Fred shouted.

"I knew that was coming," Perfidy said to Verity.

"Yes, only a ship of fools would go," Verity repeated as she looked at Dotty and Fred as they stood proudly looking out at the little blob of island in the distance.

Perfidy was growing impatient. She marched up to them and was just tall enough to tap Dotty on the. shoulder while on tip toe.

"Yes, my dear?" he said.

Perfidy was curt, "So far we have been shot at, spent goodness knows how long drifting around the ocean following an invisible map. This man," she prodded Fred in the ribs, "has proposed a plan that even a five year old would dismiss as fantasy and now we are off to some mystery island! This is serious! People are counting on us! Tell me what's going on or I'm going to lose my temper with both of you!"

She was puffing a little when she stopped. Dotty looked very seriously at her then turned to Fred and smiled, "You were right! She's great! Fire in the belly!" he boomed.

"I know, don't be getting in her bad books!" Fred said.

"Nice to see a young un with such spirit!" Dotty continued, completely ignoring the seething Perfidy.

"AAAAAHHhhhhhhhhhh!" Perfidy screeched in exasperation. She stomped over to Verity. "You deal with them!" she said then she disappeared below deck.

Verity walked over to the two men, "Excuse me, but could you be a pair of loves and share the plan? It would be awfully sweet of you." She smiled as she spoke.

Dotty looked at her. "Such a sweetheart," he said, "your mother did a good job with you!"

"I never had a mother," she replied quickly but politely. "Now, that plan?"

Dotty was a little taken back. "The plan, yes." He looked out at the island that was slowly growing bigger. "Right from the off, Spider Island has been our destination. It was essential that we find it," he said.

"What's on it?" Verity asked.

"DON'T KNOW! HA HA! Nobody does, nobody has ever managed to set foot on it!" he said with glee. "Spider Island is almost exactly halfway between Hamnavoe, and the lands to the East. The bum end of nowhere! Many traveling ships have found themselves short of supplies after long journeys and headed for the island to seek shelter and find food and water. Have you heard of the Widowmaker Spider? An amazing creature. It captures flies and sticks them on its web, see. It catches half a dozen or more and lays them out and piles them up."

"Spiders eat flies, everyone knows that," Verity said.

"The Widowmaker doesn't eat flies my dear, it has its mind on other things. Once it's laid out a tasty pile of flies, it scuttles away into some dark place or other and waits. It's very patient and doesn't move a muscle. Hours, days even, it waits. Before long a lovely fluttery bird spies the tasty treat and flies in to have a look. Nobody around, so it goes for a peck. The bird is too big to get stuck in the web so it's very pleased with its find. The Widowmaker watches and waits until the bird is just about to guzzle its last little fly. The bird is full of flies and a little slower than usual. The bird doesn't even notice that the Widowmaker is right behind it now and only has a second or two to wonder what's going on as venom pumps round its body and it's taken away to be eaten whole, beak and all!" Dotty seemed pleased with his story.

"Charming," Verity said. "What does it have to do with us?"

"Spider island is the web, on it are the flies. The Beast of the Seas waits patiently in dark places and we are a lovely little bird fluttering along!" Dotty replied. Verity shuddered as she realised the simplicity and at the same time the total madness of the situation. If the Witch of The Seas was in there, they would have to go in and get her!

Chapter 15
Rescue

'Most gods throw dice, but Fate plays chess, and you don't find out till too late that he's been playing with two queens all along.'
Terry Pratchett

The Green Witch looked at Blake suspiciously. She didn't say a word. It was Blake who spoke first. "We came looking for you," he said. Still she said nothing. Without taking her eyes off him, she moved towards the tree, and Scarlet. Blake couldn't look at her body.

"You made a mistake," the witch said at last. "You should not have come."

"Scarlet said you would help us," Blake replied.

"Scarlet is dead," she said coldly. "Do you honestly think you haven't made a mistake?"

Blake's heart was sore, he didn't answer her.

"The Witchfinder has nearly won, the world is all but lost. I am also lost my child, I don't have anything left, why did you think I would help you? Why did you think I would care?" she said as she walked to him. As she drew nearer he took a good look at her for the first time, her hair was a deep dark green as were her eyes. She reminded him of someone but he couldn't think who.

"I didn't think anything, Scarlet said you would help; she was sure of it," Blake said.

"So sure, she was willing to end herself," the Green Witch said. "She should have foreseen these events, of that I'm certain."

"That's impossible, she would never..." Blake's voice trailed away as his mind struggled to understand.

"It is odd my child, a witch does not give up her Heart Stone easily. She must have known the Witchfinder was close, that I would have spurned her. Yet there she is."

Blake looked over her shoulder at the body before shutting his eyes. "It makes no sense; she said you would help. The world is on the brink, why won't you stand with us?" he pleaded.

"My dear child, a soul that has nothing to care for, has nothing to fight for. I am sorry for your loss but you shouldn't have come." With those words, the Green Witch turned and headed slowly back the way she had come. Blake was in turmoil; this was not how it was meant to be. What had Scarlet done? He stood up and tried to concentrate. He tried to remember what Scarlet had said when he asked why she thought the Green Witch would join them,

'I have something to show her.'

What had she meant to show her? She had seemed so sure but now everything had fallen apart. Scarlet gone, the Green Witch about to vanish and Blake could hardly bring himself to think of Frances, helpless at the hands of the Witchfinder, Frances. Frances! Thoughts flooded into Blake's mind drowning him, it all started to become clear. Frances! Those big green eyes.

"YOUR BABY! SCARLET WAS GOING TO SHOW YOU YOUR DAUGHTER!" Blake shouted desperately.

The Green Witch stopped dead at the edge of the clearing but did not turn. Several vines lashed out of the trees and latched onto Blake's limbs, holding him fast. She turned and walked back towards him. By the time she reached him the vines were stretching his frame to its limits. "That is not a subject to toy with," she said.

Blake was struggling against the vines. "You said that the soul that cares for nothing has nothing to fight for. Scarlet was bringing you something to fight for!" he gasped. The Green Witch looked at him for a second then turned away. The vines loosened their grip and dropped Blake to the ground.

She spoke with her back to Blake, "Scarlet gave up her Heart Stone to bring my daughter back. Now she is dead and my child is with the Witchfinder." Her voice was distant.

"We can find her, we can get her back. You just need to be prepared for the Witchfinder," Blake said.

The Green Witch turned and looked at him with hate in her eyes, "If I find her with my child, she will need to be prepared for me!"

It was with a heavy heart that Blake left Scarlet in the wood. He had spoken to her quietly before they left and vowed to come back. The hunt for Frances had begun. It wasn't difficult to pick up the trail left by the large creatures that accompanied the Witchfinder. Blake reckoned they had at least an hour head start over them. Three important pieces of information had quickly been established. One was that the Witchfinder could not have known who Frances was or she would have surely killed her at the Hanging Tree. The second was that it wouldn't be long before she figured it out. Thirdly the Green Witch was extremely puzzled to hear that the Witchfinder had not acquired Scarlet's Heart Stone.

The trail led east through the woods. The sun was dipping down and bathed the sky in pinks and reds. The pair followed the trail till it led them out of the trees and into huge open fields of corn. The moonlight had taken over and now bathed the sky in its delicate white light. Blake put his head in his hands in frustration, "The track splits three ways. What now? How can we choose, knowing we could be wrong, even if we split up."

The Green Witch looked thoughtful. She closed her eyes. Blake looked at her. She looked quite beautiful in the moonlight.

"I felt her," she said. "I didn't know it was her, but I felt her. It's what led me to the tree, a strange feeling, an old feeling."

"Can you feel her now?" Blake asked hopefully.

The witch appeared not to hear him. "She was calling to me, she needed me, I didn't know it was you my darling, please forgive me," she whispered.

"What about now?" Blake asked again.

"She is silent. I didn't come for her, she has stopped calling," the witch said sorrowfully. Blake walked to her and put his hand on her shoulder, she flinched at first but stopped and allowed herself to be comforted.

"We will find her, I promise," he said.

"Didn't your mother tell you not to make promises you can't keep," she smiled.

"My mother never told me anything, she was never there," he replied. The witch looked at him strangely.

Blake continued, "We are on the edge of the Elysium Fields. These fields boast golden corn all year-round. Jarlton lies to the south, Hamnavoe to the north, nothing to the east," he said. "Perhaps she has headed to one of the towns."

"Perhaps," the witch replied.

"We should each pick a town, that way we have the best chance of finding her," Blake said.

The Green Witch turned and looked out to the east. "You are wrong my child," she said, "there is somewhere that lies to the east."

"I know this place, there is nothing out there," Blake replied.

"Kergord," she said, "the Witchfinder is headed for Kergord."

"Kergord is dead, it's a ghost and has been for a long time, trust me," Blake said.

"Dead, yes. I wonder? Where would be the best place to mass and hide a dead army, if not in a ghost town? Nobody would suspect until it was too late. We must hurry to Kergord." She turned and started to wade through the moon kissed corn. Blake checked his dagger, then followed.

The moon was large and hung low in the sky. The night air was still warm as the pair made their way through the fields. They made good time as they crossed country and headed to the coast. After a while Blake recognised the smell of sea air. "We're close," he said. They carried on until the Green Witch stopped in a small field on a hill that overlooked the ruin of Kergord. Blake stood beside her and looked out. The ghosts of the past could not stop the memories pouring into him. He was normally so careful to keep them at bay but standing there on the hill he was powerless to resist. He closed his eyes and was lying down on the green grass gazing at Scarlet. The sun breathed its warmth into everything and Kergord was alive and vibrant. Scarlet's sparkling ruby diamond eyes stared into his soul, she was the only one who could see his whole, she leaned in to kiss him. He opened his eyes with a start and brought himself back into the night. The next memory was happiness. He had been so careful to lock this one away but the ghosts could not stop it. He remembered how happy Scarlet made him feel and how much he wanted her. It was more than a feeling. It was something that filled every part of him, it coursed through him as sure as the blood in his veins. The happiness was soon engulfed, overpowered by guilt, anger and regret. This was why he wouldn't let himself feel. He fell to his knees and looked out at the sea. Everything had gone wrong so quickly. He had been tricked, yes, but he still knew what he had done.

"We all have to look in the mirror and see who is there," the Green Witch said. "It's not always who we want to see. Perhaps we can right a few wrongs before we are done."

"Some things can't be undone," Blake replied.

"You are right my child but a life is not defined by a single action. It's a collection of deeds, dark and light. Only at the end can we see balance. We make our choices, even when we think there are none and you have many more choices left to make my child. Nobody made you come here. You are choosing the light. But keep the darkness near, I fear we will need it before too long."

Blake stood up, his Black eyes shone. "Let's go. The Witchfinder dies tonight."

The cover of darkness made it easy for them to slink down the hill and reach the outskirts of the town. They had seen from higher up that it was busy. Nightwalkers buzzed around, the orange glow of forges dotted the streets and the clanging of steel rang in the air. Gores lumbered round the docks, lifting and loading crates onto the dozens of ships that lay at pier side. Blake had counted at least ten of the knife gloved creatures he had seen at the Hanging Tree, patrolling the perimeter. The skeleton of Kergord was now home to the things that waited in the dark.

"The only building that was left relatively untouched by the fire was the Old Stone Kirk. It seems like as good a place as any to start with," Blake said. "It sits on the corner of the market cross. I will head there. I will need you to keep our sharp fingered friends off my back."

The Green Witch closed her eyes for a few seconds. "I don't hear her," she said.

"We will see, if nothing else we can right a few wrongs, remember?" Blake answered.

"Nothing good lives here, if it's not a small girl with green eyes then kill it and kill it quickly," he said.

The Green Witch pulled up her hood and started to walk around the edge of the town.

Blake drew his dagger and scurried towards the first set of ruins. He climbed through the window of a small burned out cottage. Outside he could hear footsteps making their way along the street. He waited inside underneath the charred window frame. As the steps passed by he silently vaulted out and slit two nightwalkers' throats in quick succession. It didn't take long to drag the bodies out of sight into the cottage. He emerged and pressed himself into the shadows then moved on like a panther.

The Green Witch took no care to conceal herself. She walked along as if out for a stroll on a fine summer night. She saw the creature before it saw her. Without changing her stride she moved up behind it and walked on past. By the time the creature noticed her, the Witch had already thrown a thick green powder in its face. She walked on a few paces and stopped but did not turn. The beast writhed and fell to its knees clutching its stomach. Its skin started to bulge and stretch, until a vine burst through its large shoulder and coiled itself round the neck. Another vine burst from its left upper thigh and slithered round both ankles holding them fast. The creature choked and gagged until green soup-like liquid poured from its mouth before it crashed to the ground and groaned one last time. Upon hearing the groan, the Green Witch carried on walking.

Frances sat on a high wooden chair at a table. There was bread and cheese on a plate in front of her as well as a cup of water, which she hadn't touched. The room was clad in what looked like fresh timber that was interspersed with older, charred wood. The Witchfinder sat opposite her, staring. "Not hungry child?" she asked. Frances shook her head. "You must eat my sweetness, the bread is fresh."

Frances reached out a hand suspiciously. The Witchfinder gently pushed the plate towards her some more. Frances grabbed the bread, tore a chunk and ate greedily.

"That's better sweetness. Have a drink," the Witchfinder said.

Frances grabbed the cup without taking her eyes off the witch and drank quickly. She gulped for breath when she finished and wiped the water from her chin.

"That's better sweetness, now tell me, what was a charming little pixie such as yourself doing with Blake at the hanging tree? I'm dying to know," she said menacingly.

"I, I don't know what you mean," Frances stuttered. "You see what happened was, was that I, I mean we were headed, I mean, I don't know where they were headed. I was going to be dropped off, you see, they were taking me through the forest so I could head, er, back, yes, that's right, head back and leave them to it. That's what it was." Frances puffed slightly as she finished.

The Witchfinder listened with interest. "Has anyone ever told you that you talk a lot child? Talk a lot but say very little. Why were you at Green Amber Falls?" her tone sharpened.

"They, they found me. Yes, they found me. I was lost. I'm a runaway you see. They said they could give me safe passage." Frances was starting to feel a little more confident.

Moments passed, the Witch's black eyes seemed as though they were burning into her. The tension was broken by three knocks at the door. "Enter!" the witch called out. The door creaked on its hinges and in walked Krankle.

"The ships are ready my mistress," she said bowing her head. The Witchfinder rose and walked over to her. "Is everything as I asked?" she said quietly.

"Yes mistress, shall I signal for the move?"

"Yes."

"Did the worm talk?" asked Krankle.

The Witchfinder looked over at Frances. "The girl is a nobody, that's what she is. Leave her here for the rats," she said coldly.

"Very good mistress," Krankle snivelled.

Frances could see the pair in conversation but she couldn't quite make out what they were saying. She was sure they were deciding her fate, had Krankle come to take her, had the Witchfinder not believed her story, she thought. When she saw the Witchfinder look over at her she panicked and blurted out, "My mother is the Green Witch and if you harm me she will make you sorry!" Even before she finished speaking the words she wished she could reel them back in but it was too late. There they were, dancing their way to the Witchfinder's ears. Every muscle in the Witchfinder's body seemed to tense as she eyed Frances like a python ready to strike.

"What an interesting thing to say!" she said with a wicked grin. Frances shivered. The Witchfinder drew a serrated dagger from her robes. "What an interesting thing to say indeed!"

Frances got up from her chair and moved backwards into the corner. The Witchfinder stalked towards her, the blade glinting as her mouth gaped.

"May I have the honour Mistress? I have a score to settle with this one," Krankle said.

The Witchfinder handed her the blade.

Frances fell to her knees and closed her eyes and called out in her mind.

'Help me. Please help me!'

Krankle's shadow slowly drew nearer.

Blake crept from shadow to shadow as he made his way to the church. Nightwalkers were dotted everywhere and he had decided that avoiding attack and noise was the best strategy for the moment. His black leather coat helped him to melt into the background. He slunk round the corner of the next street. The sign at the end of the road was mostly burnt but he could make out the first few letters.

'St Sun'

He knew this was St Sunniva Street which turned into the market cross where the church waited. He looked down along the moon bathed cobbles. He waited, still, listening for any sign of movement. Nothing. He was about to move when the sound of a horn blasted through the night air. He froze again. Another horn blast was followed by the chatter of footsteps over the cobbles. Dozens of nightwalkers started to make their way quickly down the street in a steady stream. Blake didn't move an inch. It was perhaps a minute or so before the street fell silent again. When he was sure there was no more more movement he swiftly made his way down the street. When he turned into the market cross he could see the church opposite. The square was empty. Another horn blast, another stream of nightwalkers poured through the cross and headed in the direction of the docks. Blake waited and followed at a safe distance.

The Green Witch had walked nearly a quarter way round the perimeter of the village. She had met and destroyed four other knife gloved creatures. She stopped suddenly and closed her eyes. She could hear someone, Frances? It was hard to tell, the voice was so small, barely a whisper. The Witch turned and headed into the village. The voice came a little louder now.

'Help me. Please help me!'

The Green Witch started to run. Her hood flew back as she raced over the cobbles.

'Please help me!'

The Green Witch rushed through the empty moonlit streets, weaving her way towards the voice, and the church.

'PLEASE HELP ME MUMMY!'

The Green Witch darted through the market cross-straight to the church. She sprinted up the stone steps and burst through the door. She stopped in the body of the Kirk and screamed out with every fibre,

"FRANCES!"

Blake had followed the nightwalkers to the docks. He hid behind a stone wall that overlooked the pier. He gasped at the sight that met him. Vast lines of walkers crowded the pier and were shuffling into vessels which, once full, sailed away and vanished in the darkness. Gores were loading dozens of large crates onto small container ships. The boats that left were replaced and the same processes would happen again. Blake guessed there must be at least a thousand Nightwalkers waiting to board. He slumped back and sat on the rough ground and tried to think. His concentration was disrupted by a faint cry that came from inside the village. Frances! He got up and started to run back to the church.

He could see the door was open as he ran up the stone steps. Once inside he stopped and listened. He couldn't hear anything aside from his own heavy breathing. He gripped his dagger tightly and ran for the only door he could see, which was at the far end of the Kirk. The Green

Witch was sitting at the table when Blake stormed in. She sat with her back to him, staring at the corner. Blake called to her but his words were nothing more than noise to her. He moved to the table and looked at the corner. The only thing left to show that anyone had ever been there was the pool of light crimson blood which slowly made its was across the slightly uneven floor. The Green Witch stared at the corner. She was broken. Broken into pieces that would never fit back together. Blake crumpled and fell to the floor. He made a sorrowful sound from deep inside. A painful noise. It was the Green Witch who spoke first, "All is lost. Ten will now hang from the tree. The circle can't be renewed."

Blake rose to his knees. "We will battle to the end, we must!" he said fiercely, fighting back his tears.

"Even if we could win, I have nothing now," the Green Witch said calmly and coldly.

"We can't give up, we can't let this be how it ends! You mustn't think you have nothing to fight for," Blake pleaded. "Verity and Perfidy are still out there!"

The Green Witch looked thoughtful for a moment. "It's over. We reap what we sow." With that she walked out and left Blake alone on his knees in the cold stone chapel.

Chapter 16
The Witch of the Seas

'Those who rule the world get so little opportunity to run about and laugh and play in it.'
Stephen Fry, The Fry Chronicles

Spider Island loomed large. Dotty stood with Fred on the bow, looking out. They had been unusually quiet. The atmosphere was eerie even though the sun still shone brightly. Dotty held Fred gently. "Time to get below," he said. Fred looked at him then ushered the others to the deck hatch. One by one they climbed down. Fred was the last to go. He stopped at the top of the ladder and looked at Dotty one last time. Dotty nodded his head slowly and then flashed him a huge grin. Fred allowed himself one more second then, with a tear in his eye, disappeared down below, bolting the hatch behind him.

"Wait," said Verity, "how will Dotty get down?"

Fred looked at Morty. Morty looked away sadly. Fred's voice was broken as he spoke, "Dotty won't be joining us."

"So where will he hide?" Perfidy asked.

"He will steer us to where we need to go," Fred said in a small voice.

Verity began to understand. "When will we see him again?" she asked weakly.

Fred's lip was wobbling. Morty spoke up, "Sometimes things are needin' done. We is not liking it, but must is must. The heroes do what needs doin'."

Fred crouched down and started crying. Morty went over and put his small furry arms round him.

"No! We are together to the end!" Perfidy cried. "There has to be another way!"

"Someone is needin' to hold the ship steady so we is not crunched and munched to bits," Morty said. "It's the only way."

"Then I will do it!" Perfidy exclaimed. "This is my fight!" She jumped towards the ladder and climbed the first few rungs.

"Miss Perfidy, we is all fightin' my lovely, every one of us," Morty said softly. Perfidy looked down at him then turned to carry on climbing when the ship lurched violently to one side and threw her to the floor.

Dotty stood looking out at the green sea. He closed his eyes and let the sun hug him. He opened them slowly and rummaged inside his waistcoat and pulled out a gold chain with a locket dangling from it. He opened it and looked at the photo inside. It was black and white and slightly faded. Fred's face smiled at him. He was younger then. Dotty allowed a single tear to weave its way down his cheek, into his big blonde beard. "You silly old goat!" he sniffed. He pulled the cork from a bottle of Granny Arbuckle with his teeth, spat it out and drank deeply. Then he walked elegantly to the ship's wheel and grabbed it with both huge hands. Come on, he thought. Let's see what you've got. It didn't take long. The shadow came first. Dotty could see its huge mass below the water's surface. As the Beast rose, it was like an entire island was surfacing, white foamy water poured off its back as if the sea was parting. Its shadow soon cloaked the ship and made it seem like night had come. Dotty gripped the wheel tight. The Beast's massive mouth opened and started to draw in lakefulls of water. The ship was pulled helplessly in. The wheel fought hard but Dotty's huge arms held firm. "Straight down the middle," he kept repeating in his head, "straight down the middle." The Beast let out a terrible moan which shook the air. The ship jolted as it was pulled inside the Beast's mouth. "STRAIGHT DOWN THE MIDDLE!" Dotty roared. "HHHHHAAAAAA HHHHHAAAAAA HHAAAA!" It's jaws crashed shut and just like that, he was gone.

Verity opened her eyes. She rubbed her sore head groggily. Everything was a little blurry at first. She sat up and took a few seconds to realise she had been lying on the wall because the ship had ended up on its side. She was alone in the room. Stumbling to her feet she called out to the others.

"They won't hear you my child," came a voice from behind her. She spun to see the Witch of the Seas. She wore raggedy blue sodden robes. Her face was deathly pale, her fingers were long and bony.

"What have you done with them?" Verity demanded.

"Fear not little one. They are resting, safe and well. They will come to no harm here," the witch replied. She moved over to Verity and stood in front of her. She raised her hand as if to feel Verity's face but did not touch her. "It's been a long time since I saw you my child."

"I, I don't remember..." Verity stammered.

"You won't, you were a babe in arms. I always thought that when the time came, it would be you that would come for me," she stepped back a pace.

Verity was still coming to her senses. "I have brought you something, it's.." she started, but stopped once she realised she no longer had the Book of Veritas.

"A book? A blank book? That holds the secrets of the world and will save us all? Ha ha." The witch said in a slightly mocking tone.

"We were told you could read it and tell us how to keep the balance of the world," Verity said.

"The balance! I wonder who would tell you such a thing?" the witch enquired.

"A good friend," Verity replied. "Can you help me? Can you read it?"

The witch's mouth curled into a smile, "I should be able to, I wrote it."

Verity looked puzzled.

"Sit with me child," the witch said. Verity sat cross legged on the floor opposite her.

"The Witches Circle became very powerful. Some said it was too powerful. We were becoming greedy. The trouble with greed is that it never lets you have enough. The baby boys were a sign from Fate. A sign for change. Some saw a change for good, while others feared. It was not an easy thing to do but we decided to take those boys away. They were to be drowned but that wasn't to be. The Black Witch saw to that while The Grey Witch delivered her rage. She hid them away from the horror before we found her and locked her in the mountain." The Witch of the Seas looked pained as she recalled the story. "How were we to know what they would do? How could we know how they would react? We had to keep the balance of light and dark," she said as if looking for some kind of understanding.

Verity looked at her sternly, "You took their children from them, you took their love away. What did you expect, what would you have done in their shoes?"

The witch was taken aback slightly. "How dare you defend them!" she hissed.

"I can't defend any wrong doing, but I can try to understand it," Verity replied.

"But you can't forgive it," the witch snapped.

"We all make our choices, light and dark. How do you feel about your choices when the mirror looks back at you?" Verity replied coolly. "How would you feel about a little forgiveness right now?"

The witch twitched uncomfortably.

"I was chosen to be hidden away in this Beast, beyond reach because I was trusted with all the secrets. So that, even if the Witches Circle fell, it could be formed again one day, and here you are," said the witch, "you will make an excellent leader."

"I don't want to be a leader, I'm just Verity. I don't want to form a new Witches Circle," Verity said clearly.

"But it is written child, the Circle will be strong again. Witches will preside over the balance of light and dark once more," she replied.

Verity looked at her. So much had happened that should make her afraid but she felt perfectly calm standing there. Her mind wandered back to Dark Oak and Briony Grime brandishing that glass at her. She had thought there must be something wrong because she wasn't scared but now she understood why. She wasn't afraid because she was doing the right thing.

"The Witches Circle was rotten!" she said defiantly. The witches eyes blazed as she soaked up the words.

"Be very careful what you say child," her tone was threatening.

"It was rotten, and it destroyed itself," Verity continued.

"You would speak ill of your own mother?" the witch sneered.

"My mother made the wrong choice, now you want me to take her place and let it all happen again. The Circle would turn and end up back where it started, lives ruined. The only way forward is to break the circle and walk a new path," Verity said, growing in confidence with every word.

"And tell me child, in this New World of yours, who will control power, who will keep things right, who will keep the balance?" the witch asked curiously.

"Each and every soul will hold the balance, together," Verity said.

"It will not be strong, it will fail," said the witch.

"Yes," said Verity, "it might. That is the true nature of the world, is it not? If enough souls choose the darkness, the light will fail. It is up to each and every one of us to make sure that does not happen, by choosing that it won't. There is no fate but that we make for ourselves."

The witch said nothing for a moment then her face softened. "You are wise beyond your years," she said. "Your mother would have been very proud of you."

Verity felt a surge of emotion. Those nine words were so powerful, they stunned her.

"Do you truly believe in the New World? I have to know," the witch said intensely.

"It doesn't matter what I believe. All that matters is that you do what you think is the right thing. That's all we can ever do," Verity replied.

The witch produced the Book Of Veritas. She laid it in front of Verity and opened it at the first page. It was blank. "Do you know why the pages are blank my child?" she asked.

Verity shook her head.

"They have been waiting. Waiting for an author to write a story. You are the author Verity. You always have been. You need to be sure that you want to learn what you are about to learn. It cannot be unlearnt," the witch said softly.

Verity nodded.

"Very well," the witch's long bony fingers turned a large creamy page. Verity gasped to see the paper slowly fill with elegant black text. The handwriting swirled across the page, her handwriting.

'I am not perfect, my body does not look the way I think it should. I often think I'm not good enough and I let people down. I think I am not smart enough. I don't think I am good enough to achieve much so I console myself with my little lot. I am lost in a world that I don't understand and doesn't seem to want or need me. These are the shadows that make me real.

It's not until I choose to step out from these shadows that I see the truth. I am not perfect, my body does not look the way I think it should and I let people down, and if the world doesn't need me it's because that's what I have chosen. The truth is, I am lucky enough to have been given the greatest of all gifts - choice. So why should I not choose to believe that I am better than that. The world needs me, it needs all of us. I am not perfect but my life has the same story as every soul, and my story is important. I was born, I live, and one day I will move on to something else, I don't know what that will be but I hope I will be ready and happy when I do, despite all the dark thoughts that make me feel so strange. I hope that in the end, I can make things right.

Words come easily though, do I have enough strength, enough light to do the right thing? Can I make a sacrifice for others? Is it too late?

Or is it always the right time to do the right thing?'

The witch watched Verity closely as she hungrily devoured the words, agape. It didn't take long for her to finish reading. She looked up at the witch with huge blue eyes.

"Let me read the rest," she demanded.

"There is only one other page," the witch said.

"Let me see it!" Verity said desperately. The witch turned to the next page. There were only eight words.

'I am Verity. I will save us all.'

Verity was in a daze.

"Do you know what Verity means child? It means truth. You can make a sacrifice for us all. Perfidy must not know your fate. She won't understand. Do you understand?" the witch asked carefully.

Verity looked at her slowly and nodded her head. "Yes," she said quietly.

"We need to act quickly before all is lost," said the witch.

"What do we do?" Verity said.

"First things first, my child, you must know everything, there is much to tell you. Then we need to speak to your sister."

The witch led Verity through into the next room. Perfidy lay on a blanket, asleep. The witch moved over to her and placed her hand gently on her brow. Perfidy stirred and started to wake, the witch beckoned Verity over and moved aside. Verity gently squeezed Perfidy's hand. "I'm here," she said softly. Perfidy closed her eyes and smiled sleepily. Slowly Perfidy roused and sat up. Verity sat with her arm round her.

"What happened?" Perfidy asked wearily.

"You are safe," Verity told her.

The witch moved closer. "Now my child, I believe you have something of great importance," she said.

"I don't have… I don't know what you mean," Perfidy replied.

The witch smiled at her. "I know you don't. Do you know what a Heart Stone is Perfidy?"

Perfidy looked confused.

"Every witch has one. A witch's life can never truly end unless her Heart Stone is destroyed," she said.

"Do I have one?" Perfidy mumbled, sounding a little confused.

"No my child, I believe you have two, and I think the time has come for you to give Scarlet back hers!"

Chapter 17
Tomorrow's Much too Long

'Only in the agony of parting do we look into the depths of love.'
George Eliot

Verity opened her eyes and looked around. She wasn't sure where she was. The Witch of the Seas had primed her little cauldron and invited Verity to be the first to enter the smoke. The now familiar intoxication took over until consciousness left. When she woke she stood up and rubbed her neck. She was in a small clearing. An old tree trunk lay on its side in the middle and a few large rocks were scattered around. The air felt cool and crisp. The clearing didn't fit with the rest of its surroundings. She found herself thinking about Frances. She tried to shake the thoughts away but their claws dug deep. Scanning further she noticed two tree trunks that appeared to have fallen into one another propping each other up, making a kind of archway. She looked around for the others but there was no sign of anyone. She walked across the clearing and through the archway. The undergrowth grew thicker and she found herself having to push armfuls of leaves and branches aside. It didn't take long before she stepped into another clearing. She stood quite still as she looked at the Hanging tree. She tilted her head to the side a little and stared for a few moments. It was as the Witch of the Seas had described. She slowly made her way to the small frames that swayed gently in the light breeze. When she stood near enough to the first little witch, Verity reached out and held her hand. She gently pulled off the sack cloth that covered her head. The little witch's face was pale yet pretty. Her hair was blonde and dirty and her eyes were closed as if she were only asleep. She wore an Amber bracelet on her left wrist. Verity stretched up a little and whispered something in her ear, kissed her on the cheek, then headed to the next witch and did the same. Even hanging in that hideous way Scarlet still looked beautiful as Verity kissed her cheek. She reached the last witch. Even though she knew who it must be, she would never be ready to see Frances there. Tears welled up uncontrollably and ran down her face like rain as she brushed Frances cheek with her fingers. "Why you? It shouldn't be you," she sobbed. She composed herself and kissed Frances on the forehead. "I'm going to make things right. I promise."

Verity hadn't noticed the Witch of the Seas standing behind her. "Are you ready?" she said.

Verity turned. Her face was streaked with tears but there was a look of steely determination in her eyes. "I am ready," she said.

"Good, then let us begin. I would stand back a little if I were you. Scarlet might not feel too friendly when she comes back."

Verity moved away. The witch reached in her pocket and pulled out the red glistening ruby that Perfidy had given her. The witch's body obscured Scarlet so Verity couldn't quite see what she was doing but the noises didn't sound good. After a few moments she stepped away, Verity noticed the witch's left hand glistened red. Nothing happened. The air was still and quiet. Verity was about to speak when all of a sudden Scarlet let out a shriek as her body jolted.

"Good girl," said the Witch of the Seas who then walked over and cut the rope with a blade she produced from her cloak. Scarlet landed on the ground on all fours, the noose still round her neck. She stood and thrusted a hand towards the Witch of the Seas that sent her flying though the air. She turned and moved towards Verity, hands burning.

Verity panicked and cried out, "STOP!"

Scarlet stopped five yards away, eyeing her carefully, "It's me, Scarlet, It's Verity."

Scarlet shook her head as if trying to shake something from her mind then dropped to her knees, "Verity? What's happened? Where are we?"

The Witch of the Seas had dusted herself off and stood next to Scarlet offering her a hand up, "Much has happened my child, and there is much to do. We need you."

Scarlet took her hand and pulled herself up, "Then what are we waiting for?" she said.

The three left the tree and headed back through the undergrowth, into the clearing. Perfidy, Morty and Fred sat waiting. Perfidy ran over as the trio appeared through the archway. She stopped in front of Scarlet. Scarlet looked at her and smiled, "It's good to see you again my child," she said. "I knew you were the right person to trust with my Heart Stone."

Perfidy smiled and hugged her tightly. Once she let go she said, "What about Frances? You said we might find Frances."

Verity looked at Perfidy helplessly.

The Witch of the Seas said, "Frances is in much danger, she is lost and we must do all we can for her."

Perfidy looked at Verity. Verity couldn't meet her eye.

The two witches looked at each other. Scarlet spoke, "Perfidy, come with me to check the area." Perfidy followed Scarlet out of the clearing.

Once they were alone, Scarlet spoke, "The end is near. The Witchfinder almost has all the pieces she needs to end the time of Witches and create her new world."

Perfidy rolled her eyes, "Me and Verity are the last pieces."

The witch carried on, "Her number is great, her force lies at anchor off the coast of Calden. She waits now at Calden Castle."

"What is she waiting for?" Perfidy asked.

"The end," said Scarlet.

"She has foreseen that you and your sister will come to her, that she will destroy Verity and acquire the last Heart Stone pieces."

"What about me?" asked Perfidy.

"You share a Heart Stone, you are bound to each other in more ways than you can imagine. If Verity dies, so too will you. How much are you willing to sacrifice my child? What are you prepared to give up?"

"Anything!" said Perfidy.

"Your life for Verity?" Scarlet said.

Perfidy thought hard before answering, "That's part of loving people, you have to give things up. Sometimes you have to give them up."

Scarlet stopped and turned to face her, "You have grown so much my young lioness. The child who came to me in the forest is no more. A beautiful, young lady stands before me."

"How do we stop her killing Verity?" asked Perfidy.

"We don't, she must believe that she has destroyed her. You must take her place," Scarlet said.

"But you said we are bound, we share a Heart Stone," Perfidy said.

"You would need to give yours up. It would mean you couldn't come back. It would be the end."

Perfidy sat down on the soft green forest carpet. She tried to take it all in. She really did feel that she would do anything but her heart was pounding and her head spun. The thought of death suffocated her. Scarlet sat down with her.

"What do I do? Tell me what to do," Perfidy pleaded.

"Nobody but you can choose. You are free to choose as you will, without fear of judgement or persecution. That is the world we fight for."

"It's not fair, things shouldn't be this way, we are paying for the mistakes of those who went before," Perfidy said.

"In this life, we don't get to choose what's true. We only get to choose what we do about it," Scarlet said.

Perfidy stood up. "I know what I must do..." she said.

"Verity must not know your fate, she won't understand," Scarlet said.

"I'm scared," Perfidy said with large blue eyes.

"Even lionesses are allowed to be scared, Blake will be with you. He will not leave your side, together to the end," Scarlet said. "Head back to the others. I will see you again when the time comes."

"Where are you going?"

"I'm going back to the darkness. I'm going to find the Black Witch."

"She won't come," Perfidy said.

"She will when she knows her son needs her."

Perfidy arrived back at the clearing alone and found the others were nearly ready to leave. Verity came to her. They looked at each other and hugged without speaking. Both shed tears for different reasons.

"Oh woe, woe and more woe!" wailed Morty. "We is broken, what has we done!" He crumpled to the ground. "Mr Blakey gone, poor Dotty and little Miss Frances," he sobbed into his small furry paws.

A deep voice came from behind him. "What are you whimpering about Morty? It really doesn't suit you."

"Mr Blakey sir! Mr Blakey sir!" Morty leaped up and hugged Blake's chest nearly knocking him off balance.

He held Morty gladly and smiled until he caught sight of the twins. He gently lowered Morty to the ground and went to Verity and Perfidy. He knelt before them and bowed his head. "I am so sorry, I failed you. I couldn't protect them. I thought I could break the darkness by helping them but it still grips me, so tightly." His voice broke as he choked back the hurt.

Verity put her hand on his head. "You have been lost in darkness, you have not let yourself feel for so long. Yet, you kneel here now in sorrow. Look up."

Blake slowly raised his head to meet the gaze of the twins.

"I see no darkness. I see only light. A light strong enough to extinguish itself for others to shine. You have become greater than you ever imagined because you believe again," Verity said.

"Believe in what?" he asked.

"Your one true love. It has been there all along and now you feel it again, you need no longer carry the darkness."

"Scarlet is..."

"Scarlet is not dead, she heads for the Black Witch. The final fight is near," Perfidy said.

The words hit Blake as surely as a fist.

"The Witchfinder has won. She commands a powerful army, I don't know where she is?" he said.

"She waits for us at Calden Castle. We mustn't disappoint her," Perfidy said.

The group sat round in a circle while the Witch of the Seas spoke. She told them about the Circle, the children, about the fight ahead. When she finished, Fred spoke first. "Well knock me down with a wet kipper! What a tale! I was keen before, but now I really wanna knock her socks off! Death or glory!"

Morty spoke next, "I is not clever like you Mrs Wet Witch, but I is knowin' when someone has missed out the best bit of a story. I often finds what people isn't sayin' is more juicy than what they is."

"Morty's right," said Blake, "we won't win this fight. What makes you think we can?"

The Witch of the Seas flashed a knowing look towards Verity. "It was once believed that Fate would deliver a saviour. The saviour would carry a truth so powerful that it would shine light into all lives. A soul with great power, one who would destroy the enemies of the Witches Circle and save us all."

"And here she is!" Fred said excitedly pointing at Verity. "You gotta love Fate!"

"Yes here she is. Verity isn't our last chance, she is our only chance," said the witch.

"How can Verity stand alone and defeat such a force?" Blake asked.

"She won't be alone and she knows what she must do when she meets Fate," the Witch of the Seas said.

Verity looked out through the trees.

"Meets her fate, you mean?" Blake said.

"No, I mean when she meets Fate. Fate waits for us all in the other world. We must pass through the Black Light to reach her."

"How do we reach this Black Light?" Blake asked.

"Death takes us to the Black Light," she said.

Perfidy looked at Verity. "No! This is not the way, I won't let you!" she said.

"Be calm child, there is another way. There are some of us who know of secret places. Places where light and dark don't exist, tears in the fabric of the world. The Black Light can be passed through. One such tear lies deep beneath Calden.

If the thirteen Heart Stones can be recovered, Verity can take them into the Black Light and meet Fate. Only then can wrong be made right. We must provide her safe passage."

"How do we get there?" Blake asked.

"It is well hidden child. I am the last who knows how to reach it. I will take Verity," the witch said.

"Blake and I will distract the Witchfinder," said Perfidy.

"Fred, you and Morty must recover the Heart Stones. The Witchfinder has them safely hidden in the castle," said the witch.

"Wait, you is sayin' thirteen," Morty said.

"What do you mean?" Perfidy said.

"Thirteen little twinklers. One with Miss Scarlet and the nasty one has nine, right or left?"

"Right."

"Where is the other three?" Morty said.

Perfidy held out an open hand. In her palm sat a small piece of shimmering silver. It was smooth round one edge and jagged down the other. Verity did likewise holding a similar silver object. They held the pieces up and slowly moved them together. They were a perfect fit. Together they made the shape of a dazzling silver heart.

"That leaves two to winkle out. And woe betide, they is the two we has no idea where they is hidden!" Morty said.

The Witch of the Seas looked at Blake. Realisation dawned on him. He fumbled in his pocket and produced the small black pearl the Black Witch had given him. He looked at her in despair, "The Witchfinder is my..."

She nodded.

Fred's eyes were wide as he looked on, astonished. "Bloody 'ell!" he said. He proceeded to reach into his mouth with his hand. It made him gag as he stuffed it down. Between his saliva covered fingers he produced a small black pearl.

Morty gasped, "Well squeeze my acorns! That makes Mrs Black Witch..."

"Yes," said the Witch of the Seas, "the two boys who never were. Your mothers believe you are dead. We truly deserve our end for what we did."

Everyone was stunned. Blake looked angrily at the Witch of the Seas.

"You wanted to know the truth," she said.

"The truth. What is the truth? Does your truth change the world? What's gone is still gone, what's done is still done. The truth is that everyone chose their path and here we all are. In the end, we will all get what we deserve, including you," Blake said.

The witch gave no reply.

Fred stood up dramatically and thrust his fist into the air, "Come on you shower of shrimps! The world won't save itself you know! AAAAHHHHHHHHAAAAAA!"

The journey to Calden had seemed long. Not much had been said by the travellers as each found themselves lost inside. The path ahead and what would meet them was clear but beyond that, nothing could be seen. If the Witchfinder prevailed, a blinding darkness would cloak the future. Should the travellers overcome her, a blinding light would illuminate it, making everything possible. So much had come to pass. So much still to come. How were they to make sense of themselves in the world? The past clawed at their hearts, leaving its scars. Fate had been cruel, but Fate had also sent Verity. Since meeting Verity, hope had poured into their souls, making them dare to believe they could be better, leaving the darkness behind, learning to choose the light. Learning to be happy. They believed in Verity. Verity felt their hope. It used to be a burden, a weight she didn't think she could carry. Now, she felt their faith in her, it was a warm feeling; she took strength from it. They made her believe.

The moon was tinted red. It hung low in the sky. The group stood at the edge of the forest. Calden Castle sat on the opposite side of the valley, sunk into the side of the rocky hills. Verity shuddered when she saw the fleet of ships that lay at anchor in the bay far below.

"The Blood Moon," Blake said.

"What does it mean?" Verity asked.

"It's near the end of its life; a new moon will rise high in the sky tomorrow," he said.

"Which of us will see it?" Verity said softly.

Everyone looked at the sky wondering but nobody answered.

"We shall rest there till daylight. The nightwalkers will be at their weakest then," said Blake as he pointed to a small stone cottage slightly further down the hill. "I have arranged for supplies."

Inside, the cottage was bare except from a large oak table and chairs that sat in the middle of the one and only room. Several green and brown sacks lay on the table. Blake grabbed one and handed it to Perfidy then started rummaging through the others. Perfidy beckoned to Verity as Blake pulled out large hunks of bread and cheese from one of the sacks. Perfidy dipped her hand into the sack and pulled out a familiar looking shot bow. She held it up in front of her face and inspected it before putting it down.

She continued to empty the contents. Some arrows, a black tunic, black leather armour and an empty dagger belt.

"Is there everything you need?" Verity said.

"No, but there is everything *you* need. The Witchfinder must believe you are me to give you a chance of getting to the Black Light." Perfidy pulled out her gleaming dagger and held it out to Verity.

Verity looked at it nervously, "I don't know how... I can't... I mean, I don't think I could kill..."

Perfidy smiled, "It isn't in you Verity, you are strong, you want to create not destroy. I wouldn't change that for the world."

Perfidy replaced the dagger.

The group sat and ate and talked. For those few hours, the little cottage was a happy place. Morty bustled around serving bread and filling water mugs. Fred regaled the others with fantastical tales of his various adventures with Dotty, every one of which, inevitably seemed to end in some form of nakedness. Perfidy recounted stories of her younger days when Blake was trying to teach her how to use a shot bow and he ended up with a wooden arrow in his bottom. Verity laughed as she told them about Dark Oak and the time she and Frances had snuck into the kitchen and raided Krankle's chocolate biscuit barrel. All the girls were lined up in the morning and searched. They would have gotten away with it, had Frances not been discovered with half a chocolate cream crumbled in her pocket. Verity had taken the blame and was sentenced to clean the toilets with a toothbrush for six weeks. Even Blake joined in, telling them about the time when he had hidden in a net full of herring to avoid the ship's captain who was looking for him because he had tried to 'borrow' his prize lobster to cook a romantic meal for Scarlet. The disgruntled lobster had nipped Blake's hand and his yelp gave him away. Only the Witch of the Seas sat silently, listening. She looked at the group and just for a second saw a very special thing. She saw a family, the most unlikely of families but a family none the less. They would laugh and cry with each other, they would stay with one another through the good and the bad, most importantly of all, they loved each other in their own ways.

The table was quiet and the mood somber as the first blades of sunlight cut through the window into the cottage.

"It is time," Blake said.

Everyone gathered their things. Perfidy dressed head to toe in beautiful white robes and cloths. Her dagger left on the table. Verity mirrored her in black leather armour and cape, shot bow slung over her shoulder. Morty too had donned a leather breastplate and wore a little metal helmet. A small sword hung from his tunic belt.

"You look very smart," Verity said.

"Thank you Miss Verity," he said. He looked at her, "I thought you was special because it was your destiny to be that way. I was wrong about you girly peeps. You is special because you is you, no more no less. Whatever is happenin', you will always be Morty's special little one, what found me in the toiletry."

Verity hugged him tightly.

Blake stood at the door, "Come on Perfidy, it's time to go." Blake and Verity looked at each other before he left. He wanted to hold her. To tell her everything would be all right, that she would be safe but he knew none of that was true. He opened his mouth as if to speak. Verity raised her hand, kissed it and held it out to him. She smiled a sad smile. His eyes were sad as he nodded his head in understanding and then left.

"Good day ladies," Morty said as he tipped his helmet and headed to the door.

"AAAAAAHHHHHHAAAAHHHHAAAAA! I love him!" bellowed Fred as he followed. Morty gave a little bow before leaving.

"I will wait for you outside," said the Witch.

When they were alone, Verity and Perfidy looked at each other. Verity spoke first, her big blue eyes betrayed her brave front, "I know I'm supposed to be everyone's saviour, but I'm scared."

Perfidy went to her and wrapped her up with arms and love. She kissed her hair gently, "It's ok to be scared. These things have a way of working themselves out, you'll see."

"What if you knew what was going to happen?"

"What if I did?"

"Would it make you strong, or would it be the reason you faltered?"

"The darkness makes it easy to choose the wrong path."

"Choosing the right path is often the hardest choice of all, light doesn't come without a price."

"Does it make it easier to make our choices if we know where they lead?"

"Darkness blinds us. Light is blinding. I never knew where to turn but I do now."

"When did you know?"

"I knew when I met you. The moment I looked at you, I realised that everything I ever needed was right in front of me. All the holes within me were filled, all the voices that chimed in my head telling me that I was a failure, that I wasn't good enough, that I wasn't worth loving, were drowned out by your voice. It spoke so loudly. It spoke so clearly. It simply said I love you, and there is nothing in this world or the next that will be able to change that. To love you is the greatest of all gifts and there is no force that exists that can take it away from me. I will let it make me as tall as mountains and as strong as iron but in the end, the greatest love has to be strong enough to let go."

"Do you believe in Fate?"

"I believe in us. That's why we have to do what we have to do."

"Do you think we will see each other again?"

"I'm sure of it."

"I hope you're right. If you're wrong and this is it, I want you to know that you truly did save me."

"I love you."

"Let's just imagine for a minute that it's tomorrow. It's tomorrow and we are sitting next to each other looking up at the new moon. The world is full of possibility and we are excited about the prospect of choosing our new paths."

The twins sat quietly, arms round each other, both hearts weighed heavily with love and sorrow.

Chapter 18
Leaving a Piece of Youth

'When you reach the end of your rope, tie a knot in it and hang on.'
Franklin D Roosevelt

Perfidy and Blake made their way quickly and silently across the fields. They had watched the hoards of nightwalkers disembarking and disappearing towards the castle. For Perfidy, the thought of what she would do was crippling, trumped only by the fear of not doing it.

Fred and Morty had stopped and taken up hiding at the base of the hills. "How are we getting in my furry companion?" Fred asked.

"I is bettin' that you is both mad enough and strong enough to climb the face of the North Tower, right or left?"

"Right you are!"

"Alls we would need is to get to the base of the tower and Rob's your uncle!"

"Excellent! We can skirt around the perimeter all the way there. What a clever, hirsute little chap you are," Fred said.

Morty tried to look modest, "Well, I is havin' my moments."

The pair kept low as they set off to the North Tower.

"How are we going to find the Heart Stones?" asked Fred.

"You ever been pricked with an arrow Mr Fred?" Morty asked.

The Witchfinder stood on the South wall, looking out over the valley. "They are coming, look at them, so brazen. Perfidy thinks she has the beating of us with that traitorous witch. I shall enjoy wiping the smile from her disgusting mouth," her lip curled cruelly as she spoke.

"We are ready, oh majestic one," snivelled Krankle. "The walkers are positioned all around, they won't get through."

"Verity isn't with them. Blake will try to protect her. Kill him but she must be given safe passage to me. Make sure she finds me. I need to be the one who kills her, I need to be sure."

"Forgive me wonderful one, but the witches are powerful. What if they break the lines?"

"Then your failure will be punished by them instead of me!" she snapped.

Verity and the Witch of the Seas travelled straight through the valley, taking little care to conceal themselves. "Why aren't we hiding?" Verity asked.

"They know we are coming. Hiding is futile. Fear the enemy who doesn't fear you. Besides, we want them to see us, we will draw their eye giving the others their chance, isn't that right, *Perfidy*?"

"I suppose. How are we going to get in?"

"We will go to the front door and knock."

"What happens when we get to the Black Light?" Verity asked.

"If the others are successful, they will deliver the Heart Stones to us. You must carry the Heart Stones through. After that, you will have to find your own way."

They continued to Calden. The high grey walls loomed large.

Fred and Morty hid behind the wooden cow shed that faced the North Tower. Fred had counted at least fifteen walkers, and they were only the ones he could see. It was hard to tell how many could be hidden out of sight, further behind the tower.

"They is thinkin' like we is thinkin'," Morty said.

"We knew this would happen sooner or later my friend. Are you ready?"

Morty took a deep breath and gripped the hilt of his little sword. "I is never readier," he said proudly.

Fred thought about Dotty and how he would have loved this kind of caper. "Hey Morty, did I ever tell you Dotty's old story about the three wise men playing poker?" he said.

Morty shook his head.

"Three wise men are playing poker. This guy runs up to them and says, 'Hey, the world's coming to an end!' and the first one says, 'Well, I best go to the church and pray,' and the second one says, 'Well, hell, I'm gonna go and buy me a case of rum and a pack of cigars,' and the third one says 'Well... I shall finish the game.'"

"What next?" Morty asked.

"It's time to finish the game Morty...it's time to finish the game."

Now, that they were closer, Verity looked properly at the front of Calden. The large oak drawbridge lay open like the jaws of a beast. A huge grey beast that would invite them in and then swallow them up. The grey stone walls of the castle protruded from the rocky hillside as if the hill itself had tried to swallow it. Calden had been built deep into the innards of the hillside. Short of scaling the walls, there were only two ways in, the main gate and the Western Gate. The Witch of the Seas stopped suddenly and stared at the castle up ahead. "It is time," she said.

She turned to Verity.

"It is essential that the Witchfinder believes *Verity* is at the other gate, long enough for us to get inside."

The witch turned to face the gate again. She closed her eyes and lowered her head slightly. She pictured her daughter, small and delicate, forever young. Her black hair held a deep blue sheen in the sunlight. The memory stood in a plain navy dress, hands by her sides. She was smiling with big dark blue eyes, she was perfect. The witch opened her eyes and raised her head. She turned to Verity and said, "You hold the fate of us all my child."

"What if I can't save us all?" Verity said pleadingly.

"In a way, I think you already have," said the witch.

She reached to the sky and let out a terrible noise. All at once the clouds turned black and blotted out the morning sun. Thunder snarled angrily as a huge lightning bolt tore the air.

Perfidy recalled Scarlet's words, 'Wait at the West Gate. When the sky roars, walk tall and remember you are Verity, be strong enough not to fight.'

She felt vulnerable as she looked at the creatures that stood guarding the gate. She closed her eyes tightly and repeated Scarlet's words in her head, over and over, while they waited for the signal.

You are Verity.

A lightning bolt seared the sky as the clouds growled.

"It's time," said Blake.

Fred watched the lightning bolt. He winked at Morty, reached over his shoulder and pulled the shotgun from its holster.

"Time to finish the game.
AAAAHHAAAAAHAAAA!"

He sprinted towards the base of the tower. His long dirty brown coat flew out behind him. Nightwalkers screamed and ran towards him. Fred ran right for them. He held out the gun and blasted. The first of the walkers exploded where the shot hit it and sent it tumbling to the ground. Without breaking stride he cocked open the barrel and started shoving fresh shells in. He snapped it back into place and ran into the crowd. Walkers swiped and swung at him as he dodged through them. He smashed one in the face with the butt of his gun and sent it flying before spinning and raising the barrel to the head of the next nearest beast and sent a shower of metal hail its way. Two, three, four blasts. Pieces of walker flew into the air. Fred stopped and snapped the barrel open again. Smoke rose as the shells popped out. He started to liberate more from the cross belts which stretched over his chest. He was roaring, "AAAAHHHHAAA, I love the smell of shot in the morning!"

The creatures started to swarm around him. They encircled him. He reeled off four more blasts and started to reload. The numbers were too great for him to last long. "WHO'S NEXT!" he roared. "PLENTY FOR EVERYONE! I DON'T WANT ANYONE TO FEEL LEFT OUT! AAAAAHHA!"

Two more blasts, shattered bodies of close by walkers lay on the ground. He reloaded again. The creatures were near now. He held the gun out, the barrel glinted as he slowly turned in a circle. The walkers closed in, his finger twitched on the trigger. He only had four shells left in his belt. A walker broke the circle and came towards him, Fred started to squeeze the trigger but stopped when the walker stood suddenly still. Its body started to writhe and twitch. Gently at first then quite violently. Green slime started to leak from its eyes, as if it were crying. The slime kept oozing and quickly started running from its eyes, the walker twitched violently and shook, the others looked on in fear as it clutched its torso. Soon, it was on its knees, slime pouring from its nose, ears and mouth. It writhed and wretched until it eventually burst into globules of liquidly flesh. Fred looked and saw the Green Witch standing with her arms outstretched walking towards them. She raised her hands to the sky. Soon vines started bursting from the faces of the other walkers as they started to writhe and twitch. Bodies burst. Fred was showered in small chunks of skin and meat. The witch walked right up to him, her emerald eyes blazed.

"It's been a long time. I'm sorry," she said.

"You just saved my hide! You needn't be sorry darlin'," said Fred.

"You have paid so, so dearly, I want you to know that I won't lift my hand if you choose to strike me down."

"Bloody hell! And they say I'm crazy! Don't you get it yet witchy darlin'? What if I did? What if I did strike you down and tore your heart in two. What would I find? Isn't it already broken? How much more pain can I add? Don't you see? We are fighting with Verity now, the past is gone, today, right now is happening! So witchy dear, the question is not what I am going to do because I already know what I am going to do. The question is, what are you going to do?"

Scarlet stood for a while outside the Staxcian Door. She thought about her mothers. One had given her life, flesh and blood, she had given her body up for her, yet she had also given her up. The other who had found her when she was helpless and alone. Martha had sculpted her out of pure love. Scarlet felt like a traitor. She loved Martha but she could not deny the longing she felt for a blood mother. Her past ghosts were with her now. In a strange way, they gave her comfort. They had haunted her since Kergord but at least they hadn't left her, like so many other things. At least they were still there, her loyal, terrible friends. They sat with her and smiled at her. They knew just how to unlock her. All the doors inside, that she took such care to keep shut. They knew which ones to open at just the right moment, to show her things she didn't want to see. This time she gave in and let the feelings bite her with their terrible teeth and their terrible jaws. She didn't feel afraid of them now. The ghosts did not like this. She imagined gathering all the terrible thoughts and questions that she had, all her worries and insecurities. She imagined taking them and putting them all in a small, beautiful red velvet bag, just as her mummy had said, such a long time ago. She imagined the bag had an elegant wine coloured drawstring, which she made sure she pulled as tightly as she could. It felt good. Did it make sense that she could still feel Martha's love, right here, right now? Was it something physical? Surely if it was, it was the strongest magic of all. Scarlet closed her eyes tightly and searched her heart for the answer. It came to her quickly, it was as powerful as it was gentle.

'Yes.'

My love for you never really went away my sweet Blake, she thought, it's been here all along, watching, waiting. I can only hope that there's enough time left to tell you. Scarlet raised her arms and walked through quickly as the Staxcian door opened.

Blake walked out. The nightwalkers stopped to sniff the air as he emerged. Some of them licked their lips when they saw him. He strode forward, unarmed, unafraid. Perfidy looked at him and remembered something he had said to her when she was a little girl, when she had asked if he was scared of anything.

'I'm only scared of being afraid to act.'

Those words had never made sense until now. She watched him walking tall, wrapped in black leather. His hair neatly parted. Black leather gloves. Black leather coat flowing behind him. He had given up his power with his Heart Stone. Unlike the witches, his powers were gone without the stone. The darkness had held him tightly for so long, it was as comfortable as it was terrible. She watched him as he walked. His pace quickened, his strides became a run; his black fists clenched. He careered into the first wave of walkers, moving like a panther as he dodged their swipes and blows. His black fists did not feel pain as they hammered face after face, punished bone after bone, broke body after body. Perfidy watched on cloaked in white as he laid the walkers to waste. Still they came. He did not waver. He moved elegantly as he dodged the rusty blades and sharp claws.

He was puffing heavily as he snapped the neck of the last walker and looked up at the four gores that had appeared. He walked to them, his fists trembled and bled inside his gloves. Perfidy followed him. Every fibre of her ached, every fibre of her wanted to help him. She forced herself to remember the words.

'Be strong enough not to fight.'

Blake stopped a little way in front of the gores. His heart was tired and sore. You have had me for so long, you have to go now he thought. The ghosts of the past looked at each other. They seemed to be satisfied that they could leave and were a little sad as they released their inky claws. Blake gasped and fell to his knees as light radiated through his veins. He struggled and gasped for air as his body warmed and tingled. He thought about Scarlet holding him, the thought consumed him. She held him so tightly, he could not be happier. This was his truth. It was so clear now. All he had ever needed, was her to hold him this way. Everything else drifted away. He hoped that there was enough time left to tell her.

He rose and walked carefully peeling off his gloves, then wriggling his shoulders as he removed his coat. It fell as he walked on. His dripping red hands were open by his sides. To his surprise the gores grunted and then parted ways as he approached. Krankle strode through the middle of them, "Well, well, it does seem as if your bothersome ways are about to end. Give Verity up and you might just be allowed to have a quick, clean death."

Perfidy walked up and stood next to Blake. She touched his sore hand gently before standing in front of him. "Here I am you old trout, what now?"

Krankle was taken aback.

A voice pierced the air.

"Now, you do what you were born for, little fly."

The Witchfinder strode forward. She stood next to Krankle. Tall and elegant. It was clear that she had once been very pretty. "You have walked with spiders, they have led you in. It has been a long time but finally wrong will be made right," she said.

"What wrongs do you speak of?" Perfidy replied.

"You must know the truth by now my sweetness. The Witches Circle took my baby, my life, so in turn I took theirs. It's a blessing that I could deliver such justice."

"I have no quarrel with you," Perfidy said.

"Ha ha, Verity, so innocent and so stupid. There you are, you were so dangerous, hidden in dark places and dark spaces. We watched you for such a long time at Dark Oak. I had to be sure. Little did we know that little Frances is so special too, sorry, I mean was. It's time for the end Verity."

"You don't know what you think you do," Perfidy said.

"She has always been a little liar!" Krankle sniped. "We were always watching you. I knew I was right!"

Blake stepped forward and walked right up to the Grey Witch. Krankle looked panicked and the gores twitched till the Witchfinder raised her hand.

He looked at her carefully. "Your eyes are very black," he said.

"So are yours my sweetness."

"Do you sleep at night?"

"You are done Blake. Your powers won't help you now."

"What do you fight for?" said Blake.

"I fight to right wrongs," she replied.

"Killing rights wrongs?"

"It rights mine."

"You can still choose the light," he said.

"There is no other way."

"How much killing will make it right?"

"I will stop when it's done."

"Then what?"

"Then I will be a Goddess!"

"Mother is the name of God on the lips and hearts of all children," Blake said.

"I am not a mother my sweetness."

"Yes, I believe that you are right," he said sadly before moving to the side.

"Now little Verity, it's time for the truth."

"I think it is," Perfidy replied as she caught a tiny glimpse of Blake melting into the background.

With all eyes on Perfidy he slipped unseen, past the onlooking gores and slunk through the Western gate. He glanced over his shoulder and thought about turning back before heading into the courtyard.

"Time to die!" the Witchfinder shrieked.

"Yes, I know," Perfidy said.

Krankle came forward, "Leave this to me my master, I would love nothing more than to skin another young buck that doesn't know her place! I wonder if you will squeal as much as Frances did?"

She lurched towards Perfidy wielding a large knife. Perfidy stood still, stood strong. She closed her eyes, and waited. As Krankle lunged she swiftly twisted out of the knife's path, liberated it from her hand, spun round and placed it as hard as she could between Krankle's shoulder blades. When she heard the heavy frame embrace the dirt, her big blue eyes flashed as she opened them.

"You little witch!" the Witchfinder spat, "Verity isn't a killer? Perfidy?"

"At your service," Perfidy said.

The Witchfinder looked around and saw Blake was gone. "Find him and kill him, NOW!" she roared at the gores who started to lumber back into the courtyard.

"I wonder why you would come to me. You know Verity won't escape. It's her destiny."

Perfidy pulled the shot bow from her robes, "I came to take the Heart Stones from you. Hand them over!"

The Green Witch knelt down and planted a small brown seed next to the wall. She stood back and looked at Fred. A thick green stalk snaked out of the ground and stretched up the face of the tower. It didn't stop until it was nearly out of sight. She looked at Morty, "I just want to make her pay. Is that so bad?"

"It's all your hateful thoughts that has been eatin' you, Mrs Green Witch. You has made yourself pay."

"Enough girls talk, get your furry behind up there!" said Fred as he grabbed Morty and launched him skyward. "I am going to say thank you for what you did today and be on my way. I wish you lots of luck. Oh, just a thought, I bet an angry green witch wouldn't go amiss in the courtyard right now." Fred grinned before starting to scale the vine. At the top Fred struggled through the window.

"Too many Buttermilks," Morty said, raising his eyes to the ceiling.

"Don't be ridiculous!" Fred protested. "I'm as trim as I ever was. Windows just aren't as big as they used to be! Come on furry one, we have a bag to find! What now?"

"Do you trust me?" Morty said.

"To the end," Fred said.

"Alls you is doin' is leanin' out the window and stayin' very still and trustin' in little ol' Morty."

"Lets do it!" said Fred.

"Oh my sweetness! You never fail to amuse me!" said the Witchfinder.

"Hand them over," Perfidy said again.

"Do you really think I would give them to you, just like that?"

"You should," Perfidy said. Her shot bow trained on the Witchfinder.

"Do you think I would be so stupid as to carry such a precious thing with me?"

"I know you are so greedy that you wouldn't let anyone else near them."

"Such beauty but sadly so stupid. Two things my sweetness, firstly they are locked safely in the great hall, in Calden's stone chest and I would pity anyone who tried to open it! Secondly, you seem to have forgotten what happened last time you tried to shoot me."

"Yes but this time I have a secret weapon," Perfidy said. The Witchfinder watched curiously as Perfidy lowered her free arm and two small objects slid into her hand. She scribbled on the paper frantically before dropping a small piece of charcoal to the ground. Quick as a flash she pierced the paper with an arrow. She raised the shot bow and spun to face the North Tower. She could see Fred's outline at the window as she closed one eye to aim. "May truth deliver you in," she whispered before pulling the trigger.

Morty held tightly to Fred as he leant out the window. "DON'T BE MOVIN!" he shouted. The arrow whistled through the air. When he saw it, Fred braced himself.

"SHHI.."

It thumped into his shoulder and Morty hauled him in. He quickly unrolled the paper from the arrow.

"The Great Hall!" he yelped. "Clever girl Perfidy! You did it!"

"Bloody 'ell," groaned Fred.

The Witchfinder lifted her hand and clenched her fist. Perfidy felt an invisible force root her to the spot.

"You think you're so clever, little witch. They used you, they don't care about you, look where they left you."

Perfidy used every ounce of strength she had to turn her back to the witch and placed both hands over her heart. "I feel sorry for you," she called to the witch.

"HOW DARE YOU!" screamed the Witchfinder.

"I will see you again Verity," Perfidy whispered.

It didn't feel like she expected. There was a warm feeling in her tummy as the blade went through. Everything went blurry. "I will see you again," she said quietly as she lay down on the ground and slipped away.

"I will see you…"

Verity stood close to the Witch of the Seas as she swept all before them away. Walkers burst and fell and drowned in their own lungs. Verity held out the dagger but no foe was troubled by her blade. Suddenly Verity stopped, she froze. She felt strange, Perfidy! She gasped hard. The witch swiped her arms through the air and the last of the creatures fell.

The Witchfinder walked out into the courtyard. "You didn't really think you could win, did you?" she said. "How are you, Verity? Better than your sister I hope! Ha Ha Ha!"

"It's not too late to do the right thing," Verity said.

"You are so weak, just like her," the Witchfinder sneered.

"So stupid to give up her Heart Stone. I'll have it soon. And who is this traitorous wretch you have brought? Ah yes, I remember, one of the child murderesses!" She held out her hand and clenched her fist. The Witch of the Seas fell to her knees clutching her throat.

"Can you feel it!" the Witchfinder crowed. "Choking my sweetness? Would you like some water? Good! YES! Try a lifetime of it!"

The Witch of the Seas' body rose into the air. Water poured from her fingers first, then her mouth and eyes, it ran from every part of her till she hit the ground again.

The Witchfinder walked over and spat on her as the Witch of the Seas lay on the ground lifelessly. "Now young Verity, it really is time for you to go."

Verity eyed her carefully, she felt a strength that shouldn't have been there. "You are done Grey Witch. Come with me and I will help you," she said

"Haaaha, you, help me! Oh my sweetness, what a thought."

"You won't kill me," Verity said.

"Oh, won't I? And who is going to stop me?"

"I will," Scarlet said.

Verity and the Witchfinder turned to see Scarlet standing on the wall. She pulled down her red hood and her ruby eyes blazed.

"I will," the Green Witch said.

She stood on the West Wall.

"Two pathetic excuses for witches. You will be sorry you came. You are both weak, look at you. Contemptible creatures. You cannot stop me now."

"Maybe I can," said the Black Witch as she walked through the main gate.

"Even you? Of all people, you should understand," said the Witchfinder.

"You are consumed. This has gone on much too long. It must stop," the Black Witch said.

"You treacherous witch!" screamed the Grey Witch.

The Black Witch closed her fist and held it in front of her. The Witchfinder coughed then choked. Black tar oozed from her mouth. The Black Witch stared at her with no emotion. She opened her hand and let the Witchfinder gulp air back into her lungs.

"Don't direct that word at me again. I tried to save you," the Black Witch said calmly. The Witchfinder was on her knees, trying to recover herself. The Black Witch walked towards her slowly. "Drowning in blackness, that was my punishment for producing my abomination, a beautiful boy. What they didn't realise was that they didn't need to lock me away. Without him I would have drowned wherever I was, just like you," the Black Witch said.

"We are the same," spluttered the Witchfinder, "why are you against me? We are the same!"

"Oh my dear, we are not the same," the Black Witch said. She stood over the Witchfinder and offered her a hand to pull her up. The two stood eye to eye.

"It's been a long time."

"Why didn't you come for me? You said you would. I waited for so long," the Black Witch said.

"I couldn't. I had to disappear. They had to think I was gone. The Staxcian Door was watched so carefully," said the Witchfinder.

"I needed you," said the Black Witch.

"I needed you too but, I couldn't..."

"You chose your path and you have walked it, barefoot on broken glass."

"I couldn't... I was so sore. I couldn't see the light, had it been shone into my eye."

"You didn't want to see it."

"How could I! You know what they did! We were a family, we were the Witches Circle. They deserved every drop of blood I spilled."

"I would have stood with you but I would have stopped at the children. Is that why you didn't come?" said the Black Witch.

"It was the only way they would understand! They deserved it!"

"But THEY didn't did they, they were just babies like our own, beautiful little children."

"It was the only way!"

"Haven't you delivered enough pain, are you not done?"

"Done, DONE! I haven't even started my sweetness, I haven't even started!"

"You murdered their children."

"They murdered ours!"

"They didn't."

"You are lying!"

"I took them. I hid them. I made them safe. Your son came to me recently, he has grown to be so strong but so sad."

"You treacherous witch. Your tongue is poisonous!" the Witchfinder snapped.

"You have to choose to see the truth, it's not too late."

"Your only wish is to stop me and I'm afraid I can't let that happen."

Gores and walkers poured into the courtyard. "You should have killed me while you had the chance."

"I have chosen to change."

"How noble of you, then you can die here with your newfound companions as a reward."

"Which companions?"

The Witchfinder looked around frantically, "Where are they?"

Other than the gores and walkers they were the only ones left in the courtyard.

"Your child is alive."

"NO! You will not seduce me, my sweetness. You should have stayed hidden in the dark where you belong. Kill her!"

Morty and Fred made their way through the corridors to the Great Hall. They burst through the brown double doors and were immediately tiny as the Great Hall dwarfed them.

Huge stone arches criss crossed the ceiling. Giant pillars plunged up towards the roof. Massive paintings hung on the walls although the canvases had all been torn from the frames. "This is where the Witches Circle was meetin'. This is where they sealed our fate," Morty said, pointing to a large stone table in the middle of the hall.

"Where are the stones hairyface?" said Fred.

"In Calden's chest," Morty replied.

"Excellent! Let's go and liberate them!" Fred said.

It didn't take long to find three chests sitting side by side. One golden, one silver and one wooden.

"Which one?" Fred said frantically.

"I is not knowin'?" Morty said.

"There's something written on this one!" Fred said. He moved to the stone chest in the middle and brushed aside some cobwebs that revealed text chiselled onto the front of it.

'There is only one truth.'

"What the blazes does that mean?" moaned Fred.

Morty scuffled around the chests. "Look Mr Fred!" he said. He clambered onto the wooden chest and was sweeping away the dust on top with his paws. It read:

'They are not in the golden chest.'

Fred quickly did the same with the silver chest. It read:

'The Stones are not in this chest.'

They both read the last inscription on top of the Golden chest:

'They are in this chest.'

"What does it mean?" Fred said.

"I is not sure?" Morty said.

"To hell with this! Let's get them open," Fred said.

"I is not thinkin' that is a good idea Mr Fred. I is bettin' they is protected some way. If one of these is tellin' the truth, which one? Come on Mr Fred use your noodles!"

Fred read the chests again. "Ok, how hard can it be? I am a champion of the mind!" he boasted.

"Yes Mr Fred! You is! You can do it!" Morty replied excitedly.

"Right it can't be in the silver one otherwise that means the silver box is lying, see?"

"Not exactly Mr Fred."

"The wooden box has to be lying because the silver box says they are not in the silver one, which means it must be the golden one! It tells the truth!"

He read it again:

'They are in this chest.'

"Is you sure?" said Morty.

"Morty my hairy brained friend, I have never been surer of anything in my life!"

He went to the golden chest and hauled open the heavy lid. They looked eagerly inside. Once the dust settled they could see a small leathery pouch sitting in the bottom of the chest.

"HEEEE HHAWWWW! I don't mind admitting to you that I am a bit of a genius," Fred said proudly. "I mean I always try to hide it but it's difficult when your brains are this damn big!"

He picked up the bag, pulled the leather ties and tipped the contents out into the chest. Nothing but a large pile of dust poured out.

"That doesn't look right Mr Fred," Morty said.

"Err, yes, well, I think..."

Suddenly, the hall shook and a loud bellow rumbled around the pillars.

The pair were knocked off their feet as something started hammering on the floor of the hall. Chunks of stone sprayed into the air and a massive hand appeared through the freshly made hole and slapped onto the floor of the hall followed by another, and another, and another!

"Ah sugar," said Fred, sounding dejected.

The creature hauled itself through the hole and roared again. Its long fat torso was covered in black and yellow hair. Four thick scaly legs stuck out of each side. Its face was eyeless and rows of razor sharp teeth stuck out of its ugly mouth, some had pierced the skin around the lips. Its huge black and yellow tongue snaked in and out of its mouth as if it were alive itself.

"Don't worry little chum, I'll sort it. Eight legged monster beasts is a specialty of mine!" Fred said while unholstering his shotgun. He checked his shells. Four left. The creature had started to stalk its way towards them.

"Don't worry little one, this won't take long," Fred said, sweating a little. Morty drew his sword.

Fred lowered his head and muttered something under his breath. He looked back up and snapped the barrel shut with one hand. His eyes were wild as he walked to the beast. The creature thumped down its feet as it plodded to him, tongue flickering. Fred kept walking. When he was near enough he held up the gun and let off a shell. It hit the beast square in the face. It stopped and roared. He let fly with the other. A fleshy hole appeared in the beast's cheek but still it came. Fred popped the shells and slid in the last two. He reeled off one then the other in quick succession. They both found their mark and the creature fell to one side as its legs gave way. Fred stopped and looked anxiously. The creature moaned. Its face and head lay in waste where the shot had hit. Fred looked on. The creature groaned a little louder and slowly righted itself. Its tongue flashed wildly from the large hole that was now its mouth. It continued its plodding towards them. Fred dropped his head.

"This one's got the lick of me. What would you do Dot?" he whispered, "Blaze of glory I wager, eh you old queen! I miss you."

He slowly raised his head and flipped the shotgun round and grasped the barrel then rushed the beast, wielding it like a club. He managed to thump the creature once before it swiped him away with one of its front legs. His back broke as he hit a stone pillar. He groaned and tried to get up but couldn't. The beast roared and headed for him again.

"Run furry one, run!" Fred croaked. Morty was shivering behind the large silver chest. Stay at home mother Morty said. Stay in your mole hole. Nothing bad happens there. You was right, nothing bad happens there but nothing good does either, just boring and grey. Mr Fred is my friend!

"Together to the end Mr Fred! I is on my way!"

He leaped out from behind the chest and waddled as fast as he could towards the beast, brandishing his sword. Fred felt comfortably numb as he lay helplessly at the bottom of the pillar. The monster's pulped face pushed its way right up to Fred and sniffed. The black and yellow tongue slithered over Fred's body.

"Go on you filthy dog. Do your worst!" he said triumphantly.

Morty scampered as fast as he could. He was perfectly small enough to run underneath the creature's belly. He pressed his little furry ear against it.

Thump, thump, thump.

He could hear its heartbeat. Just a little further, he thought.

THUMP, THUMP, THUMP.

"There you is my lovely little sweet spot!" Morty said.

Fred recoiled as much as he could but the large slimy teeth were starting to bite at his body.

"DO YOUR WORST!" he screamed.

Meanwhile, Morty plunged his little sword into the belly of the beast as hard as he could. It's wicked jaws loosed their grip on Fred as it moaned pathetically. Morty let go of the hilt and scurried out from underneath. The beast swayed and stuttered on its feet before its legs gave way and it crashed to the cold stone floor.

"You did it Morty!" Fred said.

"Mr Fred, Mr Fred! Is you alright?" Morty spluttered as he hurried over.

"Alive and kicking," Fred replied, "except for the kicking bit, I can't feel my legs. Apart from that, I'm in the pink!"

"Oh Mr Fred! I was so trembly!" Morty said.

"You saved me buddy! Only a madman would have pulled that stunt! You risked your life, even when all was lost. Why?"

"Because you is my friend, Mr Fred. Simple as that."

"HHHHAAA HHHHAAA, you gotta love that mole! And I do! You are the best friend a fool like me could have."

"I take my eyes off you for a moment and you end up laying about, taking it easy when our world needs saved!" Blake said.

Morty spun round to see him standing behind them.

"Oh Mr Blakey sir, is I glad to be seein' you!"

"Could have done with you five minutes ago!" Fred groaned. "What are you? Some kind of glory dodger?"

Blake smiled, "I got here as soon as I could."

"How are the girls?" Fred said urgently.

"The fight is on," Blake replied, "we must hurry."

Fred's head dropped, "I can't get up," he said.

Morty showed Blake the inscriptions on the chests.

"Well you have eliminated one at least," Blake said, "so if it's not the golden chest then the only thing that can be right is that they are in the silver chest."

Morty and Fred flashed each other confused looks. The hinges of the silver chest creaked as Blake creaked it open. A small leathery pouch lay inside.

"Wait a minute!" Fred said.

Blake pulled the leather ties and poured out the contents. The bottom of the chest glittered with stones of every shape and colour.

"We need to find Verity." Blake said.

Blake had slung Fred over his shoulder as they made their way out to the courtyard. They stood at the top of a large set of stone steps. Blake laid Fred down as gently as he could before he tried to take in the scene that spread out before him. Small fires and green vines littered the rubble that lay across the courtyard. The Green Witch lay at the feet of the Witchfinder who appeared to be cutting the Heart Stone out of her chest. Verity lay nearby on her back, eyes open seemingly unable to move. The Black Witch hung lifelessly in the air, as if by an invisible noose. An inky black liquid dripped from her body that had created a pool beneath her. Blake kept looking desperately until he saw Scarlet lying face down near the western wall. He dropped the bag and ran to her.

Fred looked at the Black Witch hanging in the air. Morty held him.

"That's my mum. I ain't never knowin' her but that's my mum." Tears started to wet his cheeks.

"What is you doin' if you could get up Mr Fred?" Morty asked.

"I would get her down. I just want her down."

Morty laid him down and rubbed his little furry face against Fred's. He headed down the stone steps to the Witchfinder.

Blake reached Scarlet and fell at her feet. He scrambled along the ground and lifted her head. She groaned quietly.

"Scarlet, it's me. It's your Blake."

"I knew you'd come."

"Don't speak. Save your strength."

"What happened to your eyes?" Scarlet said.

"What do you mean?"

"They aren't black anymore, they are beautiful blue."

"Scarlet I have to tell you something..."

"I knew you would come. I feel so cold."

"Hold on, I'm here, don't be afraid," Blake said.

"I have been afraid my whole life, except when I have been with you," Scarlet said.

"Don't leave me. I need you," said Blake.

"I believe again Blake. I believe in one true love and I believe it will last forever."

"Don't leave me."

"I love you Blake."

"I love you too, don't..."

Scarlet's body felt warm as she left.

Morty jumped and slapped the Witchfinder's face.

"You is a nasty one!" he said. The Witchfinder rose from the Green Witch's body in surprise.

"How sweet!" she said as she drew her hand across her cheek and inspected the blood on her fingers.

"You has done much wickedness!" Morty said.

"And what do you think you are going to do about it, little Morty?" she said.

"I is tellin you to get that woman down," he said pointing to the Black Witch.

"Oh but she was a treacherous creature. We should leave her there and remind ourselves of that."

Morty raised his paw again but this time the Witchfinder grabbed his wrist. "You only get to do that once," she said.

Blake strode up to her. "Do as he asks," he said.

"You just don't know when to stop, do you?" she said.

Blake walked over and pulled her fingers free from Morty's arm. The moleman fell to the ground and scurried off to Verity.

"Let the Black Witch down," he said.

"Why?"

"Because you owe her, she saved your son."

"LIES!" she shrieked.

"Her own son lies watching. The Witches Circle never found us. You have been avenging a lie!"

The Witchfinder looked up at Fred gasping on the steps.

"Your eyes are very black." Blake said, "What colour did they used to be?"

"You are to be applauded Blake. I have won and I learn my son is alive yet you still think I will yield to you."

The Witchfinder pulled a dagger from her cloak and stuck it deep into Blake's heart. He gasped. His ghosts looked on sadly from afar. He looked up and met her gaze. "What colour did they used to be, mother?" he said as she let him slide from the blade.

Chapter 19
Black Light

'If you want a happy ending, that depends, of course, on where you stop your story.'
Orson Welles

Morty pressed the bag into Verity's hand and bundled her down the wooden hatch.

"Go! Run Verity! Run!" he said.

Verity ploughed through the dark tunnels clutching the bag tightly as she ran. The tunnels wound and turned in all directions. All she could do was fumble through as best she could. She stumbled into a place that seemed to have no walls. It was well lit but the light only revealed darkness. A large ink black pool stretched out in front of her.

"Beautiful, isn't it?" the Witchfinder said.

Verity turned to face her.

"The Black Light," Verity said.

"You nearly did it, you nearly won," the Witchfinder said.

"Why nearly?" Verity asked.

"You have lost everything. They are all gone. For what my sweetness?"

"You are right, they are all gone, for what? Think about what you have lost, you were a mother. What are you now, Witchfinder?"

"Nothing was lost my sweetness, it was taken from me!"

"Fate was cruel but you let it destroy you, even when there was hope," Verity said.

"There was no hope!" spat the witch.

"Yes, a sad story, no doubt, the Witches Circle was wicked and cruel. Yet your child was only murdered today. Murdered by eyes so black they would not see the truth."

"Don't try to trick me you little witch!" the Witchfinder said.

"I have no tricks for you. Blake was your son."

"NO! STOP LYING! Just stop! I have taken all I can! Just stop!"

The Witchfinder dropped to her knees.

"Just stop," she said weakly. "They took everything from me, how sore would you have been? What would you have done?"

"I can't answer that," Verity said. "I still see some light in you. We don't get to choose the truth, we only get to choose what we do about it. Let me enter the Black Light."

"I can't let you, you will restore the Witches Circle! It will happen again."

"I will do what's right."

"I can't let you." the witch croaked.

Verity walked to her and held out Perfidy's dagger. "Then there truly is no hope. Take this and finish it."

The Grey Witch stood and took the dagger from Verity's hand. Verity put her hands down gently by her sides, closed her eyes and waited.

The witch looked at her.

"I can't do it any more, I've taken all I can, I'm sorry. Goodbye Verity," she whispered.

She bowed her head and plunged the dagger in deep.

Her ghosts screamed angrily as they tried to cling to her. She held on tightly to the blade as the ghosts were forced to let go of her terrible scarred skin. Their claws had cut so deeply.

Verity walked over to her and held her dying body.

"What have I done?" she gasped.

"The darkness will be gone soon," Verity whispered as she kissed her forehead.

The Grey Witch lay back and closed her eyes for the last time as Verity gently stroked her hair. Then, she was gone.

Verity clutched the bag of Heart Stones and walked towards the pool. She walked slowly down the steps that led into it. The thick inky liquid quickly swallowed her feet, followed by her legs and torso. Waist deep, she struggled out until the inky blackness reached her neck. She took a deep breath and pressed on. The black liquid filled her mouth and nose, then blinded her eyes and filled her ears. Verity's long black hair lay on the surface for a second or two before it disappeared.

When she woke, Verity found herself in a very white, very empty room. She sat up and looked around for the Heart Stones.

"They are quite safe," came a soft voice as if from nowhere. It took Verity a moment or two to make out a white figure standing in the corner of the room. "How odd that you should come to see me," it said.

"I'm Verity, I'm a saviour," she blurted out.

"I'm afraid not my dear, you are indeed Verity but you are no saviour. You are just Verity. How did you get these stones?"

"Are you Fate?" Verity asked. Her eyes couldn't seem to focus on the figure.

"Only a few have ever passed through the Black light before their time. I wonder why you did?" it said.

"I want to make things right."

"Do you indeed? I'm sure you are aware you cannot travel back through the Black Light. If you bargain with me, you are bound to me."

"Are you Fate?"

"It doesn't matter who I am my child," it said eyeing the bag. "What exactly is your price?"

"I have already paid my price," Verity said.

"Love is a dangerous game indeed," the figure said as it walked out into the middle of the room. Verity still could not focus on it.

"Let's imagine that things were different," it said. "How much are you willing to give up, to change it all?"

"I don't know? I'll do whatever it takes!" Verity said.

"Whatever it takes you say. The Heart Stones?"

"Take them."

"Your soul?"

Verity thought for a moment. She had never had the things other people had, she had never had much and never wanted much. What about now? At the end of it all? Did she wish she had had more? More things, more recognition, more wealth?

No.

Now, at the end, she found herself longing for none of these things. Instead, she craved that touch, that look, those loving words, that forgiveness, that smile, that fierce protection, that unconditional friendship, those things that bound together to make her special.

"I came here to make things right," Verity said.

"Very well. I shall take you back," it said.

"Back where?"

"Back to the Witches Circle, back to your mother. You can tell her what to do."

"That's all?" Verity said.

"That's all," it replied.

"The Black and Grey Witch will be the mothers they should have been. The Witches Circle will grow strong because of the acceptance of the boy children. They will discover the true meaning of things, family, truth…love," it said.

"But if they grow strong again, won't the Witches Circle eventually turn and bring harm once more?"

"Yes my child it would, except this time, I hold the Heart Stones, the witches will only have the power to love each other. Some think it's the strongest of all magic because it's the one thing in our universe that won't die. That's why you are here Verity, you are the bringer of truth."

"What will happen to Perfidy, Frances, Dotty and the little ones on the hanging tree? They need to be saved! You don't get your deal until I know they are saved!" Verity said.

"Once the new events are in motion, these things will be put right. The families and lives won't be destroyed. The relationships and bonds that you hold so dear will be made again. Nobody will remember you though, not even Perfidy. Can you accept that?"

"I came to put things right."

"You are brave indeed Verity. Fate was right to send you," it said.

"You are not Fate?" Verity said.

"It's time Verity."

"Time for what?"

"The moment of truth!"

Verity woke to find herself lying in a room full of bookshelves piled high with books. A large oak desk sat at one end and a woman with black hair and blue eyes stood at the window. Verity got to her feet.

"Ahem."

"Who let you in? What do you want?" The woman said.

Verity looked at her. Finally she saw her mother. She had longed for this moment. She had spent hours imagining how beautiful it would be but it wasn't. She knew what this woman was about to decide. She was not the mother in her head. The mother in her head was brave and strong, would fight for everything that was right yet this woman would make a most terrible decision.

"I need to tell you something," said Verity.

"Well, go on, I'm very busy," she snapped.

"I am Ve…,"

"Yes."

"I am, a messenger. You must go back and tell the Witches Circle to embrace the baby boys or suffer a terrible fate. They are good and true and you need to tell the others to embrace the truth, not live a lie."

Adrianna stared at her.

"I have asked for a sign. How strange that you are here, now. How did you get in? Who is it that speaks these wise words?"

"I'm… I'm just Verity."

***

Kergord bustled and busied with the business of the day. Scarlet filled another mug of Devil's Buttermilk and plopped it in front of Zander. "That should be your last one my dear," she said.

"Don't worry," said Sandy, "it will be!" She smiled and kissed Zander's lips before heading off to wipe the last of the tables. Fred and Dotty sat in the corner, smiling at each other and holding hands across the table while two large mugs and a bottle of Granny Arbuckle lay half empty before them. Perfidy finished the last mouthfuls of her meal.

"Yum! I do love a bit of mountain rat! Don't you?" Perfidy said.

"Never had it before," Frances replied.

Morty sat opposite Blake and sipped some coffee at the next table.

"Come on Girly peeps, eat up. Your mother will be worryin' if you is not back soon, and your mother will be waiting outside to collect you, Miss Frances," he said.

Frances smiled at Perfidy as they left.

Perfidy looked sad.

"Don't be worryin', tiddler. You'll see her tomorrow," Morty said.

"I know," Perfidy smiled. She looked up at the moon. It soared high in the sky. Its bright light blazed down. "A new moon," she said. "Frances is like a sister to me. I wish I had a real sister."

Morty shuffled uncomfortably. "I isn't possibly knowin' anythin' about that. You is best heading to bed missy and be thankful you has Frances at all."

Perfidy looked at him suspiciously. "Ok," she said.

Perfidy walked up the cold stone steps, along the corridor and into her room. She got ready for bed and stood in front of her large silver mirror. There she was. She looked at herself and checked her face. She stood still and gazed at the reflection.

A sister would have been nice, she thought. She shivered as the temperature suddenly dropped. She lifted her hand to fix her hair but it froze in mid air.

Her reflection had not lifted its hand.

It stood motionless staring at her. She slowly moved her arm and waved it at the mirror. The reflection didn't move. Perfidy stared in amazement as her reflection appeared to press its hands up to the other side of the glass. It started to mouth something to her.

Perfidy gasped as she realised what it was saying.

It's Verity, save me Perfidy!

Save me!

About the Author

A H Jamieson is originally from Lerwick in Shetland.

At the University of Stirling, Alastair studied History and Religious studies as well as gaining a diploma in Education.

After university, one of life's strange turns led him and his wife to the South East where he taught in primary schools for 12 years.

Three years ago his son, or as he calls him, his 'tormentor' arrived and turned everything upside down in the best of ways. Callum was the main reason they wanted to head back over the border and settle nearer to family, grandparents in particular. Having lived in the middle of a large town for several years, the call of Scotland was proving hard to resist.

He is now enjoying living in the beautiful Scottish Borders and has added to the Jamieson family with another son.

After teaching and being an integral part of the school community for over a decade, Alastair felt it was time for a new challenge in his professional career. He says; "I would like to give something back to the education system that I benefited greatly from myself by writing some great books to inspire readers young and old."

Black Light is A H Jamieson's first novel for young adults. He has also written a series of picture books for younger children.

33919361R00123

Printed in Poland
by Amazon Fulfillment
Poland Sp. z o.o., Wrocław